Bool

CONTEMPORARY SUSPENSE
Lost Hearts Series Enhanced!
JUST THE WAY YOU ARE
ALMOST LIKE BEING IN LOVE
CLOSE TO YOU

LADY IN BLACK

Scarlet Deception Series
SECRETS OF BELLA TERRA
REVENGE AT BELLA TERRA
BETRAYAL

Fortune Hunters Series
TROUBLE IN HIGH HEELS
TONGUE IN CHIC
THIGH HIGH
DANGER IN A RED DRESS

CONTEMPORARY PARANORMAL
Darkness Chosen Series
SCENT OF DARKNESS
TOUCH OF DARKNESS
INTO THE SHADOW
INTO THE FLAME

The Chosen Ones
STORM OF VISIONS
STORM OF SHADOWS
CHAINS OF ICE
CHAINS OF FIRE
STONE ANGEL (E-novella only)
WILDER

HISTORICALS
Governess Brides Series
THAT SCANDALOUS EVENING (Pre-Governesses, includes Adorna)
RULES OF SURRENDER
RULES OF ENGAGEMENT
RULES OF ATTRACTION
IN MY WILDEST DREAMS
LOST IN YOUR ARMS
MY FAVORITE BRIDE
MY FAIR TEMPTRESS

IN BED WITH THE DUKE
TAKEN BY THE PRINCE

Well Pleasured Series
A WELL PLEASURED LADY
A WELL FAVORED GENTLEMAN

Lost Princesses Series
SOME ENCHANTED EVENING
THE BAREFOOT PRINCESS
THE PRINCE KIDNAPS A BRIDE

Switching Places Series
SCANDALOUS AGAIN
ONE KISS FROM YOU

Princess Series
RUNAWAY PRINCESS
SOMEDAY MY PRINCE

Knight Series
ONCE A KNIGHT
A KNIGHT TO REMEMBER

Medieval Series
CANDLE IN THE WINDOW
CASTLES IN THE AIR

Stand Alone Historicals
PRICELESS
TREASURE OF THE SUN
THE GREATEST LOVER IN ALL ENGLAND
OUTRAGEOUS
MOVE HEAVEN AND EARTH

Novellas
KIDNAPPED: ONCE UPON A PILLOW
LAST NIGHT: ONCE UPON A PILLOW
SMUGGLER'S CAPTIVE BRIDE
WILD TEXAS ROSE
HERO COME BACK
SCOTTISH BRIDES
MY SCANDALOUS BRIDE

LADY

in

BLACK

by

Christina Dodd

Copyright © 1993 by Christina Dodd
This Edition 2014
ISBN 13: 978-0-9960859-0-8

One

"Who the hell are you?" Reid Donovan shrugged his arms out of his suit coat.

"I'm the butler, sir."

Reid stared incredulously as with the pomp of a seasoned retainer, the butler plucked the coat from his hands.

A footman clad in simulated eighteenth century splendor plucked it in his turn.

The butler urged, "Your hat, sir?"

Reid caught the brim and sailed it across the wide entrance hall. It fell short of the painted parrot umbrella stand. "How long have you been employed here?"

"Eighteen months, sir."

"Has my grandfather cracked up at last? Or fallen into senility? It's the only explanation I can think of for hiring *you*. How old is he now?"

"Ninety-two, sir, but I believe your grandfather is in possession of all his faculties. You'll find him in the library, anxiously awaiting your arrival." Impassively the butler led the way, stopping only to pick up the hat and with butler-like aplomb placed it atop the painted umbrella stand. "This way, sir."

"I know the way to the library," Reid said between clenched teeth. "I grew up here."

"As you say, sir."

In a cold, clear tone, Reid said, "You are an interesting case."

"Not at all, sir."

"Oh, yes. Very interesting indeed."

The butler frowned, opened the library door and announced, "Your grandson, sir."

Reid strode into the book-lined room, around the desk piled high with papers and up to the withered man in the wheelchair. "Granddad, are you insane? Where did you collect that butler?" He leaned down and embraced the old man with obvious affection.

"Don't you like her?" Jim Donovan swung his gleaming chrome chair a quarter turn, and he and his grandson examined the still figure in the black silk suit. "She's a graduate of Ivor Spencer's London School for Butler Administrators. She's steady, reliable, quiet, anticipatory—"

"I'll bet." Reid Donovan swept her with the keen eye of a connoisseur.

Margaret wanted to chide them both. Instead she remained impassive and asked, "Will there be anything else, sirs?"

"Don't go yet, dear." Jim smiled at her wickedly. "Reid, a man my age has to have his pleasures. Look at her. She's a pleasure to the eye with those big blue eyes and icy blonde hair."

"Thank you, sir." Margaret allowed herself a little withering sarcasm. "I'm always glad to be valued for my ornamental qualities as well as for my efficiency. Now may I leave you to your business, Mr. Jim?"

Neither man was listening.

"What's her name?" Reid asked.

"Margaret Guarneri," Jim drawled, watching his grandson closely.

Reid stiffened. "A. M. Guarneri?"

His tone gave Margaret a start. "Yes, sir. You've heard of me?"

"Yeah, but I hadn't connected the name with Granddad's new butler." Reid scrutinized her again, a different comprehension in his eyes. "This explains a lot. Been making changes again, Granddad?"

"Been snooping in my legal affairs again, Grandson?"

"I didn't have to snoop. Your lawyer got worried enough to call me."

"Did he now?" The old man purred like an aging lion.

Reid lifted his chin. "Yes. Don't worry, I fired him."

"Did you now?" The purr rumbled ever louder.

"We can't have our legal help betraying our trust." Confused by the satisfaction radiating from his grandfather, Reid said, "You'd have done the same thing."

"You don't even realize what I've done." Jim laughed. "You're a stupid young fool."

"Young? Thanks, Granddad, but I'm thirty-eight. I've been around."

"So you're only a stupid fool. Margaret, you may go." Jim turned back to his grandson. "If it weren't for Margaret, I'd have no girlfriend at all."

Margaret quietly closed the library door behind her. She didn't begrudge Mr. Jim his fun, but the misinformation he had gleefully passed to his grandson was bound to cause her trouble—more trouble than she had anticipated when she swung wide the gigantic front doors to welcome Reid James Donovan III.

She knew about him, of course. Had even seen him, in the portraits his fond grandfather hung on the walls and the photographs he kept on his desk. She'd viewed him on television, debating the government's effect on industry. She had prepared Jim to join him in Europe and in Japan, had known a profound gratitude that Reid respected his grandfather enough to ask his advice on business matters.

But nothing had readied her to meet the man himself.

He was gorgeous. He towered five inches above her—no insignificant accomplishment. His hair was auburn, or perhaps brown with red highlights, and straight and short. A longer style would have softened that jaw line of his, would have de-emphasized the cutting edge of his cheekbones, but Margaret suspected he didn't want that. This man had a reputation for ruthlessness. He had the caustic wit and impatient energy of a barracuda. He was rich and powerful, and he knew it.

But in a very human way, she had discounted much of his mystique.

Surely it was exaggerated? Surely she was prepared? Surely to God when she first laid eyes on the man and saw the whole package—the hair and the sherry brown eyes and the vigor that motivated his every movement—surely she should not have experienced, for the first time in three years, that restless stir of desire.

He was the kind of man who made her remember men had another use besides that of an annoyance factor. He was the kind of man who scared her half to death—not that she ever showed it. The role of the phlegmatic butler suited her well, blessing her with a rigid set of rules covering every eventuality. Including this one, she supposed.

But why did Reid's eyes sharpen with determination at the mention of her name?

Reaching down, she turned off the persistent security beeper attached to her belt. The man guarding the front gate spewed his message, his voice lurching as the radio connection cut out. "Ms. Guarneri, Mr. Martin and his assistant are coming up for the daily consultation."

Margaret raised the microphone to her mouth. "Thank you," she answered, and releasing the speak button, she added a sarcastic, "Goody." Opening the door, she stepped out onto the broad porch of the gracious southern-style mansion.

The home stood on two acres of lawn on the crest of a hill—artificial, she supposed, since Houston was so flat you could stand on a box and see fifty miles in any direction—with azaleas growing in grand profusion along the winding drive.

The Houston Garden Club had once tried to get Mr. Jim's permission to add his River Oaks estate to the annual Azalea Tour, but had been resoundingly repulsed. Mr. Jim told them he had no interest in the riff-raff of Houston traipsing across his lawns or down his gravel paths. Like so many men who had fought his way to the top, Mr. Jim fiercely protected everything he had earned.

On the wide green lawn, oaks protected the wide beds of bright orange and pink and white impatiens from the blistering Houston sun.

The Donovan mansion had been built in the nineteen-thirties. A red brick exterior and tall white columns lent protection and grace to the over five thousand square feet of interior space. When Jim Donovan bought the mansion in the seventies, he had been a wildcatter who hit it big and wanted the house to prove it to the world. He'd remodeled it then, and remodeled every twenty years since. He updated the plumbing and wiring, added air conditioning and internet cable, tore up the carpets and refinished the original wood floors, and spent a fortune on expensive throw rugs from Indian, Persia, China and the rural United States.

Mr. Donovan was the quintessential resident of Houston; he worshipped tradition, as long as it was kept polished and modernized.

Speaking as the person who kept the house in order, Margaret totally agreed with his attitude.

But no technology existed that could alleviate the outdoor heat and humidity of a Houston summer. Local residents joked that from March to October, it was so hot that the trees whistled for the dogs, and a seatbelt made a good branding iron.

This was Margaret's first year in Texas; she had discovered that if anything, Houstonians understated the matter.

She hovered in the shade of the porch, but her white silk shirt stuck to her sides beneath the waistband of her skirt. Her chignon weighed heavy on her neck. Her fingers itched to loosen the button under her black bow tie and free herself from her black vest.

Her only relief from the soaring temperatures was the sight of Cliff Martin riding up the curved drive on a bicycle. His loosened paisley tie drooped across his chest, heavy with moisture. His white shirt had wet patches at the armpits. His suit coat hung over the handle bars, and his ample belly heaved as he panted. He glowed red with exertion, but Jim insisted the hired help not disturb his serenity, and so the head of their security firm rode a broken-down one-speed from his car to Donovan's Castle.

Nolan Salas jogged beside his boss, bright red and sweating almost as much, but he was thinner, shorter, almost invisible beside his boss's larger, more colorful character.

Margaret remained impassive, never revealing her amusement.

"Mr. Martin, how good to see you," she intoned in a stately tempo, and was delighted to see him roll his eyes. "Mr. Salas, how difficult to run in those shoes."

"That's true." Nolan inspected his leather oxfords. "I shall have to get new insoles."

She couldn't decide if Nolan had a dry sense of humor or no sense of humor.

"I suspect," Cliff puffed, laying the bike over in the bower of rosy crepe myrtles beside the front step, "that old man Donovan doesn't give a damn about his quiet. It's the thought of us mere mortals peddling our rumps through this heat gives him his jollies."

Since Margaret suspected the same thing, she didn't acknowledge his comment.

Pulling a red bandanna out of his brown pin-striped coat, he mopped his dripping face and said what millions of people say every day of every summer in Houston, "It's not the heat, it's the humidity."

She puckered her mouth in insincere sympathy. "April is not the month for Yankees."

"I'm not a Yankee." Cliff glared with ready ire. "I'm from Kentucky."

"Quite." To her inner amusement, Margaret found her British accent strengthened in reaction to his country twang. She opened the oak door and held it, observing with bland interest as he grappled with the idea of a female holding the door for him. Did it make him less of a man, or an employee of superior position?

She urged, "This way, Mr. Martin."

Shrugging, the hefty man shambled over and squeezed through the narrow, short entrance. "Is old man Donovan in a good mood?"

She stiffened. This oaf was trying to make her a comrade in impudence.

"Excuse me." Shoulders hunched, Nolan slid inside, and he didn't look at her as he followed his boss in; he seemed almost embarrassed by Martin's presumption.

Shutting the door behind them with a precise click, she replied, "I'm not at liberty to say, sir," and walked to the house phone. Picking it up, she pressed the button for Jim Donovan's office. "Mr. Donovan, Mr. Martin is here to report."

It was Reid, rather than Jim, who replied irritably, "Send him in, and bring in the food I ordered. It's past dinnertime in London."

"Yes, sir." As she called the kitchen and spoke with their cook, Abigail, she watched Mr. Martin fan himself with his hands, then roll down his sleeves. He slipped into his coat and tightened his tie, and stared at the dozen medieval suits of armor that lined the walls of the entry.

She stared at his profile and wondered about the sharp look of intelligence on his usually bovine face.

With a glance at her, he became once more the caricature of a southern good ol' boy. "Guess I better get in there, hadn't I? Old man Donovan might yell at me." He grinned amiably. "C'mon, Nolan."

Nolan straightened his clothes, also, used his white handkerchief to blot the moisture from his face, and followed Cliff.

Margaret stared after them.

She didn't like those men. She didn't like either one of them.

Then Cliff swung the library door open, and she caught a glimpse of Reid.

He glanced at Cliff and Nolan, then unerringly his gaze reached beyond them to her. In that short moment of the open door, he scrutinized her, seeing not the butler, but the woman beneath her clothes, a woman to be desired…but not trusted.

The door clicked shut.

She was alone in the corridor, and she found herself clutching her fist in front of her chest and breathing too quickly.

Because although she never intended for it to happen, she also saw too much: the man stripped of his businessman façade, ruthless, relentless, driven, sexual.

She could have him, and if she did—

She turned away. Walked away.

Duty ruled her life.

So why now did passion light a flame in her mind and heart…and how quickly could she extinguish it before passion destroyed a life she had worked so hard to build?

Two

Margaret hurried through the dining room and into the dim hall that led to the kitchen—and stopped. There in the shadows stood a man, posed with the stoic immobility of a statue. Pivoting on the ball of her foot, she dropped into a fighting posture.

"That's not necessary." The statue spoke with a robot's plain, flat tones. "I'm here with Mr. Reid Donovan."

"Why are you by the kitchen?" she asked.

He moved with careful deliberation, switching on the lights and staring her up and down as if she were the intruder. "I'm Reid's bodyguard," he said at last. "It's my job to come in the back door."

Still cautious, Margaret examined the man before her. He wasn't tall, perhaps five-seven, but his shoulders were so broad and square, he looked as if he was wearing shoulder pads. His hands dangled at his sides, square palms and square fingertips absolutely motionless. Cut in a flat top, his black hair completed the square box of his jaw. He was so flat, front and back, and unnaturally still—he did not blink, his fingers did not twitch—that Margaret thought he had been popped in a toaster slot, heated and popped up into the world in his present motionless form. The toaster that created him had been set on dark, for the man's skin matched his black suit.

When she was done examining him, the man slid his hand into the inside pocket of his jacket. He didn't seem to move quickly, but before she could react a wallet rested open in his spatulate fingers and his identification was revealed.

"Donovan Corporation," she said, nodding.

"Now," he said in that flat monotone. "Who are you?"

"I'm the butler."

"Yes." He agreed as if she had answered a difficult question. "You are A. M. Guarneri."

Astounded, she asked, "Why does everyone know my name?"

"It's my job to know about the people in any household Reid enters."

"He knew my name, too, but he didn't know I was the butler." Her eyes narrowed with suspicion. "Or was he testing me?"

"Perhaps as A. M. Guarneri, you are of significance. As the butler, you are not." The man bowed impassively and left, his square feet carrying him silently away.

She didn't even feel a disturbance in the air as he passed. How could that be?

And if she was of no importance to Reid as butler, why had her name attained celebrity status?

And where, oh where, had Reid dredged up that unemotional bodyguard? What an odd couple they must be, for she already knew that dynamic Reid Donovan simmered with temper and—

She interrupted herself before she could finish the thought.

No. He could simmer with whatever he wished. She didn't want to know about it. She was the butler.

Margaret continued to the kitchen, a chrome and white room, the kitchen of the future—sixty years ago. The predictions of the designer hadn't come to pass and now it was a charming anachronism, livened with blooming plants and brand-new updated appliances, and with a black cook dressed in pink and green and orange ruffles.

"Oh, Abigail." Margaret covered her mouth in mock-simulated horror. "Where did you get that outfit?"

"Can't all of us dress like a penguin," Abigail assured her, lifting pieces of chicken out of a box and arranging them on a Sevres' china platter.

The meaty aroma infiltrated Margaret's nostrils and her stomach growled about its neglect.

Abigail continued, "I copied this costume from my favorite old movie."

"The Carmen Miranda you made me watch?" Margaret surveyed her friend from head to toe. "That turban and the feather earrings—"

"The perfect finishing touches, aren't they?" Abigail grinned at her, white teeth flashing in her dimpled brown face. Raising her arms, she whirled in a circle, showing off a trim figure.

Abigail was vibrant, intelligent, one of the most gorgeous women Margaret had ever seen, and if Abigail had desired, she could have owned her own restaurant. She didn't desire. Abigail knew exactly what she wanted: she wanted to cook for Mr. Jim, she wanted time to enjoy life, and she wanted to be outrageous.

She succeeded on all levels.

"You forgot the bananas," Margaret said.

"I didn't forget them. I thought fruit on my head would be over the top."

Margaret laughed, a great release of merriment, until she collapsed onto the bar stool. "I always think you can't top yourself, and then you prance in wearing another bizarre concoction. I wish I had your self-confidence." She watched as Abigail scooped red beans and rice out of a Styrofoam container into a serving bowl and pulled biscuits out of a paper bag and placed them in a basket. "What *are* you doing?"

"Reid called down to me as soon as he got here and had me order him southern fried chicken from N'Awlens Chicken Ranch Take-out." Abigail glanced up at Margaret and grinned at the dumbfounded expression on her face. She licked her fingers with flair. "Spicy variety."

Margaret sighed. "I didn't even know I was hungry until I smelled it. It's your night off, then."

"That's why I wore my newest creation to work. Whenever Reid comes into town, all I have to do the first night is pick up the phone and dial the Chicken Ranch—they deliver. Second and third night too, until Mr. Jim complains."

"Mr. Donovan's so stuffy, I never thought he'd eat take-out chicken."

"Mr. Donovan? You don't mean—are you talking about Reid?" When Margaret nodded, Abigail's jaw dropped. She swiftly recovered, and said, "Stuffy? He hasn't got a stuffy bone in his body."

"Chauvinist, then." *Offensive* might be a better word. *In your face. Too aggressive.*

Too handsome.

Too sexual.

Oh, damn. She didn't want to think about that.

"Chauvinist! Why, girl, that man doesn't care about sex or social station or age. Not as long as you do your job. You know what he did? Mr. Jim wanted to hire me and Reid wanted to hire this Frenchman. Reid suggested a cook-off, with the guy cooking the first night, and me the second. After Reid tasted my shrimp étouffée, he called me to the dining room and went down on one knee and begged my pardon for doubting me and asked me to work for his grandfather." Abigail threw back her head and roared with laughter. "I was twenty-two and embarrassed, but he was so kind. Been here eight years now." She nodded at Margaret. "For the salary he pays, who am I to find fault if he wants chicken takeout on his first night home?"

"He seemed less pleased to see me," Margaret informed her. "Perhaps in eight years he's become a snob."

"No," Abigail flatly denied. "Any man who comes down during a dinner party to dance me around the kitchen is not a snob. If he's angry, it must be you."

"Marvelous. He looked me over and decided in an instant—"

"Looked you over?"

"Yeah, like a man-to-woman overview?" Margaret still couldn't believe it. "It's been a long time since any man dared."

Abigail stepped back and looked her over, too. "Mm. Interesting. That man will dare anything. Might do you some good to—"

"Don't start, Abigail." Margaret stood up and straightened her lapels. "I'm not on the market."

"Not every man's going to die, you know." Abigail centered the platter on the serving cart. "How long has it been?"

"Two years and seven months. The look Mr. Donovan gave me was not a polite summing up of attraction. It was…carnal. Then after he heard my name, it was more like shrewdness." Pulling a handful of silverware from the drawer, she lined knives and forks next to the platter.

"Let me do it." Abigail snatched up the utensils Margaret had arranged and laid them in a geometric design. "Maybe he's perturbed about the threats to his granddaddy. That's enough to throw anyone out of sorts."

"I'm a mite out of sorts about it myself." Margaret grinned with sudden wry amusement. "But dear old Mr. Jim did me no favors. You know what he said? He said, 'If it weren't for Margaret, I'd have no girlfriend at all.'"

"Why, that cranky old fraud." Abigail's brown eyes twinkled, her skin had a sheen, and she seemed to glow with pleasure.

Margaret considered those suspicious symptoms. Whenever Abigail glowed, a man was involved. Since Abigail obviously admired Reid Donovan, but seemed ready to push Margaret at him, only one other choice remained. "Abigail?"

"Hm?"

"Who was that man in the hall?"

"Who…?" Abigail did a great imitation of being blasé. "Oh, you mean, Nagumbi?"

"That was the name on the ID," Margaret agreed. "Who is he?"

A smile played on Abigail's lips. "Mr. Reid's bodyguard. Didn't he tell you?"

"Yes, of course he told me *that*. Has he been with him long?"

"For years and years." Abigail put her hands on her hips and eyed the cart as she explained, "When Mr. Reid was just out of high school, he wanted adventure and Mr. Jim didn't see anything wrong with that. But they've got money and Mr. Reid was going places where the locals make a living off of kidnapping Americans. So Mr. Jim hired a man who'd been around the world to make sure no one interfered with Mr. Reid's adventures, and also make sure Mr. Reid didn't plan adventures so brainless he'd never come home again. That's Nagumbi."

Margaret squinted at the beaming cook. "Is Nagumbi always so vivacious and quick-witted?"

"He's a challenge, that one is." Abigail hummed a measure of *Call Me Maybe* as she arranged the plates on the cart.

"A challenge? He's too old to challenge you."

"That's what he says, too. But all that means is he can't run fast enough to hide."

"You ought to be spanked."

"I've been telling him that, too."

Unwillingly, Margaret laughed. She patted Abigail's shoulder. "I'll see if I can arrange a fake—"

The intercom roared with blunt impatience. "Where the hell's my chicken?"

Abigail flung a handful of linen napkins on the cart as Margaret grasped the handles and wheeled it past. "On its way, Reid," the cook called. "She had to fix the wheel on the cart."

"Who?"

With satisfaction, Abigail said, "The butler did it," and winked at the groaning Margaret as she fled the room.

Three

As Margaret pushed the cart into the library, she heard Reid say sharply, "Where do the police stand on all this?"

"Kidnapping is a serious charge." Cliff sat on the edge of his seat, his hands clasped between his knees.

Nolan Salas was nowhere in sight.

Cliff looked earnestly between Reid and Jim on either side of him. "The police are concerned, of course, but they can't keep up the constant surveillance necessary for complete confidence in his safety." He stared as Margaret rolled the mahogany cart into the center of the male triangle.

Stepping back, she leaned over Jim Donovan's shoulder and murmured, "May I serve you, sir?"

"Yes," he said testily, leaning back and allowing her to snap his tray onto the handles of the chair. "If this spicy chicken doesn't burn my mouth off before I can swallow it."

Reid lifted his head from his avid contemplation of the dinner. "That'll be the day, Jalapeño Jim." He pronounced both *J*s with an *H* sound.

Margaret cleared her throat of sudden, unexpected mirth.

Who knew Reid had a sense of humor?

"Didn't Abigail order any corn on the cob?" He demanded attention with nothing more than the disquieting stare of his sherry-colored eyes.

"I couldn't say, sir." Placing the silverware by Jim's left hand, she laid a plate filled with beans, biscuit and a chicken wing on his tray. "Would you like me to call down?"

"Aren't you the butler, Margaret?" Reid asked caustically. "Don't you plan the meals?"

"Normally, yes, sir. But—"

"No buts. This is your responsibility."

"Don't be an asshole, Reid," Jim interrupted. "Margaret's got nothing to do with this dinner, and you know it. You can have corn on the cob tomorrow night—with your damned spicy chicken."

The old man and his grandson went eyeball to eyeball, and neither seemed willing to back down until Cliff chuckled. "These women! Always switching roles to suit themselves. Firstly they want us to open the doors for them and secondly they covet our jobs. They make life difficult for us men."

Reid and Jim broke apart and glared at the intruder in unison.

Jim said, "I'm not so old I can't keep track of male and female without a schedule."

Reid said, "Life's difficult enough without drawing battle lines between the sexes. I've got no patience for that."

Cliff, you jerk. Margaret stripped the skin from Jim's chicken wing. *Outside you try to line up the employees against the employers; in here you try to line up the men against the women. Divide and conquer.*

"Cliff, want some dinner?" Reid asked.

"No." Cliff put his hand on his distended belly. "Too much spicy food gives me heartburn."

Reid's gaze flicked at Margaret, then roamed the room. "Will Salas want some?"

"We ate right before we came," Cliff said.

Margaret hoped that was true, or poor, skinny Nolan Salas was going to starve right before her eyes.

Actually, the smell of the chicken was making her anticipate her own dinner.

"What I want to know"—Reid poked around the chicken parts—"is how that second extortion note arrived on my grandfather's desk."

"Easy. The extortionists have an inside accomplice." Cliff fumbled with his inner suit pocket and drew out a short, battered cigar.

"I thought you were giving those up." With bright eyes, Jim watched as the man flicked his lighter and ignited the wide tip.

"I am." Cliff puffed until the fire crept up the cigar and fumes billowed from the sides of his mouth. "Sometimes the craving's too strong."

"You must be nervous," Jim suggested. "You don't have to be nervous with us."

The annoyed security man chewed the end of his cigar and brown flecks of tobacco escaped onto his lips.

Jim watched with wicked satisfaction. "Margaret, get the file on my little problem."

Margaret went to the antique walnut file cabinet and opened the appropriate drawer.

Reid paused, a spice-flecked chicken leg halfway to his mouth. "*Little problem.* Is that what we're calling it now?"

Jim dug into the red beans and rice. "What's the matter, boy? I've been in worse situations."

"You've never been ninety-two before, though, and Granddad"— Reid shook the leg at Jim—"I'd like to see you make ninety-three."

"You weren't worried about me at eighty-two, and I was damn old then. Why, there are actually men who give up and die at eighty. But the women don't." He winked at Margaret as she placed the file marked KIDNAPPING at his left hand. "That's why I stick around. Women positively fawn on an old man like me." He corrected himself. "A *rich* old man like me."

"Yes, don't forget the rich part." Reid glanced meaningfully at Margaret—then proceeded to piranha his way through two biscuits.

The library was now the finest room in the house, created when Mr. Jim took the original small dark chamber filled with shelves and leather-bound books, tore out the walls on either side, and expanded to fill as much space as was contained in most private homes.

He had made the original room his sitting room and office, and there grouped a comfortable sofa and three easy chairs in front of the fireplace, used only on the few days a year that Houston experienced winter weather. Close by, his desk, a behemoth antique walnut creation that matched the file cabinet, faced the windows that looked out over the gloriously colorful back garden.

There, in the grassy expanse, blazing orange impatiens and giant green elephant ear leaves surrounded wide-branched old oaks. At the heart of the garden, as a cool alternative to the August heat, a waterfall tumbled over jagged rocks and into a pond where shimmering silver koi swam among the lily pads.

The view from all the windows was beautiful. The library itself was spectacular, with broad, rich paintings on the walls, precious first editions protected by glass enclosures, and art glass sculptures illuminated by hidden lights.

Mr. Jim had spared no expense when it came to the workmanship used to create the shelves, the coved ceilings, the display cases. Yet the place would never be showcased in a magazine or one of the rich and famous TV spectaculars.

Bound books of every kind found their homes on the shelves and surfaces of Mr. Jim's library. Well-read paperbacks nestled next to sixty-year-old *Encyclopedia Britannicas*. Stacks of mysteries and romances and fantasy tumbled over onto the Persian rugs. Mr. Jim wouldn't let Margaret pick anything up, or move anything at all, and when she suggested bringing in a professional librarian to catalogue the books, he had refused in horror. He claimed he knew the location of every volume in here—and as far as she could tell, it was true.

He read his books. He loved his books. He wanted no one messing with his books.

And Mr. Jim always got his own way.

Margaret made sure of it.

"Admit it, Reid, it's the stroke that put me in this wheelchair that scares you." The stroke that put Jim in the wheelchair had scared everybody.

"I'll admit it." Reid had loosened his gray tie and the first two buttons on his starched white shirt. He had rolled up his sleeves and he looked comfortable and at home here. But still fierce. Still forceful. Power rolled off him with a palpable, irritating constancy, like lava off an active volcano. "You're all the family I have. You raised me and trained me, and no criminal is going to end your life."

"No, boy, no criminal's going to end my life." Jim used the last of the biscuit to sop up the last of the beans.

"You say that like a vow, yet you're helpless in a way you've never been before." Reid crumbled his third biscuit between his fingers. "What are you going to do if someone grabs you? Roll over their feet?"

Jim took the file in his unimpaired left hand and thumbed through it. "I found the first note on April twenty-first, but it could have arrived on my desk any time the week before—"

"That's precise," Reid observed.

"My desk is a hell of a mess," Jim said proudly.

Reid looked over at the mass of papers scattered across the polished surface. "Sure is. You want me to sort through your paperwork while I'm here?"

"I've been saving them especially for you," Jim said.

Margaret maintained a stoic expression. At least—she hoped she did.

Jim's secretary had retired twenty years ago, and since then he griped about how quickly technology moved, but he had learned to handle a computer, a scanner, a fax machine, and a printer. He knew how to Skype and text. What he hadn't learned was how to file the constant flow of paperwork that inundated his desk, and lately, he had only allowed Margaret to assist him when stacks threatened to topple.

Now she knew why. He wanted Reid to do it.

He liked to keep Reid close; that was why, although Reid hadn't visited during the whole time she had been in residence, he kept a utilitarian desk tucked into a cubbyhole in the left wing of the library. Margaret imagined the two men working and laughing, shouting insults and consulting spreadsheets…

Nolan slipped back into the library, slid into a chair against the wall, placed his feet together, and observed them with such acute concentration Margaret wondered if he *was* hungry.

She lifted the plate of chicken toward him and silently offered it.

Nolan shook his head.

Reid asked his grandfather, "Any fingerprints on the extortion note?"

"Margaret's. She was helping me tidy up—she found the note." As she removed his plate, Jim patted her arm.

She flicked him a disgusted look, and picked up an ashtray, her eyes fixed on the cigar clasped between Cliff's fingers.

"Margaret found it?" Reid subjected her to a long, cool stare. "Has Martin Security investigated Margaret?"

Cliff snapped his fingers.

Nolan Salas rose to his feet and in a singsong monotone, he said, "Born and raised in California, graduate of Berkeley School of English Literature. Married at twenty-three to Dr. Luke Guarneri, moved to Houston where she worked at a now defunct oil company. Dr. Guarneri worked for MD Anderson Cancer Research—"

Jim glanced at Margaret's rigid face and slapped his table with the flat of his hand. "That's enough—get down to facts. Did you find anything suspicious?"

Cliff finished the report. "Only that she speaks with a British accent after having lived in England for only one year."

Margaret dove to catch the ash falling from the end of the noxious cigar.

Nolan winced.

"Thanks, honey," Cliff said.

"I'd say an English accent is prerequisite of the job," Reid said dryly. "If I need any information before tomorrow, Mr. Martin, I'm sure I'll be able to reach you?"

"Oh. Of course, anytime." Cliff remained seated, not realizing he had been dismissed.

Margaret moved to the door and opened it.

Nolan scuttled out.

A painful flush lit Cliff's nose and ears and turned into a rash on his cheeks, and he abruptly stood and crushed his cigar in the ashtray. He nodded at Reid and then Jim. "I'll keep checking on everything for you. In terms of reliability, my firm is fine for several reasons. Firstly, I keep close tabs on everyone who works for me." He stuck his hands into his pockets and rocked back on his heels. "Yes, sirree, acts of a hostile nature like this one are my personal domain."

"I appreciate that," Reid said.

Cliff continued, "Secondly, at Martin Security every individual matter receives my personal attention. I'm a man who follows through on my responsibilities."

Rising, Reid moved toward the door. "That's a reassuring thought, Mr. Martin."

Cliff followed with the ungainly lurch of a football linebacker. "Thirdly," he stepped into the hallway, "I hand-pick every man who works under me."

Margaret flicked a glance at Nolan.

The poor guy watched Cliff Martin as if the association pained him.

Probably it did. But in these days, employment was tough to find and working for a jerk was better than not working at all.

Margaret prepared to follow the two men to the front door.

Reid laid a restraining hand on her shoulder. "That's great, Mr.

Martin." Leaning close to her ear, he said quietly, "Have the footman show him out. We need you here."

"As you wish, sir." Relieved when he released her, she signaled Simon and watched as he urged Cliff Martin and Nolan Salas past the suits of armor and out onto the porch.

He returned to his post and gave her a thumb's up.

She nodded and returned to the library, shut the door and took up her post against the wall.

"Are you sure *he's* not our villain?" Reid spoke to Jim, but a flick of his gaze included Margaret.

Did he want her opinion? Or was he studying her…again? Was he watching her reactions to his suspicions and his accusations?

Jim inspected his grandson. "You mean Martin? Naw, it's not Martin. He's too stupid."

"He is that," Reid muttered, then raised his voice. "But is he really? If he's smart enough to run a successful security firm—"

"His daddy paid to set him up in business," Jim said.

"So?" Reid waved a hand at himself. "My granddaddy set me up in business, and I've done all right."

"True." Jim nodded. "I never thought you'd do so well with those electronic gadgets, but you saved my ass when oil crashed."

"Thanks, but I doubt you would have been in a soup line regardless of your losses." Reid glared at his grandfather. "You're not going to distract me. I want to know about Cliff Martin. He admitted this is an inside job. So I want to know—who recommended *him?*"

"Manuel recommended him," Jim said.

"Uncle Manuel?" Reid visibly wavered. "Are Manuel's contacts in the Houston Police as good as ever?"

"He'll be around. Why don't you ask him?" Jim asked.

"And force the old guy into a Hispanic hissy-fit? No, no—if Uncle Manuel says Martin Security is fine, I'll believe him until I learn different." Reid leaned back in his chair, and used both hands to push his short dark hair off his forehead. "But I don't know how I'll stand Cliff Martin. Is he always so wordy?"

"Martin?" Jim chortled. "Only when he's nervous—or you try to get him to leave. Aggravating, isn't it?"

"Ghastly. Nothing annoys me more. I'll avoid both his nerves and his leave-takings from now on." Reid grimaced. "And his cigars. Where does he buy those stinkers? Walgreen's?"

"Turn on the ceiling fan, Margaret," Jim said.

She turned the rheostat to the lowest setting.

"The stench does hang in the air, doesn't it?" Jim was amused.

Everything amused Jim now. He had been a giant man, and a man among giants, moving the world according to his business acumen. He had enjoyed life, savored love, laughed at danger, but now all he could do was watch. It didn't bother him; he didn't mourn his lost freedom. He observed the comedy of existence with a rascally twinkle in his faded blue eyes.

And Margaret loved him for it.

"Come here." The abrupt command shifted her attention to Reid. Reid, whose eyes glowed with virility and who gave off that lava-like heat.

Do not notice.

She immediately shifted her attention to the set of elk antlers over his head. In a slow, stately stride, she moved toward the two men.

Apparently, slow and stately didn't cut it with Reid, because he snapped, "Knock off the butler shit and sit right there."

Four

Reid pointed to the hot seat vacated by Cliff.

Margaret stopped. "Sir, it isn't proper—"

"If you're afraid he sweated in the chair, sit over here." He pointed to the chair set at right angles to his, separated only by an end table. "That's better, anyway. You can put your plate down if you need to."

"Plate?" Margaret said weakly.

"I could hear your stomach growling clear over here. Don't you schedule yourself dinner hours?" Reid scowled. "Sit down and have some chicken."

Margaret glanced at Jim.

Her boss sat there, watching and obviously hugely enjoying himself.

She would receive no help from that quarter. "Sir—Mr. Donovan—butler protocol prohibits eating with one's employer."

"Sit!" Reid's roar blasted her off her feet and into the designated easy chair. He surveyed her outraged form with satisfaction. "So that's how to handle you."

She stiffened. *Handle her?*

He paid no attention to her outrage. Picking up a dish, he hovered over the platter. "White or dark?"

She thought frantically, wondering which would be easier to eat.

"A leg," he said. "Biscuit?"

Crumbs on her black skirt.

"I'll slather it with butter and honey, too." He placed a big scoop of red beans and rice beside the leg. "There." He handed her the loaded plate.

She had so lost this round. "Spoon? Fork?"

"You can't eat this stuff with a spoon and fork. It takes one of these." He held up a combination plastic spoon/fork, with rounded bowl and short tines. "It takes a spork."

She couldn't help herself. She corrected him. "A foon."

"Right." He laid it on the table by her elbow, then with a sensitivity she would never have suspected, he faced his grandfather and gave her the privacy she needed to eat. "Let me see the most recent note."

Jim handed it over.

Reid scanned the copy. "Who's got the original? The police?"

"Yes, and they IDed the printer." Jim's eyes snapped. "It's my old printer. I haven't used the damned thing since I got the new set-up in the office. I only keep it for emergencies."

"You only keep it because you never throw anything away," Reid corrected. "What are you going to do about it?"

The kind old man whom Margaret knew disappeared, replaced by a cold, determined autocrat with iron in his soul. "I'm going to get the bastards. When have I ever let anyone take me like that?"

At this moment, his grandson resembled him, determination, iron, and all. "Yeah, I figured. What happened after you received the first note?"

The autocrat faded. "First I had to calm Margaret down. She was running around here squawking like an outraged chicken over a three-egg omelet."

Reid grinned and glanced at her, then leaned over and wiped the side of her mouth with his napkin. "Whoops, that didn't do much good," he murmured. "My napkin's almost as greasy as the chicken. Here." He picked up a clean napkin and swiped it across his tongue, then scrubbed at her face.

She sat perfectly still, trying to remember what had been said in the London School of Butler Administrators that could apply to this occasion.

Her mind was blank.

"There." Reid examined the white linen. "No makeup. Where did you get that gorgeous skin? You must be Scandinavian."

"No, sir. American." She had the satisfaction of seeing his audacity take a check.

But he recovered promptly. "Except for the British accent."

"As you said, sir, it's part of the job."

"What do you think of our esteemed security man?" He shot the question at her like a bullet.

She perceived his deadly flair for interrogation. Relax the victim, then go for the throat. She put her plate down and wiped her hands, gathering her wits. "Martin Security was recommended to us by Mr. Manuel over six months ago and my—and the police concurred. Martin Security been operating in Houston over four years. Cliff Martin is the son of Frank Martin, owner of the largest chain of security firms in the world. When I found the first note—"

"What did it say?"

"I'll never forget." She closed her eyes, and it sprang into her mind.

> *To Whom it May Concern,*
> *Good health for the elderly carries a big price tag, and it's easy for a man in a wheelchair to develop a flat tire.*
> *All you have to do is slip once, and I'll have the old man and you'll have heartbreak. Wouldn't it be easier to pay for life insurance ahead of time? I'll give you a call when you're not busy.*
> *I do know when you're busy and when you're not.*

"He knows when you are sleeping," Reid sang. "He knows when you're awake. He knows if you've been bad or good…" He gave the nonsense a sexy intonation.

She laughed, the white receding from her face.

"You didn't answer the question," he said. "What do *you* think of Cliff Martin?"

Picking up her plate once more, she answered, "He seems very capable," and tore a big chunk of dark meat off with her teeth.

"When she hasn't got her mouth full," Jim advised Reid, "she says just because Cliff Martin smokes a smelly cigar doesn't mean he can't rely on his personality to drive people away."

Reid laughed. "What about his friend? What about…what's his name?"

"Nolan Salas." She glanced at Jim for guidance. "His father sent Nolan to Cliff to be trained. He intends that Salas will open an office in Bombay."

"For someone like Frank Martin, looking to fill an important position, Salas is an odd choice," Jim said. "He almost fades into the scenery. Half the time, Cliff doesn't seem to know he's there. The other half, he's using him as a gofer or a clerk."

"Salas seems inoffensive," she said. "But Cliff seems like a good ol' boy and I occasionally get glimpses of someone very different. Really, don't we all have hidden agendas and secrets we hide?"

"I know we do." Reid smiled at her—the sweetest, sexiest smile she'd ever seen outside of the movies—and she forgot to chew. Good Lord. She'd put him in a little slot under *Barracuda*, but perhaps she needed to change that.

A slot labeled *Trickster*, perhaps? *Deceiver*?

Enchanter?

She brought her teeth together in a hard collision. She was nothing more than a widow-woman looking for the hottest stud in pants.

He knew it, too. Look at that knowing grin, look at the way he watched her legs swing nervously and studied the hand twitching down the already lowered hem of her skirt.

But she could divert him; she could knock that smirk right off of his face.

Taking a deep breath, she stared into his eyes and said, "I'm the one who found the second extortion note, too."

Five

Margaret's arms flexed and extended, flexed and extended, the weights held steady in her hand. The early morning sunlight, tinted green by the dense foliage, crept through the windows of the daylight basement and dimly illuminated the large gym with its mats, machines, and torturous chrome exercise equipment.

Pausing, she turned off the overhead fluorescent lights.

Her arms ached with the repetition, and she shook the kinks out with flicks of her wrists.

She had done her sit-ups on the inclined board, worked her neck and back, twisted from the waist, and struggled with her calves and big thigh muscles. Her shorts and t-shirt stuck in patches to her body, and wisps of straight hair stuck out from the braid at the back of her neck.

Unable to stall any longer, she moved to the stainless steel machine that was Hollywood's answer to the rack. Sitting on the padded bench, resting her spine against the back, she hooked her knees around the stainless steel rest and pushed in with all her might. A spring resisted her efforts, and when she reached the innermost point, the spring urged her thighs apart again. But she controlled it, compressed and released her muscles in a slow, steady rhythm until her breath caught in her throat and her teeth clenched in agony. Then she did it…again. And again.

She was concentrating so hard, she didn't hear him arrive.

"Why are you exercising in the dark?" Reid asked.

Margaret jumped. Her knees snapped out. "Damn!" She rubbed her thighs.

Reid strode out of the darkened stairwell. "Sorry. I thought you heard me coming down."

"No, sir, I didn't." She sat with her legs lax for a moment, panting, and then began again.

"How could you?" He stepped in front of her and grinned. "That contraption destroys your senses—all you can hear is the pounding of blood in your ears."

Margaret reached for her proper butler demeanor, but apparently it had oozed out her pores. "Demolishes the entire nervous system," she agreed.

His voice deepened and turned velvet. "But it develops marvelous inner thighs."

She cast a quick glance at him. A mistake.

He studied her legs as they opened and closed with the most rapacious...

And he was absolutely naked.

She turned her head away. Then, unable to resist, she glanced again.

Shorts. He wore a pair of shorts. Sinfully brief, gloriously tight, toasty brown shorts that blended with his gloriously tight, toasty brown body.

She would have sighed with relief, but her breath was engaged.

His mouth twisted with amusement.

She wondered if he knew what she thought. That made her close her eyes, in physical and mental discomfort, and when she looked up again, he was gone, off rummaging through the weights on the rack.

He hefted iron until he reached a good number...for a gorilla. "These should do it," he said. Coming back, he stood right in front of her. Stretching his arms over his head, he bent his elbows until the weights touched his back. He straightened his elbows, and bent his elbows, and straightened his elbows... Tricep curls. He was exercising his triceps, and like a wave coming in to shore, the muscles in his chest and stomach rippled. The thin arrow of auburn hair pointed along his breastbone and down his stomach, disappearing beneath the partition of his waistband.

Margaret's eyes ached with the exertion of watching; still working her thighs, she found herself mesmerized.

"You never told me," he said, "why you exercise in the dark."

"It's not dark." She nodded toward the brightening windows.

"Besides, I hate fluorescent light."

"All the effort my granddad put into constructing the perfect gym, and you don't like the lighting?"

"Fluorescent lights remind me of a hospital." She snapped her mouth shut.

Damn, how had he conned her into admitting that?

"We need to talk," he said.

She silently disagreed.

He continued, "About the kidnapping threats."

Her exhale was less a pant than a gasp of relief. Paranoia dogged her; obviously he could care less about her experience with hospitals. "What do you want to know?"

"You diverted me last night with your little admission—"

She stopped with the thigh press. She'd done a few too many. Tomorrow, she would be sore. "Admission?"

"You discovered both notes." Taking the weights to the rack, he replaced them and picked up larger ones. Two gorillas-worth.

Oh, God, what was he going to do now?

Bicep curls. Slow and steady. He said, "By the time I stopped yelling, you had disappeared with my grandfather. A clever maneuver, and I salute you, but I still don't know the whole story. How did you find that second note?"

"I was watching for it. The, um, note, I mean." Okay. She needed to concentrate on the conversation, and not on the gun show going on right before her eyes.

She groped for her water bottle. She took a long, slow drink. She wiped her forehead with her towel.

She was sweating from working out. Not from watching him. From *working out.*

"Did they put the note on his desk again?" he asked.

"No. They connected it to the front door in the classic method." She swallowed. Why was her mouth still dry? "With a knife."

"Dammit," he said reasonably. "Any fingerprints?"

"No."

His arms bulged with a casual rhythm, deceptively effortless. "Where was the outside security?"

"Unconscious in the library—laid out on Mr. Jim's desk, for Lord's sake, bleeding from a head wound."

"*In* the library?" He lowered his arms and let the weights dangle. "Whoever it was, was inside."

"Oh, yes. The guard is still in the hospital in satisfactory condition, and he swears he glimpsed a tall, fat woman in a plaid skirt."

"Plaid?"

"One of the authentic Scottish kilts is missing." She started with the thigh press again. Stupid move, but Reid made her want to show off. Or rather—show him up. "Mr. Jim had a fit because *Someone was mucking around with his collection.*"

"The contents of the note?"

"Were considerably more menacing. The note rambled, seemed bitter and personal, printed on Mr. Jim's printer." Margaret sat straight with outraged honesty. "I swear to you, that printer was guarded every moment."

"Couldn't it have been the same kind of printer, but a different machine?"

"No. The police analyzed both notes. The drum on Mr. Jim's printer has a smear, and it shows in blurry text."

"Why hasn't the drum been replaced?"

Margaret tucked the straggling bits of straight hair behind her ears and pushed her bangs off her forehead. "Because he's too cheap to let me call a technician, even if we could find one who would work on that antiquated piece of junk."

"That's Granddad," Reid agreed. "So it's someone you left guarding the library."

"Impossible. I stand by my people."

"—Or the villain printed up several notes all at once. I read the police report, of course. The note seemed to be addressed to me this time, and it asked for one million—"

"Two," she corrected.

He smiled sardonically.

She realized he'd been testing her.

"Two million," he said. "But the police reports don't mention a lot of things. Like why the hell haven't we changed security firms?"

"You heard your grandfather last night. Mr. Jim's dear old buddy in the Houston Police maintains Martin Security is above suspicion."

"Isn't Uncle Manuel retired yet? He and my granddad used to get in trouble together." Reid's mouth quirked. "A *lot* of trouble together."

"He's retired, but he keeps a finger in the pie. When he suggested Martin Security Mr. Jim hired them sight unseen." Margaret wondered in torment how many times she had pressed her knees together. Her muscles quivered with strain. "Mr. Jim and Mr. Manuel gather in the library and chortle about the old times. They're two wicked old men." Remembering who she was and who she was talking to, she hastily tacked on, "Sir."

He ignored her courtesy. "Maybe, just maybe, Uncle Manuel's slipping."

"That occurred to me, too, so I checked it out. My own contacts with the Houston Police Department insist Martin Security is the best." And she trusted her guys.

"The police report seems vague, but there's a pattern. Have there been other kidnappings in Houston?" If he'd read the report, he knew the answer.

She told him anyway. "No kidnappings, just extortion. Whoever this is, he picks his victims well. Aged or disabled members of wealthy, doting families."

"So, how long have you been trying to seduce my grandfather?"

In shock, she relaxed. Her legs sprang apart. One of the abused muscles protested in a mighty spasm. "Oh, my God." She clutched her leg in anguish.

He dropped his weights onto the bench. "Let me." He loomed over her and pushed her hands aside. With long fingers, he captured her inner thigh and began to rock it back and forth. "That's quite a cramp you have here. Can you bend your foot? Straighten your leg?"

She groaned with heartrending pain as she lifted her leg and bent her foot toward her calf.

"That's good." Dropping to his knees, he pressed his palm hard against her skin, smoothing and massaging.

The cramp fought back, spasming again.

She tried to wiggle away from the renewed agony.

"I dreamed of having you writhing beneath my hands, but not like this." His voice sounded amused.

Margaret glared right into his close, knowing eyes. "I'm not seducing your grandfather. He's ninety-two! He's partially paralyzed."

"I know. But I got your attention."

"How childish."

"Whatever it takes. I wanted to see how you'd react." He grinned when her mouth dropped open. "I learned quite a lot."

She wondered how he'd managed to live so long. "I'll bet you did."

"But it still leaves the question—why did he change his will and leave you such a large bequest?" He no longer sounded, or looked, amused.

Her spine melted onto the cushioned back. "Is that why you've been acting like a complete..." The serious set of his mouth stopped her. "It's not what you think."

"Are you not A. M. Guarneri? Did you not realize my grandfather left you a sizable sum in his will?"

"Not exactly." Now she knew why he'd pre-judged her so harshly, and she wasn't sure she wanted to clarify the situation.

"Not exactly A. M. Guarneri? Or not exactly a sizable sum?"

"I'm A. M. Guarneri, all right. While I appreciate every penny, ten thousand dollars is hardly going to keep me in furs and caviar for the rest of my life."

He snorted. "Ten thousand. Very funny. I'm willing to listen to any logical explanation, so tell me—why did Granddad leave you such a large amount of money?"

"It's quite normal, sir, for an employer to leave a sum of money for the butler." And that was the truth. She understood his concern, but she was irked to have been measured on the basis of her looks and her name.

"Fine. Look me in the eye and tell me the facts."

Her gaze faltered. Her mind worked furiously, trying to come up with an explanation that would pacify him without telling the whole truth, but time was a luxury he didn't grant her.

"Stop trying to think up those little lies." His eyes sparked. "You're obviously an amateur at the parasite game. Don't you know you're supposed to have your story ready ahead of time?"

"Next time, I'll remember," she snapped.

"Normally I'd have approached you slowly, with tact, but this business with Granddad's money has freed me from that baloney. I want you, lady, and you gotta know I'm a better deal than my grandfather."

"My leg's fine." She tried to push his hands away from the inside of her leg, but his grip changed on the now-slack muscle, to a sweep of callused fingertips on tender skin.

"I've got as much money, I'm a hell of a lot younger, and I will give you a ride you'll never forget."

Shivers slid down to her toes and up her spine to the roots of her hair. That light caress of his hand possessed more power than a bottle of Mr. Jim's best port. And that voice. Vibrant and appealing, saying words that shocked and excited her. She didn't know what to reply, so she took his wrist and pushed it away.

His long fingers tangled with hers, and he stared at their entwined hands and then into her confused gaze. He said, "Or maybe you don't care about my money or my looks or how good I am in bed, because I haven't got one foot in the grave and the other on a banana peel?"

Without volition, her other hand flew to his face—and stopped an inch from his cheek.

He hadn't moved, hadn't ducked, simply waited for the blow.

It was frightening to see him measure her reaction to his words, her reaction to her own violence. Frozen with dismay, her palm trembled from the heat of his skin, too close to an irreparable mistake.

"Go ahead," he urged in a whisper. "I'll know what you're capable of. You'll find out what I'm capable of."

Tears filled her eyes. She dropped her head, then her hand. "I'm done with the machines." Her voice sounded husky, and she cleared her throat to continue. "I have to finish my routine." Still he watched her, kneeling against her calf, and she jiggled their clasped hands until they parted. "Please? Move?"

He inched back, giving her enough room to get up off the machine —but only just enough. With the wobbly legs of a colt, she sidled one step away, and then another. It was a test, an experiment doomed to failure…but an experiment she had to try.

He let her almost get out the door. "What do you do for the rest of your workout? Swim?"

"Um. Yeah."

He said the thing she feared. "I'll go with you."

"No, you can't," she said quickly. "I swim laps."

"You really should use the pool as a cool-down after working with weights," he advised.

"Aerobic exercise is just what I need." And she thought, *You can't go, because I'll work too hard trying to show off. If you'd just go away, I could strip to my suit and take a leisurely swim.* "You'll get in my way."

He raised one eloquent eyebrow. "It's an Olympic sized pool."

Six

Reid and Margaret entered the house through the kitchen.

Margaret's face was crimson, she knew. Chlorinated water trickled into her eyes and down her back. Her plain racer's swimsuit heaved on her ribs and her cover-up stuck in wet patches. The air conditioning felt like the blessing of a god.

"I'd slow down on those laps if I were you, Margaret," Reid suggested. "Don't you know that swimming so hard after a workout isn't good for you?"

Panting, she glared at the odious man at her side. He wasn't wheezing; he wasn't broken by their half-hour uninterrupted traverse up and down across the Olympic-sized pool.

Why had she done such a foolish thing? She'd always been so scornful of otherwise intelligent women who became blithering idiots when faced with a man.

And Reid was *just* a man.

An attractive man.

Citing the already blazing Houston sun, he'd pulled on a plain white t-shirt before he leaped into the pool. What nonsense to stare at him while he stood on the checkered linoleum with the wet material etching every muscle and highlighting the suntanned skin beneath. He'd swum in his gym trunks, and they didn't cling like a second skin because they were wet.

She was relieved; she'd thought they would. And angry; she'd wanted to see.

He touched her shoulder. "Staring at my body won't answer the question. Don't you realize you could injure yourself exercising too much?"

When she thought what a fool she'd made of herself trying to keep up with him, her temper rose, drying her with a flush. She opened her mouth to blast him, to knock him off his high horse—

"What in heaven's name are you doing trying to race Mr. Reid in the water?" Abigail's voice interrupted Margaret's foolish impulse.

Margaret swung on her. Dressed in a pink silk wrap, Abigail held a plate of toast in one hand and orange juice in the other, and she stared from one to the other with incredulous eyes.

"I saw you out there, churning up the water." Abigail nodded to the window with its view of the pool. "Are you mad?"

"What are you doing up at this hour?" Margaret badly wanted to distract her friend.

"I'm hungry. Why didn't you swim like you always do?"

Desperate, Margaret protested, "You never eat so early."

"I do if I just got in, nosy." Abigail set the food on the counter and stepped over to pluck at Margaret's cover-up. "Girl, didn't you know Mr. Reid was a swimming champion in college?"

"No." Margaret stared stonily at Abigail. "I didn't."

"I bet this wretch didn't tell you." Abigail crowed and dug her elbow into Reid's ribs.

Margaret snatched her hem out of Abigail's hand and wrung it out.

Abigail turned on Reid. "Are you the one that made her swim so hard this morning?"

"No." He stared right at Margaret. "I suggested that she take it easy."

If it was possible, her face turned redder.

Abigail said, "Hmm."

Margaret turned on her heel and fled.

Reid flipped his power-red tie through its knot and studied the copy of the second note as it lay on his grandfather's desk. He paid special attention to the wording:

> *To Whom it Concerns Most Dreadfully,*
>   *Keep the knife. It's a little memento of my esteem. Old Man Donovan isn't nearly as worried as he should be. Probably because he has no one who cares for him. Or*

does he? I know there's a man who treasures his grandfather very much and who should be more than willing to cough up just a little of his cash to ensure his safety. After all, it would be sad to see such a crippled gentleman become more crippled.

I know I can thank you in advance for the sum of two million dollars. Remember, if you wait until he's taken, the amount goes up. All you have to do to get the cash to me is say that you want to. I've got ears everywhere, and I'll tell you where to put it.

"I'll tell *you* where to put it, you simpleton," Reid muttered.

This note reflected the extortionist's personality, unlike the first, more formal demand. It wasn't concise, as if the criminal had been in a hurry when he typed it. Jim Donovan wouldn't have missed this clue, Reid knew, and he bounded across the hall toward the suite of rooms at the back of the house.

He knocked at his grandfather's door and pushed it open. Stepping into the sitting room, he stopped short. From the bedroom, he heard the light laughter of a woman interspersed with Jim's gravelly voice, and he shook his head in disbelief.

No, it wasn't possible. The woman whom he had just grilled in the gym, had just swum two miles with, the woman who had almost slapped him—she could not possibly be rolling around on Jim's bed.

Reid had questioned her, harassed her, embarrassed her, and she'd responded with such poise and sincerity he'd believed every word. He'd been considering motivations—other than money—she could have for inveigling herself into Jim's affections. He'd wondered if she could possibly be as ingenuous as she appeared, and wondered more what he would do if she proved herself.

Ask for a date? Bring her flowers? Send her love letters? Hell, he'd been considering every one of those wistful courtship gestures. But now… His curiosity embarrassed him, but that didn't stop him from tiptoeing to the bedroom door and peeking around the corner.

"Dammit," he swore, disgusted with his own gullibility. "What the hell is going on here?"

Two faces, one wrinkled and overwhelmed with age, one firm and fresh and loving, turned toward him. Two different faces, one identical amazement.

"Damn," Margaret said. She slid off the bed. Her feet were bare. Tossed across the bedside chair, her black suit coat and vest gave testimony to her shame. The two ends of her black bow tie hung from her collar, and her shirt was unbuttoned: only the top two buttons, but enough to condemn her in Reid's eyes.

Jim's surprise melted beneath the blistering stare of his grandson, and he cackled with outrageous joy. "You interrupted us, boy."

"So I see." Reid weighted each word with outraged significance.

"I was dressing him." Margaret held up Jim's pants as evidence, then stuffed them behind her.

"Why?" Reid asked aggressively.

"Why? So he can be dressed. So he'll be able to leave his room." She shrugged. "That's why."

"How altruistic of you." Striding forward, he braced his hand against the bedpost. His eyes swept his grandfather, clad only in a pair of boxer shorts. "And here I thought you wanted to cover your tracks."

She sucked in a gigantic breath of air and prepared to release it as dragon's fire.

But Jim smacked the side of her arm. "Stop your jabbering and get back up here. It's already ten o'clock in the morning, and I'm not at my desk yet."

Swiveling on her heel, she stared at her employer. Cold reason returned. "Of course, sir." She located the crumpled pants, climbed onto the foot of the mattress, and held one leg of the trousers up.

He slipped his left leg in.

She grasped his right ankle—the ankle incapacitated by the stroke —and shoved it into the other leg. Grasping the waistband, she tugged it up over his knees.

Jim grunted with exertion as he tried to help her by raising his hips, but he only rolled to one side.

"I can get it, Jim," she soothed in a whisper, lifting his rear and scooting the pants up.

"I'm too big for you to handle." He chortled at his own joke, embarrassed to have his grandson observe the extent of his disabilities.

"Yeah, yeah." She settled the waistband. "I've handled you before."

"I can hear every word you're saying," Reid boomed from behind her.

She jumped and rolled her eyes.

"What can I tell you, boy?" Jim asked in a normal voice. "I'm a man, she's a woman. I'm divorced and she's a widow. I'm rich and she likes it."

"Your ass is grass and I'm the lawn mower," Margaret said in an identical tone of voice as she buttoned his waistband. "I have to zip you up, and I hold your life in my hands."

"You mean—" Jim mocked himself.

"Yes." She smiled with all her teeth. "If you don't shut up, I'm going to castrate you with the zipper."

He sighed. "I tremble. Why don't you threaten to remove something useful?"

"You could bleed to death," she assured him, "long before I call an ambulance."

"Is that how a proper English butler speaks to her employer?" Reid mocked. "Or have you progressed beyond the stage of offering respect?"

"*Simon* and I help Mr. Jim get dressed every morning." She glared at grandfather and grandson impartially. "Simon does the intimate stuff—

"My underwear," Jim interrupted.

"And I do the rest."

"Why doesn't Simon do it all?" Reid interrogated.

Looking as innocent as a wolf picking wool from his teeth, Jim said, "Because he takes all the pleasure out of it."

"Because he's young, healthy and efficient," Margaret said through her teeth. "He's so efficient Mr. Jim is exhausted by the time Simon finishes shoving him around. Clean up your dirty mind, there's nothing else to it."

Jim sighed with gusty chagrin. "Ah, darlin', if I were eighty again, you'd not be able to make that statement."

She couldn't help it. She laughed. "You're incorrigible."

Jim grinned and lapsed into silence.

She finished dressing him, aware that Reid scrutinized every move. "There," she said, sitting back on her heels. "You're done. You want to rest before I ring for Simon to get you in your chair?"

"Let my censorious grandson help me," he decided. "He ought to be good for more than glaring at us."

Reid stepped around to the bedside. "What do you want me to do?"

Margaret examined Reid bitterly. Here she sat, in compromising circumstances, without the protective armor of her butler outfit, and he—he was perfectly clad from the shoulders of his designer suit to the tips of his Italian shoes. She wondered with aggravation whether he owned casual clothes. Clothes worn not to intimidate, but clothes merely to slop around in. Was she destined to see him only in suits with the correctly knotted ties?

"Bring the wheelchair and set the brake," she told him.

Of course, he also pranced about in those brief and terrific gym shorts. Either way, he was formidable, and she acknowledged the disadvantage. Clothed, he portrayed a handsome, impressive tycoon. Unclothed, he was just a man…just a handsome, impressive man who oozed sex appeal.

Hoisting Jim up by his shoulders, she steadied him as they maneuvered him into the chair.

Reid took the full weight of his grandfather as he lowered him the last few inches. "Whew, Granddad, it's a good thing you're skinny." He wiped imaginary drops of sweat from his brow.

Jim, who had done no more than be lifted, panted and groaned and shifted. "So they tell me." Groping, he extracted a handkerchief from his shirt pocket. "I hate this uselessness. Having to be carried like a…like an old man." He smiled weakly. "If I didn't have something to think about, I'd be insane."

"I'll get your pills," Margaret said, swinging into the bathroom. She returned with a glass of water and four pills in her outstretched hand.

Jim took the water and one capsule, and shook it admonishingly at his grandson. "Don't get old."

"What's the alternative, Granddad?"

"Bound to a chair, to a schedule of medication—"

Margaret grasped the handles of the chair and pushed him toward the hall.

Reid remained where he was.

She felt his gaze burning a hole in the back of her head. She didn't care. Her responsibility was to Mr. Jim. "Feeling sorry for yourself?" she asked him.

"Being realistic. You know what happens if I don't take these pills? You know what happens?"

"What happens?" She humored him.

With outstretched finger, he pantomimed a knife slicing his throat. "I'm going to die soon anyway. Might as well improve the world while I'm here."

"Finish your pills, or you won't have the chance to improve the world," she ordered affectionately, wheeling him into the library. "Now, do you need anything else?"

"A great-grandchild. Think you can handle that?"

Seven

Margaret laughed with unthinking glee, and then glanced toward Jim's bedroom where her latest encounter with his grandson had taken place. She blushed from the tips of her toes, up. "Lord, no," she choked. "Not if that's my choice for the father."

The old man reared back, offended. "I don't see what your problem is. Reid is handsome, virile, rich—"

"I know." She squatted beside the wheelchair and stared with meaning at Jim. "I already heard that once this morning—from him. This list of his finer qualities never seems to mention humility or modesty."

Relaxing, Jim waved a dismissing hand and snorted, "Pff! A modest man would have no effect on you. Admit it, you've noticed him, haven't you?"

"Like a snake notices a mongoose." She rose and buttoned her shirt tight against her throat. "Did you remember I've got a luncheon date today?"

Jim nodded. "I remember, I remember. I'm not senile yet. Just *you* remember I don't want another man horning in on my territory."

"Oh, the date's not with a man." She smiled at him affectionately. "It's with *two* men."

"Modern women." He sighed. "Don't even know how to make a proper assignation. Why don't you take Reid so he can size up the competition?"

"No," she said precisely.

He didn't seem surprised. "How many more days until you make me a happy man?"

She chuckled. "Three more days."

"What time?" he asked.

"Ohh"—she tapped her lips with her finger—"late afternoon, if everything goes well."

"I can't wait."

"Me, either." They exchanged conspiratorial grins, then she asked, "Can I get you anything before I straighten your bedroom?"

"Nah." He rolled himself to his desk. "I can keep myself out of trouble right here."

"That'll be the day," Margaret muttered as she slipped out the door.

Stopping at the hall mirror, she tied her bow tie before entering Jim's suite of rooms.

As she feared, Reid waited for her, one hip perched on the mattress. Stern, humorless, he exuded dignified concern for his grandfather. "I want to know what's been going on here."

Margaret slid her feet into her correct black shoes and considered how to reply. She buttoned her vest and pushed her arms into the black coat.

Unable to ignore the training of a lifetime, Reid caught the collar and helped her.

"Thank you," she murmured. Reaching into the bed, she fished out the old man's pajamas and straightened the sheets.

"Are you trying to impress me with your efficiency?" he drawled. "The maids make the beds in this house."

"Not this bed, sir." Cool competence, she decided. That was her best strategy. "I make this bed. Your grandfather is uncomfortable with his occasional loss of control over his bodily functions."

"Ah." Reid thought about that and watched her tuck the blanket in tight. "I hired a nurse."

"He doesn't need a nurse—and he hated her. Not long after I obtained this position, she quit." She stared him right in the eye, challenging him.

"You take a lot on yourself," he said, irate with guilt and dismay.

"I'm the butler, sir. A trained butler hires and directs the staff, lays out the master's clothes, selects the wines, takes care of the dogs, packs for trips, approves the menu, pays the bills, does the marketing. In return, a trained butler gets a good salary, a two-bedroom apartment in the main house, and insurance benefits." She paused delicately. "Mr.

Jim has been, er, subtly inquiring about my preference in cars. For Christmas, I assume."

Reid nodded. "That sounds like him."

"Now, Mr. Jim doesn't have dogs, he doesn't take many trips, he doesn't eat much, can't drink wine, and his staff is so devoted to him, supervision is minimal. An accounting firm takes care of the bills. But my job is to keep the master happy, and if caring for Mr. Jim with my own hands is what it takes, I'll do it." She turned away as if that settled the subject. She finished the bed. Reid no longer seemed hostile, she decided; reflective and calm, as if he weighed her words and intentions against her actions and awaited the result of his computations.

"What if he gets seriously ill?" Reid asked.

"I'm approved by the Red Cross in first aid and CPR, and at the first sign of trouble I'll call an ambulance. I can dial a telephone as efficiently as a nurse." Her voice contained not a hint of sarcasm.

He heard it anyway. "What makes you so much more desirable than…what was her name?"

"Mrs. Adams." She wondered if his choice of words was deliberate, and concluded it was.

"That's it. What makes you a more desirable companion?"

"Mr. Donovan." Crossing her arms across her chest, Margaret looked stern. "Your grandfather is ninety-two years old, but he is a sharp old devil—sharper than most men of thirty-eight."

Reid's barracuda's grin told her he'd understood.

"He's moved mountains in his time, been a potentate of the business world—and he resents being told, *It's time to take our bath, now.*" Margaret's imitation of the nurse was deadly, complete with a singsong voice that rose an octave.

Reid winced.

"Mr. Jim can be led and cajoled, but he cannot be forced." Margaret bared her teeth in remembered fury. "Mrs. Adams almost brought on another stroke with her heavy-handed administration."

"So you fired her."

"Certainly not." She placed her hand on her chest and drew back. "When the grandson of the master hires an attendant, the butler hasn't the power to fire her."

"You made it so uncomfortable, she didn't want to stay."

In Margaret's heart, the first stirrings of apprehension changed the tenor of her breathing.

Reid seemed so nonchalant, one hand in his pocket, the other grasping the bedpost, and he examined the carpet beneath his shoe intently. His pose reminded her of a movie she had seen when she was young and impressionable; a movie that still haunted her nightmares. In the scene that terrified her, the villain stood with his head bowed before the cocky heroine until that moment when he raised his eyes—and they glowed red.

But when Reid raised his eyes, they were not dyed with hell's fires. They were cold as the moon afloat in the bleak night sky. He said, "Think about it. If the butler can make life so distasteful, a nurse flees, how can the grandson of the master influence the butler's decision to seek a new position?"

Chilled to the bone, she rubbed her hands up and down her arms. "Are you threatening me?"

"I don't make threats. If I choose to make *you* uncomfortable, you'll go."

A spurt of anger warmed her temporarily. "Mr. Jim—"

"Would you involve my grandfather in our quarrel?"

"I…no." Her anger faded. "No, if we can't work together, I'll not involve Mr. Jim. But if you force me to leave, it will hurt him."

His smile was a mere curl of his mouth. "Why do you think I'm going to let you remain?"

Eight

"You're right, Jim, the boy *is* looking a little poorly." Manuel Alcadio Quesada Vargas puffed on his pipe and stared at Reid from mellow brown eyes. "Do you suppose it's our weather?"

"Nah." Jim jerked a sheet of paper out of the box and crumpled it up. "He was born here. He's tough."

"Spent too much time away from Houston. Look closely at him. His neck's hardly red at all." Manuel blew a stream of smoke high into the air.

There, surrounded by piles of paper, Reid worked on his laptop.

"It's not the weather." Jim lobbed the paper ball toward the trash can and missed, and pulled another sheet out of the box.

"Maybe he hasn't kept up with his southern fried chicken."

"Believe me, he has," Jim said with heartfelt sincerity.

Manuel puffed until the smoke circled his chin like a Santa Claus beard. "Only one other thing could make a big, strong man like Reid look so feeble, but I don't rightly believe it."

"Believe it."

"You can't tell me it's women."

"I can, too."

"Women have Reid on the run?"

"Woman," Jim corrected. "One woman. You know what he's doing now?"

Reid raised his head at last. "Perhaps my green expression results from that tobacco you insist on smoking." He adjusted a miniature desk fan around so it blew toward Manuel.

The old men ignored him as if he were an insignificant gnat.

"What's he doing now?" Manuel asked in deep fascination.

Reid leaned down and scooped paper projectiles into the trash. "Or maybe it's the mess around my desk that's distracting me."

Jim tossed another ball toward the can. "He has dressed me every morning for the past three days."

"Oh, my." Manuel's eyes sharpened as he examined his godson. "Well, the family that dresses together…"

"Confesses together." Reid glared at his grandfather.

"The boy doesn't do nearly the job Simon and Margaret did," Jim said. "They were a hell of a lot more fun. *She* was a hell of a lot more fun."

"I can imagine." Manuel nodded sagely. "What else is he doing?"

"Brooding."

"Brooding?" Manuel's eyebrows shot up, almost onto his shiny pate. "You mean like sighing and languishing?"

"Nah. Women sigh and languish. Men ponder and endure." Jim nodded solemnly.

"Fascinating case study." Manuel scratched the back of his head. "What's Miz Margaret up to these days?"

"Sighing and—"

Irritated, Reid interrupted. "Since when is the butler called *Miz*? All the butlers I've ever met are called by their last names."

"Ha!" Manuel snorted, replying to Reid at last. "You wanna call the butler *Guarneri*? It sounds like what you say when somebody sneezes."

"Ah-choo!" Jim said.

"Guarneri!" Manuel replied.

Reid stood. "If you want to spend your time babbling about the sexy blond sweetheart who happens to be our butler — "

Jim smirked. "She's a widow, a respectable one, and she'd make you a fine wife."

"Wife?"

"You two would make beautiful babies for me to hold. I'm not getting any younger, so you need to get with it pretty soon. Come to think of it" — Jim stroked his chin — "*you're* not getting any younger, either."

"What is this, some little plan you and she cooked up to trap me?" The thought of the butler plotting his downfall irritated the hell out of Reid.

"No, no, Margaret hates the idea. I suggested it after she'd had a chance to look you over." Jim folded his fingers together over his skinny belly. "She laughed and refused."

"She laughed?" For some reason, that thought made Reid angrier, and he paced toward the window and stared into the garden, rife with afternoon shadows.

"I believe she compared you to a snake," Jim offered.

"That little—" Reid turned, observed the gleeful smile on his grandfather's face, and sighed with exaggerated patience. "All right, you old codgers. You win. I needed a break, anyway. I'm going to the kitchen to con a snack out of Abigail. *She* still likes me."

"The boy got an inferiority complex?" Manuel wondered. "Nobody likes him?"

"Oh, I like him." Jim gave up his basketball game and started shredding the paper. "And you like him."

Manuel nodded.

"But now, Margaret...I don't know if Margaret likes him."

Reid strode to the door, but he didn't bolt fast enough.

"No, sirree," Jim drawled. "Like isn't nearly strong enough a word for what Margaret feels for him, or he for her. Why, when they're in the room together, the attraction gathers so thick, I get aroused purely from the emanations."

Manuel choked on a puff of cigar.

Reid halted in the hall, waiting to see if the old man recovered.

In a rasping voice, Manuel gasped, "I better stick around, then. I can use all the help I can get."

"Woo-ee," Abigail whistled. "Don't you look nice!"

Margaret whirled in a circle, her ice green jacket hooked over her shoulder by one finger, a la Frank Sinatra. Her matching skirt clung close to her thighs, and her kelly green shirt accented the suit with a touch of wild color. "Will I do?"

"You sure will. You think those shoes are high enough?"

Margaret stuck out one three-inch heel and examined it. "I'm only five foot ten. I have to take care, or I'll be overlooked."

"I'll remember that." The diminutive cook grinned.

Margaret moved to Abigail's side and rubbed up and down against her arm, like a cat scratching its back. "What do you think of this?"

"Silk?"

"All the way."

"Well, that shade sure looks pretty with that white hair of yours loose all over your shoulders. You want to borrow my nail polish?" Abigail lifted one hand out of a ceramic bowl. Drops of some ominous clear liquid dribbled off the frosted white fingernails and onto the eating bar.

"No. What's in there?" Margaret peered into the bowl. "Ice cubes?"

"Sure. If you really want to set your polish, you dip your nails in cold water."

Snapping her fingers, Margaret said, "I remember. I did that once, and all I got was ripple marks on the polish."

"You've got a lot of class, Guarneri." Drying her hands on a towel, Abigail leaned back in her bar stool and grinned. "So today's the big day. Excited?"

"Excited? Me?" Margaret assumed a debutante slouch, then threw her arms in the air and whooped. Pulling Abigail up, she whirled around the floor with her, humming the Tennessee Waltz.

Abigail laughed until her breath caught, complaining, "Why don't I ever get to lead?"

A rough male voice invited, "You can, if you dance with me."

The ladies spun around.

Reid stood propped against the doorjamb, an insolent grin on his face and a smoldering passion in his eyes as he examined Margaret's outfit. He noticed it was silk, he noticed the green flattered her coloring. More than that, he noticed the split up the back of the tight skirt and the above-the-knee cut that looked so devastating with her long, slender legs. He noticed—and resented—the catch in his breath at the sight of her Slavic cheekbones and blue, blue eyes.

He resented the touch of caution underlying her swiftly smothered desire.

"Very pretty," he said. "Going somewhere?"

She slipped into her jacket, looking down at her hands as she buttoned each button.

It hid the thrust of her breasts against the fine silk of the blouse, and he resented that, too. "Well?"

"I have to go out for a few hours," she said softly, "Sir."

She didn't want to tell him where, he noted. She had the nerve to believe it was none of his business. "It's not possible. I need you in the study."

"I cleared it with Mr. Donovan weeks ago."

He hated when she sounded clear and cold, and used logic against him. "Will you be back in time to direct the serving of the evening meal?"

"No, but the staff is well trained."

"This must be very important."

"Yes."

He paused, giving her a chance to expand.

But the lady had ice in her veins.

He directed the blowtorch of his personality toward her. "Did you forget that little matter we discussed last week?"

Margaret's eyes frosted until they were cold blue. "About the nurse?"

"Exactly," he purred.

"Oh, I remember." She sauntered over to the shoulder bag flung on the floor. "It's simply of no concern to me."

The blowtorch heated to a mild red. "No concern? Is unemployment of concern to you?"

"As a social issue, yes. Regarding myself, I don't foresee unemployment in my future. May I go now, sir?" She turned on her heel and walked away from him, heading for the back door of the kitchen.

With a bound, Reid stood beside her, jerking her around to face him. "Don't turn your back on me," he ordered.

"Let go of my arm."

With slow deliberation, he grasped her other elbow and turned her to face him. "If you leave now, don't come back."

"Mr. Donovan hired me," she said. "Mr. Donovan will fire me."

"Yes." He released her. "He will."

They stared at each other intensely, one cold as the Arctic seas, one hot as the volcanoes beneath them.

In simultaneous motion, they nodded curtly and strode in different directions: Margaret to the car that would drive her to the airport, Reid to the library.

Abigail stood in the middle of the kitchen floor where they left her, rubbing her arms and smiling. To the assembled pots hanging above the stove, she said, "This woman gets in a room with those two, and it fairly warms my female parts. I wonder what that big hunk of a bodyguard is doing tonight?"

Nine

"Did you bring her?" Jim called. "Did you bring my girlfriend home?"

An ebullient child of nine years danced through the doors of the library. "I'm here, Sir Gramps." She headed right for Jim's open arms. "I missed you."

Standing against the fireplace, Reid stared at the tanned little girl wrapped around his grandfather. Her short black hair curled with wild abandon, her black eyes snapped with vitality. She hopped on one foot as she squeezed him, too excited to stand still.

His grandfather trembled from pleasure, and his faded eyes teared as he held her. Then he pushed her away. "Go on and kiss your Uncle Manuel before he busts a gut."

"That's right, what am I, chopped liver?" Manuel braced himself for her titanic hug.

Jim dabbed his eyes.

"Chopped enchiladas," the girl said.

They laughed, comfortable with the banter.

"Stand up now," Jim instructed. "Let me introduce you."

The child straightened, clasped her hands in front of her, and observed Reid with composure.

Taken aback by the forthright stare of such a young girl, Reid held out his hand.

"Reid, this is Amy Guarneri," Mr. Jim said. "Amy, my grandson, Reid Donovan."

Amy grasped the offered palm and shook it firmly. "How do you do, Mr. Donovan?"

From Amy, it was more than a polite phrase. It was a sincere inquiry of concern backed by a solid guaranty of curiosity.

"Later, Amy," Margaret's gentle voice broke the child's intense concentration. "You can cross-examine Mr. Donovan later."

For the first time, Reid's gaze was drawn to Margaret.

She stood framed by the doorway. The three hours since she stormed out of the kitchen had changed her. No longer the proper butler or the hostile woman, she seemed strangely softened. The jacket had vanished, the tie on her blouse dangled. Her skirt was shifted a quarter turn so a side seam ran down the front, and the slit opened at the side. She held her shoes in her hand and smoothed the loose hair off her forehead.

She was, for the first time since he met her, totally unselfconscious in his presence.

At last, Reid's brain began to perk. "Amy Guarneri," he mused aloud. "Amy *Margaret* Guarneri?"

"Not Margaret," Amy corrected. "Margot. My mother's name is Amelia Margaret—see? They sound alike, but we each have our very own name."

"Doesn't anyone ever get mixed up?" Reid asked.

"Oh, no. Only a dummy would mix those two names up," she assured him.

He nodded slowly in agreement. "Only a dummy." He looked up at Margaret, but she wasn't smirking—which spoke volumes for her control. If anything, her eyes held the sympathy of a fellow diner on hasty words.

Their gaze lingered until Jim chuckled and said, "You look done in, Margaret. Was the plane late?"

"I wouldn't look done in if it had been late," Margaret said wryly. She nodded at Amy. "It's chasing after *that* monkey that did it."

"Mah-om!" Amy clarified their relationship, the relationship Reid could hardly comprehend. "I'm not a monkey."

"No, but you certainly have more energy than I've ever had." Margaret limped into the library and sank into an easy chair on one side of the fireplace. Dropping her high heels on the floor, she declared, "I should have worn running shoes."

"Ah, Mom!" Amy launched herself into her mother's lap. "Aren't you glad I'm back?"

In an excess of silliness, Margaret leaned her back and smooched her neck. "Yes, I'm glad you're back," she said, grinning at her squealing daughter. "Yes, I missed you. Yes, I can hardly wait for you to go back to school…next week!"

Amy made a face and kissed her, hugged her and hopped up.

The two buttons at Margaret's bosom dangled loose.

"Amy, what did you do in California?" Jim asked.

"Heather and I—"

"Heather's her cousin, eight years old," Margaret informed them.

"Yeah, my cousin. She's my"—Amy screwed up her face in concentration—"my father's sister's daughter. She and I played a lot. The best thing we did was play a trick on Grandpa." She giggled and danced a little jig. "You know that green shaving gel? You know how really slick it is? We put some on the doorknob of the shed and Grandpa grabbed it and thought it was—"

"Oh, Amy," Margaret said with horror.

"But that's not the good part." Amy charged on. "The good part came the next day when we flipped Grandpa for the last two Moon Pies. You know what he did? You know what he *did*?"

"Tell us what he did," Jim invited, his wrinkled mouth twitching at the corners.

"He used a two-headed coin, so he knew we'd win and when we bit into the Moon Pies they were filled with shaving cream." Amy grimaced in remembrance.

The adults burst into laughter.

"Mine was aloe vera." The grimace twisted tighter. "Heather's was *Old Spice*."

The adults laughed harder.

Amy began to giggle again. "Isn't that funny?"

Reid leaned over Margaret's shoulder. "How does she giggle and talk at the same time?"

She turned her festive, shiny face to his. "It's a preadolescent trait," she assured him. "She's priming herself for puberty."

"How do you keep up with her?" he asked.

"I don't. Look at her." Margaret stared at her daughter with a mushy smile. "If she were a puppy, her tail would be wagging."

Reid stepped back and considered the butler.

Things had changed now. Margaret had changed, he had changed, the situation had changed.

His suspicion of her part in the kidnapping scheme was largely unfounded.

Her relationship to his grandfather was obviously a myth, developed by Jim Donovan for the pleasure of watching his grandson jump to conclusions.

The mixture of skepticism and anger had added to Reid's desire, and no qualm had undermined his plan to ravish this villainess.

If the relationship between the butler and the master's grandson was to ripen to something more, he would have to think, and think hard, about the ramifications of consorting with a working widow with a child. A working widow with a child and his matchmaking grandfather's goodwill.

A working widow who could very easily command Reid's heart with her combination of fire and ice, duty and spirit.

Was he willing to take the chance of being trapped? Or was the shoe on the other foot? Would he have to trap her?

He wasn't a fool; there might be an attraction humming between the two of them, but Margaret wouldn't have him if he was presented on a silver platter. He'd have to work and scheme and cajole to get her. A smile lifted one side of his mouth, but it disappeared at his next thought. —

He'd have to put his whole life into keeping her.

"Excuse me." Reid straightened from his slouch beside her chair. "I have work to do."

He smiled on them impartially and strode out the door, leaving three adults and one child staring after him, and a huge pile of papers on the desk.

Ten

"In the dark again?"

Reid's voice should have surprised Margaret, but it didn't. He lingered in her mind like bubbling yeast, sometimes overpowering and sometimes barely noticed, but always there.

Margaret kicked and recovered, kicked and recovered. The loose fitting white pants and wrap shirt of the martial arts, the *gi*, were damp from her efforts. Her hair was once again plaited into a single braid. "Is there hidden meaning in that comment?"

"Not at all." Reid stepped into her peripheral vision, off to the side of the mat where she practiced her repetitious exercises. "But it's early, and it's almost dark here in the gym."

"I don't need the lights for this kind of workout," she puffed, her bare feet lashing in the cutting kick.

He stepped in front of her, an indistinct shadow of male essence silhouetted against the dim windows. "I came to apologize."

Margaret planted both feet firmly on the mat. "Sir?"

"For my assumptions."

"I wish you wouldn't."

"Why?"

"Because it's easier to dislike you when you're an unjust boor," she said frankly.

He chuckled, a low chuckle of amusement and relief. "All the more reason to apologize. I don't want you to dislike me. That's too paltry an emotion for us."

"Paltry emotions are fine. They're safe and clean and uncomplicated."

"Ah." Pacing away from her and then back, he offered, "My apologies, nevertheless. For making assumptions about you, and for ignoring your protestations—weak though they were. I had no reason to believe my grandfather's bequest was anything but his own doing."

"He loves Amy, and she loves him. He fills a void in her life, that need she has for an ever-present male." Margaret shrugged with sheepish embarrassment. "So he wanted to leave her something. I told him no, and he said half a million, and I said no, and he said one hundred thousand, and I said no, and he said ten thousand, and I said fine. I really should have told you who the bequest was for as soon as you accused me, but I thought you'd be suspicious until you met Amy."

"Amy *does* vanquish suspicion. You held him to ten thousand, huh? Ten thousand?" She nodded, and he laughed and shook his head. "So that's what he told you. Ten thousand. That old coot. Hardly enough money to have him kidnapped for." Holding up his hand, he stopped her comment. "I don't normally blunder into situations without formulating the facts in a logical manner. The only excuse I need to present you is the obvious one—that I was worried about my grandfather. But there is more to it than that. I wanted you."

Margaret sank into an unrehearsed knee bend.

"I wanted you, and a cold-blooded seduction seemed less despicable if you were a wanton bitch pushing Granddad toward a stroke."

She straightened up hopefully. "Does this mean the seduction is out?"

He chuckled again, another low, warm chuckle. "No, it means the *cold-blooded* is out."

Resigned to weakened joints, she began a series of knee bends.

"I'm not proud of persecuting a woman for no more good reason than unfounded suspicion and well-founded desire. Excuses are unacceptable, in my employees and certainly in myself. You can calculate your effect on me by the lies I was willing to tell myself." The brightening morning ignited behind him, and she could discern the shape of his body clad in slacks and a shirt. "Do you accept my apologies?"

Shadow hid his cool gambler's features, and she couldn't help presuming a deliberate maneuver on his part. He frightened her more now than he ever had. Any man who could examine his own motivations with such cool clarity required careful handling.

"I have to apologize, too, sir." She paused in her workout. "I lost my temper yesterday in the kitchen—something I haven't done in years. I deliberately provoked you."

"Why do you suppose you did that?" His voice echoed smooth and comforting, like a psychiatrist guiding a patient.

"I don't know," she said sharply, her trepidation gone in a blast of temper. "You're the brains here. You tell me."

But he didn't. He looked around. "Where's Amy?"

"She's off to SplashTown with Sophia, her bestest friend in the world."

"I remember those days. In the week before school starts, you have to play hard to get in all the fun you won't have during classes."

"Yes. Tomorrow night we go to school and meet her teacher, and buy her supplies from the PTA. The rest of the week is more play and although she doesn't care, she has to have new shoes. Her feet are growing so fast…" And why was Margaret telling him about her daughter's feet? Reid Donovan was a playboy billionaire. He didn't care about Amy and her growth spurt.

But he nodded. "I know what you mean. One summer, my feet grew three sizes." He watched her, then asked in a tone that indicated only a slight interest, "Are those karate exercises?"

She wasn't fooled. "A little judo, a little aikido, a little karate. My martial arts master teaches me whatever he thinks I can handle."

"What do you do it for?"

"Sir, I'm a butler for a very wealthy man. It behooves me to be able to protect your grandfather—and myself—should the situation arise. For chauffeurs and body servants of every type, there are special schools that teach methods of defending the master against trouble." She was patient. Deliberate. *Irritated.*

"Wouldn't it be easier to run and leave the master, as you call him, in trouble?" Reid asked.

She didn't blame him for his cynicism, but she'd learned the lessons at that special school very well. "To most kidnappers and extortionists, the servants are unimportant encumbrances to be disposed of without thought. If I fail to properly care for Mr. Jim, it's likely I'll be the first victim."

He frowned. "Granddad wouldn't ask you to give your life for him."

"That's why I work to do my best to stay alive. I assess everyone who comes on the grounds. I personally check in any deliveries, and if the delivery is made by someone new, I use a portable metal detector on them."

Reid shrugged out of his shirt and hung it on the stationary bicycle. "What would you do if you found a greedy anarchist prowling around?"

"I'd call in reinforcements. All of the staff are at least slightly trained in fighting, and they're strictly trained in how to call the police."

"What if he comes on you while you're alone?"

The thought made her tense. "He'd better be a better fighter than I am."

"Isn't that likely?" Reid's belt swooshed out of his belt loops. Margaret suddenly remembered that she was here to train. One fist against her chest, one fist outstretched, she switched hands in a lunging punch. Left, right, left, right: ignore, the man, without, the clothes. "Only too likely. That's why I practice."

"When do you take lessons?"

"During the school year. I simply work to remain in shape during the summer months."

"Do you fight in your classes?" He clenched one fist, watching as the cords of his wrists tightened. "Bouts with your classmates? Your teacher?"

"Of course." The rasp of his zipper echoed loudly in the room.

Okay. Enough was enough. Margaret snapped, "What in the hell are you doing?"

"I have a little martial arts training." He flung his pants after his other apparel and stood in his shorts and socks.

Most men would look stupid.

He looked like the man she wanted standing in her bedroom.

"I wouldn't mind a bout," he said, and before Margaret could refuse, he quickly added, "If you don't mind dealing with amateurs."

"Of course not, but—"

"Think of the chance to beat up the boss's kid," he suggested.

"Very tempting, but—"

"Or are you afraid I will flatten you?"

No, she wasn't afraid he would flatten her. She was good, and she knew it. For a woman who hadn't begun training until her thirties, she was remarkable. But she didn't trust this sneaky, conniving bastard.

"I bet I can beat you," he teased. "Bet you a hundred bucks."

"A hundred? You must think well of your fighting," she answered, wrestling with her conscience.

He rummaged in the supply closet and pulled out a *gi*. Shaking out the crumpled white pants, he slipped them on and flung the jacket back onto a shelf. "I left these last time I had a lesson here. Must be two years. So what do you say?"

"All right." She drawled it reluctantly, almost sure she could beat him and almost sure she could afford the hundred dollars if she didn't. "Am I being hustled?"

He spread his hands in appeal. "There's only one way to find out." With cool determination, he strode over and turned on the fluorescent lights.

Eleven

By the end of the second bout, Margaret believed Reid had *wanted* to hustle her. He worked so hard, feigning and kicking, but he didn't have enough varied fighting techniques.

He was good, she gave him that. He had almost beaten her the last time, until a brilliant defense on her part had opened the way to an equally brilliant offense, and she flattened him with a right reverse punch. It was as satisfying as he had promised.

Extending her hand, she pulled him to his feet. "Good job. I thought you had me that time." She could afford to be gracious in victory.

"Yeah." He put his hands on his knees and puffed. "The agony of defeat. The ashes of embarrassment. But I still think I could have you, now that I know your technique."

"I know yours, too," she pointed out.

"Yeah, but you have one big hole in your defense." His palms touched flat on the floor as he bobbed down and then placed his hands on his knees again.

"Come on. You're just a sore loser. A hundred dollars for the first bout, two hundred for the second." She stretched her fingertips up high.

His shoulders slumped as he stared at the mat. "One more bout."

"I've already beaten you twice."

"Just one more."

"No!"

"One more, and we'll make it interesting." His head was still bent, not looking at her.

"How?" she asked, in spite of the good sense that urged her to quit.

"We could bet something we both really want this time."

Warning bells chimed in her brain, but her surging adrenaline ignored them. "Like what?"

"What do you want more than anything in the world?"

"Stability." He glanced up, measuring her sincerity against her answer. He was interested—more than interested, fascinated.

She shifted, and wished she had considered before she replied.

To her relief, he only said, "You have it. You'll run this house as long as it stands. That's what you *need*. But what do you *want*? Summers off? A sailboat? A guaranteed college education at Harvard for your daughter?"

Her quick inhalation told him what he wanted to know.

"That's it? The college education? Okay, you fight for the education. I'll pay for four years and make sure she gets in. You know you can trust me to do it."

That was true, she realized. She could trust him: she *did* trust him, but... "What do you get if you win?" she asked suspiciously.

His gaze was on the mat again. "You."

"Oh, no." She laughed and stepped back. "We're not going to play that game."

"You don't mean you think...?" He glanced around with every appearance of shock. "No! I need someone to go with me to look at houses."

"At houses?" She vacillated between embarrassment and disbelief. "Why are you looking at houses?"

"Why does a grown man look at houses?" he asked reasonably.

"To buy?"

"Yes." He drew it out as if he couldn't comprehend her disbelief. "To live in? For investment?"

"That's it," he agreed.

"The Houston market's insane right now," she said, still doubtful about his motives.

He rubbed his eyes with elaborate weariness. "Buy low, sell high. Some free real estate advice for you."

"Thanks." She watched him closely as she spelled out, "The terms are these. If I win, Amy gets a Harvard education. If you win, I help you find a house—or houses? Is this a trick to make me spend time with you?"

"Suspicious, aren't you?" he chided. "No, it's no *trick*. Let's forget another match, shall we? My wallet can bear a three-hundred-dollar loss."

So it *had* been a clumsy male contrivance, an attempt to keep her close by his side. It embarrassed him, and she couldn't help teasing, "I thought it was your ego you were concerned about."

He winced. "Never mind. Forget the match. I'm tired, and so are you."

Her audacity flared to life. "You were so sure you could win."

"I could." He didn't sound as if he meant it.

"Remember the hole in my defense?" she taunted. "Remember how you know my techniques? One more match. To see who's the champion of the world."

"Well," he said grudgingly. "Okay." He lifted his hand from his knee and grasped hers to shake it. From his downcast position rose the phoenix. He shed exhaustion like a snake's skin. He stood straight up, his body sparkling with vitality. His sherry brown eyes shone alert and satisfied. His bright, even teeth flashed in a smile that sent chills up her spine.

Twelve

She'd been suckered.

"Match refused," Margaret said.

"No." Reid stepped back and bent in the standing bow.

Automatically Margaret returned the *rei*.

"I'm not letting you chicken out now," he said.

"I'm not chickening out. I'm getting smart."

He dropped into the right back stance. "Fight or don't fight. The bet stands."

She barely ducked his high blow, defending herself with a return punch. The bout developed rapidly, moved smoothly, pushed her to the limit. She had no more breath with which to protest. She still attacked with finesse, she still parried spontaneously.

But Reid dealt with her with heated efficiency.

This was no longer sparring. This was fighting.

The end arrived in only moments. Reid dropped to the floor and knocked her leg out from under her. In a series of moves she had never seen before, he had her pinned, helpless beneath the male body that swarmed over her, surrounded her, settled on her. He held her wrists above her head.

Her heart pounded. Adrenaline raced through her veins. "What was *that* move?" she demanded.

"Break-dancing," he said with smug satisfaction. "My master in New York advises putting an element of surprise in the arts."

"Sandbagger." She tugged at her wrists.

"Not at all." He grinned at her, nose to nose. "I saved myself for the championship bout. Every strategist knows that."

"You didn't know we'd have a championship bout," she objected.

"Yes, I knew. Sooner or later, I knew we'd have one."

"Who's your master in New York?" she asked suspiciously.

He named a well-known champion, adding, "Servants of rich men aren't the only ones who take special training. If possible, the men themselves take the training. It's so much better than having to rely on others for defense."

"Naturally," she said in disgust. "You wouldn't like having to depend on someone else."

"I wouldn't want someone else to give up their life for me." Leaning closer, he whispered, "Especially not someone as attractive as you."

His breath fanned her face. He overwhelmed her with himself.

She didn't like that. "Let me go."

"Of course." He immediately released his grip.

She brought her hands up to his chest. The shock of his flesh against her hands made her sputter like a Victorian maiden. "Now get off me."

"Of course," he agreed again. But this time his obedience wasn't so prompt. Showing off with the sizzle of an adolescent, he let her feel his weight; feel, too, the excitement she engendered in him.

Furious, dismayed, and unwillingly exhilarated, she made her second stupid mistake of the day. Stiffening her body, wiping all expression from her face, calling on every ounce of her butler-stuffiness, she said, "Please get off me, sir. This isn't proper."

She saw his flare of anger, heard his leonine growl.

She had provoked him. She had known she would. She had known she would pay the price. But wildness in her exalted at the thought of defying him, and when his fingers snagged her chin, she jutted it toward him and stared right into his eyes.

He was not impressed. "Don't play games with me."

"*You*—don't threaten me."

"Don't turn away from me."

Of course, she did so at once.

His voice was a low purr in her ear. "Don't turn away from me. Not with your body, not with your mind. I have ways to make you pay attention that aren't as pleasant as this." Laying his head into the curve of her neck, he kissed her. His recently shaved chin was a soft burr against her skin.

She turned back to him.

Their mouths met; he pressed them together.

She kept her lips tightly closed.

Their noses touched, tip to tip, and his eloquent eyes stared into hers, communicating his amusement. Lifting his head, he ordered, "Breathe."

She sucked in air.

"Good, now open." He put his head down to hers once more. His lips fed velvet coercion to her mouth, brushing and urging until he passed the threshold of her teeth and submerged his tongue.

He tasted delicious, like melted hot fudge, rich and smooth and delicious.

Margaret hadn't realized it, but she was starved for sweetness.

He chuckled at her awkward eagerness. Raising himself, he untied the belt and the ties of her jacket and spread it apart. Her exercise bra bound her breasts, but the chill of the air conditioner made her nipples poke at the sweat-dampened material. He watched with fascination as her chest rose and fell under the twin demands for oxygen and composure. When he raised his eyes, they resembled melted pools of heated sherry.

The odor of a healthy man assailed her nostrils, the cool mat warmed beneath her, the firm padding laid her before him like a feast. "You can't mean to do—*this*," she whispered hoarsely.

"This?" he teased. "What do you mean—*this*?"

She ignored his nonsense. "You'd be forcing me."

"If we had sex right here and now, you mean?"

The phrase was coolly professional, the kind of wording a psychologist would use. Yet it was explicit, too, and raised images in her brain, sketches easily filled by her impressions of him, and his kiss, and their fight. She knew how his body worked. She knew how rhythmically he moved. She knew his hips were narrow, his shoulders broad.

She knew he was not only capable of an erection, but that resting here against her had given him one that flattered, enticed and infuriated.

"No sex," he agreed, "for your mind isn't ready. Although your body has been ready since we met." He smiled with all his teeth. "Hasn't it?"

How did he know? How did he know about the damp that wet her thighs, about the frustrated longing to climax with the mere application of his tongue?

He leaned back. "You have bruises on your ribs," he muttered, his voice husky with regret. "I apologize. I thought my control was better than that."

"You have bruises, too. I'm sorry." Although she shouldn't be. She should have kicked him harder, longer, more boldly. If she had realized how skillfully he had fooled her, she would have really hurt him...her fingertips lightly brushed purple mottled marks on his chest, then traveled the smooth flow of ribs that led toward his waist.

Sexual heat had dried the sweat on his skin, leaving him warm and dry and...*warm.*

He didn't move. He didn't breathe.

He was far too easy to touch.

Yet his eyes were bold as lions, speaking in silence of his delight.

She took her hands away. "Sorry," she muttered again.

"Don't apologize," he said. "And don't stop."

She flushed from the tips of her rosy breasts to the top of her ears. Her eyelids drooped, her nostrils quivered with every breath.

"Coward," he whispered. The sight of her nourished him: her white-blonde hair bound in a short braid, her bright blue eyes, her fair Nordic skin. His gaze lingered on her face and traced her generous lips. She glowed with exertion and arousal, and the sensations and the scents made him want to take her, claim her, bind her to him in every way he could.

Unselfconsciously, she lifted her fingers to her mouth and with a flick of her tongue, she tasted them. Her eyes widened in surprise.

That fine body had lost the stiffness of dignity and the vigor of combat, and it was soft, pliant, feminine. She looked similar to the way she had when Amy ran her through the wringer and transformed her into a mother.

He'd done the same thing, seeking different results; he'd transformed her into a lover. No longer the proper butler, no longer the aggressive fighter, she looked like a woman.

His lips curved with devilish pleasure. He liked this feeling of power. Margaret was so self-contained, so marvelously reserved, and now she trembled in his hands like a tender leaf in the wind. Pulled by the lips parted so sweetly, he kissed her again, in promise, then stood and pulled her to her feet.

She floundered, unbalanced by passion, missing her social graces and her suitable role.

"I've watched you, Margaret. You and I are tuned to each other's thoughts, to each other's motivations and ambitions. My grandfather and I are like that—always on the same wavelength, speaking without words. Some of my top men are like that. But I have never met a woman who could manipulate me. You're the first."

"I am not honored." Pulling her jacket together, she fumbled for the ties. "And I don't want to be on your wavelength."

"I know you don't."

Outside the room, they heard someone running down the stairs.

Reid ignored the sound. "I don't like having you inside my mind, either, but sometimes fate — "

Someone hit the door. Someone tried the knob.

"Reid?" Nagumbi's voice. He sounded grim.

Quickly, Reid turned her to face him and brushed her hands aside. Leaning down, he picked up her belt, wrapped it around her waist and knotted it.

"The door's locked!" she said. "How did it get locked?"

"I locked it. Nagumbi picks locks."

"Get the door," she said, struggling to take control of her clothing.

Reid shook his head. "He wouldn't interrupt us if it weren't—"

"Reid?" Nagumbi's voice sounded again.

"—Important. And I'll not have anyone looking at you." Raising his voice, Reid called, "Coming." He twitched at her top until it was arranged to his satisfaction, and raised his rapier gaze to her face. He saw it all—distress, embarrassment, worry—and he touched her cheek. Walking toward the door, he reached it as the knob began to turn. He yanked it open.

Nagumbi's bland voice sounded a knell of doom. "Your grandfather has been kidnapped."

Thirteen

Reid snapped the door wide, slamming it against the wall. In contrast to his display of temper, his voice was firm and quiet. "How did that happen?"

Margaret moved to the door, and mixed with her dignity was a new element of determination, resolve and fury. "How long has he been gone?"

"I just got a call from the police." Nagumbi answered her as if she had the right to know. "He was taken thirty-two minutes ago at the Romania Bakery."

"It's one of his favorite's." She nodded for him to continue.

"The police are hot on Mr. Donovan's trail. They expect a break right away." Having given the essentials, Nagumbi turned and started back up the stairs.

Reid went to his pants, rummaged in the pocket.

"What do you need, sir?" she asked.

"My goddamned phone." He glanced up. "Must be in my suit jacket." Hopping on one foot, then the other, he put his pants on as he headed up to the first floor.

Margaret grabbed his shirt and followed.

They caught up with Nagumbi in the kitchen.

Reid took his shirt, and took the lead. "Who nabbed him?"

"Two men," Nagumbi said, "their faces concealed by ski masks."

They swept past Abigail, who stood worried and wide-eyed, and headed for the main part of the house.

"Where was the chauffeur?" Margaret asked.

Nagumbi said, "I wasn't given a complete answer to that question."

"What do you mean?" Margaret tugged at his sleeve.

Nagumbi stopped and faced her.

Her hand fell away under his intense stare, but she insisted, "Do you mean the chauffeur didn't resist the kidnappers?"

"The officer didn't mention any struggle." Once again, Nagumbi followed Reid.

Margaret followed close on their heels. "Was the chauffeur wounded?"

"No," Nagumbi said.

Margaret fell back to the rear. She listened as Reid shot questions at Nagumbi, but nothing they said enlightened her or eased her worry.

She had hired the chauffeur. She could have sworn Mark Phan was reliable. He'd protected a former employer from an attack by revolutionaries in the streets of Rome. He'd had a toughness she associated with fearless youth.

So why the hell had Jim Donovan been taken without a fight?

Just wait until Mark got back here. The police interrogation would be nothing compared to the grilling he'd get from *her*.

Yet under her indignation brewed a different worry.

Had Mark betrayed them all, and sold Mr. Jim to the kidnapper?

Reid, Nagumbi and Margaret swept into the library in a purposeful triangle.

Nagumbi and Margaret stopped, flanking the door.

Reid headed for his desk. "Where is my goddamned jacket? I need my phone."

"Who do you want to call?" Margaret asked.

"Uncle Manuel."

"His number is programmed into the house phone." Going to Mr. Jim's desk, she dug the corded phone out from under a stack of papers and punched line two. The speaker phone lit. The dial tone sounded. She punched Manuel Vargas into the auto-dial. The ringing started.

Reid rounded the desk. He lifted the receiver, effectively cutting off Margaret and Nagumbi from any information.

As he waited, his gaze roamed the room with restless energy. His lips were tucked tight in anger. His eyes lit on Margaret and paused, neither warming nor frosting.

She was no longer an enemy to be defeated or a woman to be seduced, but an entity trapped in the weights and balances of events.

The driving passion was gone, as was the animosity. Until she earned his trust, he'd wait for the truth.

Right now, she didn't blame him.

The man had lost his grandfather.

When Manuel picked up, Reid's focus changed from her to the conversation at hand. "Manuel," he said into the phone. "They've got Granddad, and I want you to find out what the police are doing about it." He listened and nodded. "About a half hour ago. Yeah, let me know..."

Someone pounded on the front door.

Reid pulled the phone away from his ear.

Nagumbi stepped out into the hall.

Margaret strode past him.

Simon, the footman, moved with stately splendor to the door, never hurrying his pace as the pounding got louder and louder.

Margaret cursed the training she'd force-fed him; one never hurried, no matter how frantically one was summoned.

She was hurrying now.

But Simon won the race. He swung open the double doors and like water spilling over the dam, humanity surged in.

In the midst of the tide of blue uniforms, one motorized chrome wheelchair rolled, and a furious voice roared its frustration. "Damn you all, you had the perfect setup and you let them get away. Too afraid to wait to close in, now we have to—"

Jim caught sight of Margaret and snapped his mouth shut. Color mounted his forehead and he seemed almost choleric, forcing himself to cease his harangue, and unhappy about it. "Where's my grandson?" he snapped at her.

"In the library, sir." She stepped aside and gestured him in.

He rolled toward the entrance.

When he came even with her, she placed her hand on his shoulder and squeezed.

He paused, and without looking at her, he patted her fingers. "No need to worry, dear. I was never in danger."

She stepped back, suddenly trembling with reaction.

Jim rolled into the library, officers trailing behind.

She looked helplessly at Nagumbi, but he was staring after Jim, a frown on his brow. Spinning on his heel, he marched away, as if he wanted to find answers and didn't expect they'd be in the library.

Everything was out of kilter. Everyone was reacting oddly.

Margaret shook her head to clear it and stepped back into the library.

A pale Reid held his grandfather's hand and at the same time demanded a report from the police.

Jim again spit invective at the officers for rescuing him too soon.

The police were milling about, mostly staring at the assortment of medieval weapons lining the walls. One very harried HPD spokesman, a Detective Morris, was trying to explain to Reid why the kidnapping had happened in the first place.

Jim kept interrupting him with snorts and insults.

Going to Jim's desk, Margaret picked up the buzzing receiver and put it back on the cradle. In her opinion, if this was the way HPD handled their cases, it was a wonder the insanity rate wasn't higher among the victims.

Two things were very, very clear.

Reid was furious that Jim had been taken.

Jim was furious for being released.

Reid demanded to know where the cops had been during the kidnapping.

Jim wanted to know why they'd arrived before there could be identification of the mastermind behind the threats.

In exasperation, Reid demanded, "Where was the chauffeur we hired to protect Granddad when he went out?"

A silence fell, then Jim and the HPD spokesman said together: "He was shot." "He was chicken."

Reid's eyebrows shot up, while his suspicion perceptibly lowered the temperature in the room.

Jim and Detective Morris looked at each other in dismay. Jim gestured in defeat. "You may as well tell him the truth."

"Yes, I suppose." Detective Morris looked square in Reid's face. "When it happened, the chauffeur ran and one of the police mistook him for a suspect. When commanded to halt, he did not, and the officer fired on him."

Reid wasn't buying. "I want to interview him in the hospital."

"Unfortunately"—Detective Morris took a deep breath—"he was killed."

Margaret made a soft sound of consternation—appalled at the loss and confused by this performance so contrary to her reading of Mark Phan's character.

Reid must have heard, for he glanced at her. "Killed? The officer shot to kill?"

"No." Detective Morris blotted his forehead with his handkerchief. "The victim tripped and fell into the trajectory of the bullet."

"Who hired this clumsy coward?" Reid asked.

"I did." Margaret straightened her shoulders and stepped forward. "When we got the first extortion note, we retired your grandfather's former chauffeur, and I hired Mark. I wanted someone specially trained—at the same school that trained me—to defend an employer."

"You did a fine job choosing your man," Reid said sarcastically.

"Yes, sir. I'm sorry." She was sorry. Sorry she had been so wrong. Sorry that the personable young man was dead.

"I can't figure it out." Jim rubbed his chin with his arthritic fingers. "I count myself a good judge of character, and I didn't read him as a coward. I wonder if the kidnappers bought him off?"

Detective Morris flipped out his iPad and typed officiously. "We'll check his bank account."

Reid frowned.

Margaret could almost hear Reid's thoughts: if she hadn't hired a coward, then she'd hired a thief instead. "Have his parents been notified?" she asked.

"Not yet, ma'am," Detective Morris said.

"I'll call them," she said.

But Detective Morris took her arm. "In these instances, the police prefer to notify the next of kin. If you would please refrain from making contact until we've taken care of the formalities."
Margaret nodded her agreement.

Reid rubbed the bridge of his nose between his two fingers as if a headache was in the offing. "You'll send me the report of your interrogation as soon as you're done, of course."

"Interrogation?" Detective Morris stepped back. "Of whom?"

Reid raised his head and fixed him with a cold gaze. "Of the kidnappers."

"They weren't apprehended."

"What?" Reid put all his considerable power behind the shout.

"They weren't—"

Reid's voice dropped to a quiet deep-freeze. "How the hell could you let them get away?"

"They, er, abandoned your grandfather and escaped on foot through the arboretum in Memorial Park." Detective Morris spread his fingers with apologetic humility.

"Bunch of incompetents," Jim growled.

"I've been raised to respect the police," Reid said coldly, "but I'm inclined to agree."

Jim wrestled his hand from his grandson. "I was talking about the kidnappers."

At a signal from Detective Morris, one by one the officers began their retreat from the library. "I'm sorry this has been handled so badly," he said. "I believe that Mr. Donovan is well protected by the security firm you have here, and we'll recommend another chauffeur. One who has been cleared through our department."

Indignantly, Margaret said, "I checked with your department when I hired the chauffeur we have now." She corrected herself. "The chauffeur we *had*."

Detective Morris paused in his flight. "It would seem our information was wrong."

"All his references checked out," she said. "His former employers adored him."

"Then, I would say, someone offered him enough money." Detective Morris smiled nervously at her, then around the room. "Everyone has their price."

"It's too bad he won't have the time to spend it," Margaret sniped.

Detective Morris looked pained.

The officers looked angry.

The exodus out the door continued.

As the room emptied, Reid turned to her. "You defend your friend well."

"Mark Phan wasn't my friend, but he didn't deserve death on the assumption of guilt." Her gaze lit on Jim's damaged clothing. "You look like you've had a little rough handling yourself, sir. What happened to the buttons on your shirt?"

Jim glanced down. "The kidnappers tore it."

"And you've got cords hanging off your wheelchair." She leaned down and picked up the yellow and blue wires. "Did they tear that up, too?"

He looked as distinctly uncomfortable as she'd ever imagined the old reprobate could look. "I can't imagine how that happened."

"Something must be broken on the chair. Can you go forward, backward, turn?"

"Everything seems to be working fine," he assured her.

Kneeling beside him, she followed the wires to nothing. "It looks like they tore something off."

"I can't imagine what it was." Mr. Jim sounded angelic.

Reid knelt beside Margaret. "What do you suppose…? I didn't realize Granddad had controls there."

"Nor I," she agreed. "I'll have it checked in the morning." She stood and brushed her knees.

He stood, too, and when she straightened, he looked into her eyes.

The dreadful events of the past moments faded, and the memory of those moments in the gym washed over them.

In her mind, she saw his chest, bare and carved with muscle, and the low-riding pants of the *gi* that concealed and teased. She remembered how his hair had become mussed. She raised a nervous hand to her own and found wisps of it evading her braid and hanging about her face. Afraid she looked like an abandoned hussy, she popped the band off the end and finger-combed her hair.

From the expression in Reid's eyes, that didn't help. If anything, the sweep of moonlight blond against her shoulders seemed to guide his gaze down, to linger against the dips and rises of her figure.

"Well, would you look at you two." Relaxing back into his chair, Jim subjected them both to the X-ray of his vision. In a clear, thoughtful voice, he asked, "Did you two reach an understanding while I was gone?"

Margaret gawked at him.

Reid warned, "Granddad."

"No," Jim decided. "If you'd reached an understanding, Margaret would have a soft, blurred look, and Reid's temper would be a bit better."

She wanted to halt Mr. Jim's ramblings, and she was willing to lie to do it. "Sir, you know what I think about employees becoming involved with their employers, and you know what I told you about Mr. Reid

Donovan." Her tone was firm, her gaze unwavering, right until she spoke Reid's name. Then her voice cracked and her eyes dropped.

"By God, Margaret." Jim struck the arm of his chair with his palm. "You look like you discovered *something* about my grandson you like."

Her gaze jerked back to his, and he was grinning—grinning as Reid had when he'd won the bout. Grinning, as if he was the cat that had carried off the biggest canary and wanted to gloat over it. His blue eyes zipped back and forth between his butler and his grandson in lively amusement, and he pursed his wrinkled lips. "You two been fighting like a couple of men?"

Margaret stared at Jim. If she kept her attention fixed on the elder Donovan, she could refuse to meet Reid's eyes, refuse his demand for her attention.

Jim cackled. "Who won, Margaret? Did you wrestle him into submission and put those nail marks on his shoulders, or did he toss you and beat you to the floor?"

That made her look at Reid. She saw the red crescents on his skin and the way he reminded her, using his eyes and his body and the tilt of his head, that she still owed him his forfeit.

"Strip him of his clothes, and he's not such a bad fellow," Jim advised her.

"Damn you, Jim." Wheeling around, she left for her quarters. Her knees felt too shaky to run, but she abandoned her butler's dignity and accelerated to a rapid pace.

Reid transferred his attention to Jim in disgust. "Thanks, Granddad. I always know I can count on you to throw a ringer into the works."

He strode out, heading for his room, and left the old man alone slapping his knee and gasping with delighted laughter.

Fourteen

"But Reid's birthday is *next month,* Mom."

"I don't care, Amy. I'm not *his* mother."

"He hasn't got a mother. He's an orphan."

"My heart bleeds."

"Mah-om!" Amy sighed. "That's mean."

Margaret blended the blusher over her cheekbone. "*I'm* mean."

"No, you're not. You're the best mother in the whole world. You take care of me all the time." Amy tucked one knee into her elbow, and let the other foot dangle. She sat on the toilet lid, watching her mother make up her face in preparation for another day as the Donovans' butler, and she nagged.

Sometimes, it seemed to Margaret, Amy was the best nagger in the world. Especially when someone's well-being was involved. Especially when it was an act of kindness. Especially when she knew she was right.

With the earnest goodwill of a child, Amy said, "Sometimes you don't like what I do, but you love me no matter how awful I am. You teach me all kinds of things about relationships and to be self-confident and do what I know is right in my heart. You tell me if I can't say something nice don't say anything at all, and—"

Margaret put her cosmetic brush down beside the sink and turned to face her daughter. "Amy, don't you have anything better to do on a Saturday? Don't you have homework?"

"I already did it. Homework is light the first week of school. You know that."

Margaret did know that. Damn it. "Why are you regurgitating everything I've ever told you?"

Her little blackmailer smiled with all of her considerable charm. "Because we need to give Reid a birthday party. Mr. Jim's not planning *anything*. He hardly even *remembered* it was his birthday. He says he *never* gives Reid a party. He says he *never ever* even *gave* Reid a party when he was little. He says Reid hardly *remembers* it's his birthday. You'd never let *me* go without celebrating *my* birthday, and I'd never let *you* go without celebrating *your* birthday. It's a *shame* to let anyone go without—"

"Amy." Margaret interrupted the unceasing flow of rhetoric. "Don't you think you should call him Mr. Donovan?"

"Who, Reid?"

Margaret nodded.

"Okay." Amy nodded back. "It's a deal. I'll call him Mr. Donovan and we'll give him a party."

"Oh no, my dear." Margaret leaned into the mirror and wiped color across her lids with her fingertip. "I'm not making deals with anyone else. I learned my lesson on that." There was a crushed little silence, and she glanced sideways at her daughter.

Amy's shoulders sagged and she was studying the tip of her swinging shoe.

Margaret knew it was foolish, but she tried to reason with her. "Look, honey, what kind of a party could we give someone like Mr. Donovan? He's rich and he's old enough to be your father." *That* was a stupid thought to implant in her daughter's mind, and she rushed on. "A thirty-eight year old man doesn't want balloons and paper hats and treat bags with Mickey Mouse on them. He'd want a naked woman jumping out of a cake."

"Bet he wouldn't," Amy muttered.

"Even if he liked Mickey Mouse, he'd probably be chagrined if we made him sit at a table with a paper tablecloth. He would be annoyed if we invited his friends to come and watch him blow out thirty-eight—"

"Thirty-nine."

"Okay, thirty-nine candles. And when we spilled red punch on his"—Margaret's lips pursed in thought—"expensive rugs, he'd probably be very angry. Hmm." And maybe, just maybe, he'd stop looking at me like he can't decide whether to drag me off to jail or drag me off to bed. Maybe he'd talk to me, instead of gloating over me. Maybe he'd remember his position and stop giving the household ideas by the way he watches me. "You know, Amy, you might have an idea there. Who do you suppose he'd want? Batman or Smurfs?"

"Avengers?"

Simon flung open the dining room doors, and Reid wheeled Jim in.

Jim set the brake.

Reid skidded to a stop.

Both Jim and Reid looked absolutely flabbergasted.

The guests savored the expressions of total amazement for a split second, then yelled, "Surprise!" Everyone took a breath and laughed, yelled, "Surprise!" again, and broke into little groups, streaming over to greet the birthday boy.

Margaret watched as Reid looked around at the assemblage. His closest friends were here, some with their families and some alone. There were babies chewing their feet, adults leaning on canes, and every age in between. She'd culled the names of twenty-five of Reid's buddies, consulting Nagumbi and Abigail and Manuel, and subtly sounding out Mr. Jim. She'd stood by the phone, ever vigilant of RSVPs. Twenty of the twenty-five had come. The other five had sent greetings and presents and disappointed excuses.

Still the seconds ticked along before Reid truly grasped what was happening. "This is wonderful," he gasped. "This is for me?" He looked around the room with the wide eyes of an eight-year-old who had had his greatest desire fulfilled. "This is *wonderful*."

Margaret surveyed the dining room with self-righteous pleasure. Plastic balloons crept along the vaulted ceiling, their brilliant colors inching toward the return air vents. Mylar balloons bobbed, tied to the back of every chair and marked with a guest's name. The paper tablecloths were weighted down by plates of cupcakes and bags of treats and whistles and hats. The center table held a sheet cake. A gigantic wall hanging showed the birthday boy and his best friend in a smiling fantasy drawing. The friend had round black ears and a black bow tie and wore a cheerful grin.

Everything—*everything* shouted M-I-C...K-E-Y...M-O-U-S-E. Every available space held a picture of Mickey. The balloons were shaped like Mickey, the cake was a miracle of Mickey frosting, the cupcakes were stuck with tiny Mickey toothpicks. The hats had ears, the whistles squeaked when blown, the treat bags held Mickey gum and

Mickey candy and Mickey cards.

She turned back to Reid and found his eyes lingering on the one guest he didn't know; the one present she'd brought for him.

She'd met Chantal at one of Mr. Jim's functions during the past year. Chantal was young—in her middle twenties—and charming. She was tall, but not as tall as Margaret, and lush—her puberty had obviously been a resounding success. Her clothes hugged every curve and shouted good taste. Her auburn hair curled in a mad riot down her back, and one teeny wisp teased her brow. One look from her brown eyes caused previously sane men to abandon their talk of finance and follow her like begging puppy dogs. They found, to their horror, that Chantal could talk finance with the best of them. And politics, and the current state of the Houston economy. The woman was a freelance reporter, selling her investigative articles online and to the news services.

The woman was not only beautiful, she was smart.

Worst of all, in Margaret's view—she was nice.

Genuinely nice. Other women liked her. Ruefully, but they liked her. The first words she'd spoken to Margaret were a compliment on her black uniform and how well it accented her blond hair. Margaret had taken that with a grain of salt, but when Chantal had sought her out to ask if she could go down and applaud the cook, Margaret had surrendered. She'd become a member in good standing of the Chantal Fan Club, and now she was her biggest supporter. How could she not? Beautiful, smart, and nice; three of the biggest clichés in the English language as redefined by Chantal.

They were friends, and when Margaret had invited her to lunch and begged her to come and vamp Reid, Chantal had agreed. Without vanity, she'd been sure she could lure Reid into her coils, and from what she'd heard, he'd be a pleasure to keep. "But, Margaret," Chantal had warned, "as worried as you are about this—are you sure you want me to take him?"

"Take him and welcome," Margaret had replied, and now she watched as Chantal shook Jim's hand and obtained an introduction to his grandson.

What a triumph. Margaret had embarrassed him with a party and tossed him a distraction, all in one smooth maneuver.

Boy, was she glad.

Margaret could see the gleam in Reid's eyes from here. He lifted Chantal's hand to his mouth and stared at her with such open appreciation, Margaret wanted to, to…arrange some party activities.

Reid found Amy in the crowd surrounding him, and he lifted her onto her toes and hugged her.

When he put her back on her feet, she laughed and chatted and pointed about the room, and Margaret knew what she was saying. *I sent the invitations,* Amy was confessing. *Nagumbi arranged the Mickey-o-gram. Manuel and his wife had insisted on providing the Hispanic delicacies. Abigail decorated the Mickey Mouse cake herself.*

Mommy—Amy's accusatory little finger shot her way—*Mommy coordinated everything just for you.*

Reid's eyes met Margaret's across the room, and she wanted to gasp and sigh. He didn't look angry. Perhaps he was a marvelous actor, but he looked happy. Amused, astonished, pleased, and warmly endorsing her kindness.

Uh-oh.

She kept staring at Reid, and he kept staring at her until the rasping voice of Mr. Jim asked, "Why the hell wasn't I told?"

Margaret looked down at him, surprised he'd reached her side without her noticing. She looked up at Manuel, who stood beside his friend, and grinned and twisted the end of his mustache. Hands outspread, she shrugged at both of them.

"Were you afraid an old man of ninety-two would slip?" Mr. Jim demanded.

"No, not you." She shook a finger at Jim. "You'd never slip *accidentally.* You're too sharp for that. You'd do it on purpose, out of loyalty to your grandson, and no one was going to spoil Amy's surprise."

"I'd have never thought it, but you may be right. He seems to like this childishness." Jim raised his head and stared at the Reid-and-Mickey banner. "Who'd you get to paint that?"

"Norma Van. She couldn't come. She has a showing in New York this weekend, but she insisted she wanted to do something, and now Reid has a Mickey Mouse painting worth thousands." Margaret chuckled.

"She's a lady," Jim answered, bestowing his highest compliment.

"Most of these people are great," she agreed.

Jim turned his wheelchair to face her. "You don't have to sound so shocked. What kind of friends did you think Reid would have?"

She didn't answer—for what could she say that wouldn't sound rude? Looking across at Reid as he worked his way through the crowd, greeting them all with a special smile or a smack on the back or a tender hug, she wondered what she *had* expected Reid's friends to be like.

Not what they were. She'd found their lack of arrogance surprising—surely Reid's wealthy good friends should be snooty? Shouldn't the head of the largest oil corporation in the world be a bit stuck-up? Shouldn't an exiled prince of Bulgaria be too good to chat with a butler? Shouldn't a Japanese magnate shake her hand with less enthusiasm? Shouldn't the French chief of a big city police department complain about her security? But no — all of them displayed an unselfconscious delight, exclaiming how glad they were that Reid was at last having the party he deserved.

They'd taken the rooms she assigned them, and when the mansion had run out of bedrooms they'd agreed to stay at a hotel without a grumble. They'd lavishly praised her great idea and exclaimed about her innovation. They weren't like any rich people she'd ever met—and she'd met quite a few. Why, some of these friends weren't even rich. None of them were haughty.

It seemed that Reid's business associates could be as rude as they liked, but his intimates had to be real folk. She ignored the doubts that circled her brain. She ignored Mr. Jim and Manuel, too, watching her with their bright eyes and analyzing her every expression.

Stepping forward, she clapped her hands and called, "All right! It's time for birthday games. Amy, get the birthday boy his ears and his whistle."

"That's not fair," the corporation president called. "Reid gets real Mickey Mouse ears with his name sewn on."

"Reid is the birthday boy—" Margaret said.

"Yeah," Reid interjected.

Margaret continued, "—And you haven't got your treats yet, so behave yourself or you won't get a surprise. Now, everyone put on your hats."

Every one of them pulled the elastic bands under their chins and settled the pointed paper hats on their heads.

"You'll have to take the whistles out of your mouths to play this game," she said. "We can't have you running with a whistle in your mouth—you'll fall and shove it down your throat."

"Thank you for sharing," one voice called from amid the laughter, and they all grinned at Margaret as if she were the head cheerleader and they were the school pep team.

She said, "We're going to play musical chairs."

Fifteen

"I must complain about your unprofessional attire."

Margaret looked down at herself, her smile fading. "What? Why?" she stammered. Her black skirt sported a spot or two of frosting, her white shirt looked a little wilted, and her jacket had been discarded in the excitement of the piñata, but other than that, she thought her appearance was conventional.

Reid reached up and touched the maroon scarf she'd knotted around her neck. "Rather radical, isn't it?"

"Oh," she faltered. She'd forgotten about the bow Amy teased her into wearing. "I thought that at a party—"

He studied her with a lazy pleasure. "It's too much. That black and white suit is severe enough to scare many a mighty man, but the color throws out a hint of temptation. It might give the braver fellows I call my friends ideas, and I want to keep them as friends."

She didn't say anything.

Well, what could she say? She didn't want to pursue that comment. His sherry brown eyes were too pleased, too contented, too possessive.

"Pierre has already commented on the cool lady in the black suit," Reid said, "and her hint of passion beneath."

"Pierre?" She visually searched the crowd until she located the tall, debonair Frenchman. "Ah, the policeman. He's charming."

"All the women say that about Pierre." Reid leaned close. "Beware, he's a wolf in sheep's clothing."

"Thank you for the warning," she said ironically.

He contrived to look hurt. "Are you insinuating *I'm* a wolf in sheep's clothing?"

"Not at all. You don't even own a set of sheep's clothing."

He chuckled. "How well you know me. What do you think of the rest of my friends?"

A warm smile lit her face. "They're marvelous. Pleasant and witty and interesting."

"All of them?"

"All of your friends are at least one of the above," she assured him.

"They like you, too." A deep contentment colored his speech. "They seem to be under the impression you're a dear pal first and a punctilious butler second."

"Well." She studied her nails. "I can't imagine what made them think that."

"Maybe it's all the effort you put into organizing this party."

The warm note of pleasure made her squirm with guilt, and she avoided his eyes. "Don't make more of this than you should. It was Amy's idea."

"She says you did all the work."

"No, no. I'm great at delegating responsibility. Everyone did their part, and besides, I've organized a lot of parties." She darted a look at him, but her disclaimer seemed to make no impression. "For Amy, you know. I can do it with my eyes closed."

"Good." He sounded eager and pleased. "You'll do me another one next year."

"I will?" She pivoted her head around and glared.

"Please?" Butter wouldn't melt in his mouth. His eyes gleamed with soulful pleading, his mobile mouth pouted.

"You remind me of Amy."

He didn't look at all abashed.

So she said with slow emphasis, "You remind of an eleven year old girl."

"Does that mean you'll do it?"

"Do you live to sucker me?" she asked.

He bent until he was eye level and gave her a big, smacking kiss.

Heads turned at the sound.

Margaret felt the heat of a blush climb from her toes to the roots of her hair. "Pushing, pushing," she murmured. "You act like a child, I'll treat you like a child."

Straightening up, he smirked with accomplishment. "I am not a child. I thought I'd proved that to you."

She turned to march away, but a strong arm at her waist stopped her. "Stay here," he commanded. "I won't tease anymore."

Glancing around, she saw too many faces observing them with intense good-will. "Fine." She leaned her elbows against the antique oak buffet behind her—and upset two of the glasses stacked there.

They clanked.

She jumped.

Reid caught the glasses before they fell and shattered. "No harm done," he said.

Margaret wished she was far, far away.

A silence fell between them.

"I don't want to be that young anymore." Reid sounded reflective, and Margaret followed his gaze. He stared at Chantal, chatting vivaciously to Mr. Kioto.

"Why do you say that?"

"Look at her, hustling for a story. Her greatest happiness is standing on a pier in the Gulf of Mexico during a hurricane. Or interviewing some politician's ex-girlfriend. Or getting the goods on a financial scandal." He cocked an eyebrow at Margaret.

"She promised to keep everything she heard tonight confidential," she assured him. "In return, I told her she could make as many contacts as possible."

"I know I can depend on you." He blessed her with a slow rub between the shoulder blades, one that made her want to stretch and purr. He looked back at Chantal and grimaced. "She lives a miserable existence."

Margaret snorted.

"Yes, she does. I know, because I've been there."

"It made you very successful," Margaret observed.

"Yeah, that's why God gives you driving ambition when you're twenty. When you're forty, you don't want to contend with it."

She couldn't help it. She laughed. He sounded so doleful, so wise.

"Okay, Miss Smartaleck, didn't you have a driving ambition when you were young?"

"Of course. I wanted to travel, to see the world. I was going to be a teacher of English in far-off Pakistan. Or Kuwait, or France, or Hong Kong. I wasn't fussy."

He leaned up against the buffet and crossed his arms across his chest. "What derailed that ambition?"

"My husband. He came along, and my sights narrowed considerably." She grinned, entertained by the memory of her younger self. "I wanted to get him through medical school so he could discover the cure for cancer and we'd be on easy street and save the world at the same time."

"And then?"

Her smile faded, and she didn't answer for a long time. She wandered, lost in her memories and her old pain. "Then I found out what really counts in life." She rubbed her arms with her hands and realized she was staring at Chantal. "So," she said brightly. "What do you think of her? Isn't she gorgeous?"

"Gorgeous," he agreed. "She looks like she went to the Golden Globe Awards and won twice."

Stupidly, Margaret almost told him Chantal wasn't in show business, when his meaning came clear. She choked, coughed, and wished he hadn't tapped into her sense of humor so precisely. Gaining control, she queried, "Isn't she irresistible?"

"No doubt irresistible. Especially for men who are jaded and older and look for the cure in the adoration of a much younger woman."

She detected the bite of sarcasm.

He took her chin between his fingers and pinched it. "Unfortunately for you, my darling, this method of distraction won't work."

She had the depressing feeling he had read her mind. "What do you mean?"

He smiled that five-hundred-watt smile straight in her face. "I've got my mind set on one woman who is, I admit, younger than me. But not too much younger. Not obscenely younger. She's warm and kind and gives great surprise parties. I'll leave little Chantal to a man who's more her age." He pointed to Jim. "Like Granddad."

"That's *horrible.*"

"Did that destroy your little plot? Did you ask Chantal to tempt me? She tried. She tried valiantly. But she's no fool—unlike some people I could name—and she knows a lost cause when she sees one. So let's have no more tossing of fair maidens at my head, and I won't toss myself at you." He released her chin and patted her cheek. "At least, not for the moment."

Margaret remained silent, stubbornly refusing to agree to his pact.

"Perhaps I misread the situation. Did you want me to toss myself at you?" He moved closer to her side, sliding his arm behind her on the buffet.

"No!" She jumped away and upset the glasses again, and this time they hit the floor—hundreds of dollars worth of shards and splinters flying into corners and seeking the fringe of the rug to hide in. She stared at the glittering catastrophe and groaned, "Oh, no."

Reid shook his head. "Drunk on red punch."

Margaret pretended she hadn't heard him. In the blink of an eye, she switched from being a woman to being a butler—or mother. "We've got to get the kids out of here." She pushed the button on the intercom and spoke to the answering Simon. "We've had an accident. Get a cleanup crew in here, and have the caterers set up the buffet in the ballroom." Releasing the button, she snapped her fingers and pointed. "Amy, you put your shoes back on and herd the other children into the entry."

Her daughter pulled a pitiful face. "But we haven't opened the presents yet."

"I'll have them moved. Now do as you're told, please."

To her relief, Reid stepped forward and announced, "Due to this ghastly mess, we're moving the party so we can eat and open presents... and dance."

"Wh...?" Margaret whipped her head around, but it was too late. Reid was ushering the smiling, chattering group out into the hall, and he turned and winked at her with sly humor.

Sixteen

Reid stripped off his suit coat and white shirt, flinging them on the floor amid cheers and laughter. Reaching into the box lined with tissue paper, he reverently raised his new Mickey Mouse t-shirt and slipped it over his head. It went well with the new red Mickey Mouse tie, knotted around his neck, and the new Mickey Mouse watch on his wrist.

Margaret leaned across to Mr. Jim. "If he doesn't stop blowing that Donald Duck whistle, I'm going to scream."

"Scream all you want, my dear." Jim patted her fanny and laughed when she jumped. "After what you've done for my grandson, you could answer the door in a Mickey Mouse *costume* and I wouldn't care."

"It's not such a big thing." Margaret shrugged.

"But it is. Look at him. He looks like he did when he was a boy, before his parents died."

"They died?"

"Of course. Did you think he was hatched?"

"I didn't know when he came to live with you," she answered patiently.

"When he was eight. His parents were both scientists. Mad scientists, I believe, and teachers both."

"Where did they teach?"

"At a high school in the Seattle area."

"A high school?" Margaret was surprised and amused. "I would have thought you'd have bought them a college."

"James and Brenda were idealists, believing the future of the world lay in the youth of today." Mr. Jim's mouth quirked. "Couple of fools in love."

"Car wreck?"

"Hiking accident."

"Was Reid with them?"

"Oh, yes." He shook his head sadly. "They had the school Science Club out identifying plants in the mountains, and some youngster decided to dance beside the cliff. James lunged for him. Brenda caught at James. They both flew off the precipice."

Nudged by the sardonic twist of his mouth, she queried, "The boy didn't fall?"

"Of course not. But James was killed instantly. It damaged Brenda enough to keep her in the hospital for a month."

"Then what happened?"

"Then she died, too."

Margaret had known what he was going to say, but even so she was shocked. "Good God."

"So an eight-year-old boy came to live with a sixty-one-year old man." He raised one withered hand and rubbed his eyes tiredly. "I did the best I could."

She checked him with a suspicious gaze. Mr. Jim had been known to use his age and his infirmity to deliberately touch the heart, but she acquitted him of manipulation now. He wasn't watching her for her reactions; just sat with pursed lips, remembering.

"I wasn't retired then. I had a hell of a big corporation to run. I hadn't had a boy around for years; I'd forgotten how rambunctious they got. But one thing I did remember." He raised one crooked finger. "I remembered James at that age. I remembered how he'd wanted to be with me and how I'd never had the time, and I resolved not to make that mistake again. I took Reid everywhere with me."

"That must have been something to see."

"At the tender age of ten, the boy could discuss municipal bonds with the best of them, and he predicted his first oil well strike at eleven."

"And you?"

"I played G.I. Joe."

She sputtered with laughter. "Good for you."

He tilted his head and looked at her sideways. "I never could decide if it kept me young or aged me fast."

"You're still here at ninety-two," she pointed out.

"He brought one thing to me, for sure. It had been so long since I'd had it, I'd even forgotten to miss it." He smiled mistily. "That snot-nose brat brought me love."

Margaret sought Amy with her eyes. Her daughter had found a friend from among the other girls, and those two girls had attracted a following of younger children. The little ones paddled after them like a hatching of ducks after their mothers. "That's all kids are good for," she scoffed, her heart in her eyes.

"Amy's having a good time, isn't she?"

"She never met a stranger," Margaret admitted.

"Same with Reid. If he has any fault, it's that he recognizes people through his intuition and immediately makes his decisions about them. It used to drive me mad. I warned him he'd get hurt."

"Did he?"

"No, not him. He warned me about a business associate and I ignored him. You see, I based my perception on previous actions and known factors. I got taken for a bundle. That's when I realized that the little bugger might have a disturbing tendency to be right."

Margaret laughed.

Taking her hand, he stroked it. "But I never even thought to give the boy a birthday party. He never said he wanted one. But when he walked in this afternoon and saw this nonsense—I guess maybe he missed a normal life."

"Perhaps he missed some of the aspects of a normal life," she corrected. "He loves you, and the way you raised him made him the man he is."

"You think I did a good job?"

She reassured him, her voice too warm and her expression too kind. "I think you did a marvelous job."

"Good." His mouth curled with satisfaction. "I took care of him for the first half of his life." He turned his wheel chair and headed for the door. "You take care of him for the second half. Come and help me get ready for bed. I'm tired."

Like a prickling on the back of his neck, Reid knew when Margaret re-entered the ballroom. Shifting so he could see the door, he viewed her and sighed with pleasure.

She was so beautiful.

He shook his head and laughed at himself. She wasn't actually stunning, he supposed. Tall and shapely and well formed—so what? The women he'd escorted all fell into that category. What caught a man's attention was the way she moved; fluid grace bred into every bone. It made him think of long summer nights filled with slow, careful lovemaking. The light stroke of a hand, the gentle use of teeth and tongue. Fires lit and tended with care until they flared out of control.

Shifting uncomfortably, Reid returned from his erotic dreams and focused on Margaret again. Her skin shone unfashionably pale, like the base of his grandfather's china lamp. She wore little makeup—some blusher, he guessed, and mascara to cover her white lashes—and it told on her when she was weary. Like now.

He checked the ballroom with his eyes. When she had disappeared and he'd discovered she'd gone to care for his grandfather, he'd taken over the job of butler.

Under his command, the buffet had been removed and was now nothing but a comfortable memory. Most of the children had been put to bed or worn to the point that they were happy watching a Disney video. The candelabra had been dimmed, and his iPod played a pleasant combination of jazzy tunes and old-fashioned melodies.

Abigail had snared Nagumbi and somehow convinced the stiff, respectable bodyguard to dance with her.

Uncle Manuel had caught up with his little dynamo of a wife and the two moved together like the ballroom champions they had been.

Couples swayed, wrapped in music and communicating heated, leisurely ideas.

This was the end of one very successful party, and Margaret had done it all: all for him.

Now he would give her her reward.

Cruising the edges of the floor, he coasted up to her and murmured, "Dance with me."

Seventeen

Margaret jumped and brushed at her ear, tired enough to be cranky when he breathed on her neck, tired enough to have missed his approach. "Sir, I have to start the cleanup."

"When we make love, will you call me by my name?"

She glared.

"Or will you moan, *More, sir, please, sir?*" He laughed at her.

"I have to organize the cleanup," she enunciated clearly.

"It's done. I delegated some of that authority you bragged about." He put his arm around her waist, but she resisted.

"Everyone's coming for breakfast," she said.

"Let 'em eat Eggos."

"That is not what the Donovan guests expect."

She sounded so fussy, so unbearably stuffy, that he abandoned his plans of subtle seduction and did what he did best. He bullied her. His hands reached out for her hips, and he pulled her close. "To hell with the Donovan guests."

The touch of their bodies jolted her from her fatigue and her orneriness. Her eyes widened as she looked up at him. "Sir."

He rubbed the dark patches beneath her eyes. "Your mascara has smudged."

He rubbed himself against her.

"Reid!"

He could see her awareness grow, and it reaffirmed his first impression. Margaret needed to be swept from her feet before she could be handled.

"You want to dance with me right here and now, in front of all these people?" she asked.

"What people?" He looked into her eyes. "I don't seen any other people. Only you."

She took a long breath that brought her closer to him.

Closer…and he took advantage.

She looked down at their joined bodies. "I don't dance like that—or at least, I haven't since I learned better."

"It doesn't *get* any better than this. Or at least, not while you're dancing," he mocked.

She tried a bargain. "I'll dance with you if you'll be good."

He smiled a wicked smile, and dancing wasn't all that was on his mind. "I'll be good if you'll dance with me."

He stepped out to the blatantly romantic tune, crooned by Michael Bublé.

The sound system surrounded them in the romantic rhythm. The other dancers were silent. The room was large. There was no danger of collision and no reason to speak.

With a yielding sigh, Margaret slid her arms around his shoulders.

What a chauvinistic thrill it gave him to know he could take her initial reluctance and turn it to tapioca! It gave him an even greater thrill—a pure masculine thrill—to know why she was reluctant.

She wanted to stay away from him. His fire was too warm, too enveloping. She feared the burn, yet desired the warmth.

God, he *was* warm. When he looked back over the past few weeks with a dispassionate eye, he could account for the true reason he'd been antagonistic when he'd first seen her.

She was the one. *The* one.

Like any man, he hadn't been ready to admit defeat. Especially to Margaret, a woman who failed to realize what a prince she'd snagged. His previous, much more flattering for his own ego philosophy, had been pretty matter-of-fact.

Women had invented marriage.

Women did the chasing.

Like black widow spiders, women captured unwilling male victims and tangled them in their snares.

When he'd thought about it—and he really didn't bother to think about it much—that's how he suspected he'd go; strung up by some devious woman.

Instead, here he was, madly pursuing a woman who didn't like him, didn't admire him…she only wanted him. And she didn't like wanting him *at all.*

She wanted to remain phlegmatic, caught in the workaday world. Most definitely, she didn't want to dance close, their bodies purring as they rubbed against each other…

So she kept her head up, away from his shoulder. She kept her upper body curved back; if his fingers hadn't been flexed on her hips, their bodies would have met nowhere in the dance.

But when they touched, the world changed. The air around them glistened and quivered.

She breathed deeply, dipping toward his neck, smelling the pheromones his passion created for her.

He pressed his hand against her cheek until she laid it on his chest. He rubbed his chin on the top of her head, and her perfume came up in subtle, seductive waves. Unable to resist, he hummed a deep and mellow accompaniment to Michael and the band.

He rubbed one of his hands up and down her spine, sliding too far down her buttocks, then, before she could react, sliding back up to fondle her ear. Either extreme made her uncomfortable; she'd stiffen a bit. But the part in the middle felt divine, if her boneless lassitude was anything to judge by.

Like a psychic in a grocery store tabloid, he read her thoughts with uncanny accuracy.

She wanted to forbid him; she *would* forbid him, just as soon as the music stopped.

But his iPod drifted from one song to the other with nary a break between."You know what I've been thinking?" Reid used a rumbly voice, new to Margaret and meant to soothe.

It worked. She relaxed against him.

Cuddling her close, he repeated, "You know what I've been thinking? I've been thinking how well we fit together."

"Sure," she breathed.

"When we make love—"

She lifted her head.

He pushed it back down. "When we make love, we'll fit exactly as well."

"No." But it was merely a whisper.

Reaching between then, he released her tie and let it float away. "I've always wanted to be part of a family. Like Dick and Jane, Spot and Puff, Mother and Father. That's the American ideal, isn't it?"

"Um? Oh, yes."

"There's you and me—that's Mother and Father." He felt the tension invade her limbs. "And Jane—that's Amy. Spot and Puff, we can get at the pound—and Dick. Well," he chuckled softly, laying tender lips on her forehead, "Dick would be *our* project."

She jerked back.

He let her go.

"Are you crazy?" Her eyes flashed with an indignation all out of proportion to his fantasy. "That's one sick proposition. What would happen to Amy and me when you got tired of playing house?"

"How long do you plan to live?"

"Forever. The question is—how long do *you* plan to live?"

He'd touched a nerve; that he could see.

Her nostrils flared, her chin squared defiantly, but her lips quivered.

With firm hands, he gathered her back against his chest, and he led her in the dance until he felt the iron in her spine subside. "The ghost of the husband raises his head," he guessed.

"He's not a ghost."

"He's not alive, either."

"I mean," she said, sounding provoked, "I'm not haunted by him."

"Has someone suggested you were?"

It was a trap, and he felt sorry to have set it, but if this was the explanation of her skittish behavior, he needed to know.

But she didn't reply, and she kept her face turned away from him.

He said, "That's an answer all its own."

She set her jaw. Nothing more would be forthcoming from her.

Intent on bringing her back to him, he whispered, "You certainly know how to freeze a proposal."

Her face skewed around to his, her expression incredulous. "What do you mean by that?"

"Think about it," he ordered.

With trembling hands, she pushed her hair out of her eyes and glanced up at the ceiling, then at the other dancers. Her eyes lingered on Nagumbi, trapped in a glittering Abigail's arms and showing an unwilling enjoyment. She felt a kinship for him, and in a quavery voice, she said, "You do a mean fox-trot."

"Um." He touched her lower lip with one fingertip. "The music's still playing."

She ignored that. "I guess you had a lot of lessons when you were young, huh?"

"Not too many." He'd not push anymore tonight. He tucked the silky strands of hair behind her ears, lingering to stroke the outer shell and the curve of her cheek.

"Well, thanks for the dance." Swinging her arms, she rolled her eyes. "I...enjoyed it."

"I...enjoyed it, too."

His eyes were smoky, his face was kind, and his mouth was very, very amused. "See you around," he whispered, and he turned without another word and found himself in Chantal's arms, weaving romance in a dance.

Margaret stared after them.

She was glad he danced with Chantal. Maybe Chantal's looks and sexuality would knock some of that nonsense out of his head. Some of that scary nonsense. Yes, she was glad that Reid had gone and found himself another partner with no fuss.

Then she turned up the lights, went to his iPod and put on some good ol' rock and roll, and livened up the party enough to keep it going until two in the morning.

When at last the guests drifted away, some out the door, some up the stairs, Margaret nodded goodnight with acute satisfaction.

Beside her, Reid said, "You missed one party game."

Margaret pressed her palm to the small of her back. "Believe it or not, I missed several. It only *seemed* like we played every game in existence."

"See ya, Margaret." Abigail headed down the hallway, her sequins sagging with exhaustion.

Nagumbi stood looking after her, and then moved with his natural majesty in quite the opposite direction.

Moving behind Margaret, Reid pushed her hand aside and began a slow, rotating massage.

She stepped away.

He followed, and massaged again.

She wasn't strong enough to step away again. All the muscles along her spine contracted, vying for attention, and she groaned pitifully.

"Hostessing a party for forty rowdy and happy adults—not to mention a pack of wild kids—is not an easy job. But it's over now," he said.

"Worrying about security has been no picnic, either."

"Granddad's fine."

"I know." She broke away from him and turned to face him. "But do you know the trouble I had convincing Cliff Martin he couldn't come in and mingle with the guests?"

Remembering the smelly, vulgar security man, Reid said with heartfelt sincerity, "God forbid."

"I heard a million dire warnings, including a threat to go to you with the plans."

Reid's face tightened in anger.

"But police advice and common sense prevailed at last, along with persuasion from Nolan Salas, whose designated job is apparently being the voice of reason. He reminded Cliff that you fired your father's lawyer after he informed you of the changes to his will."

Suspicion sharpened Reid's voice. "How did Salas know that?"

"I think you said so when he was in the library with you." She frowned as she tried to remember. "Didn't you?"

"I thought that was before they came in." He couldn't remember the exact sequence of events, either. "But perhaps I repeated myself."

"Perhaps." She rubbed the side of her face with careworn concentration. "If you don't mind, sir...um, Reid, I'd like to go to bed."

"Are you going to start calling me Sir Reid now? Don't you think that's a little formal?"

She laughed uneasily and backed up.

His hand shot out and caught her elbow. "You never asked which game we didn't play."

"Huh?" Befuddled, she shook her head to clear it. "Look, if we didn't get to a game you liked, write me a list." She tried to pile guilt on his unrepentant head. "I've already contracted to do your party next year."

"But I can't *wait* for next year to play Spin the Bottle." He took one Giant Step forward.

She had thought she was too tired to react, but her heart leaped.

"Uh-oh."

He leaned down to her mouth.

It wasn't fear that motivated her heartbeat. It was excitement, belatedly recognized and all the more powerful for that. Putting her finger on his chest, she warned, "You didn't say, *Mother, may I?*"

He kept coming. "Yes, I may," he murmured against her lips. And he kissed her. He branded her. He blurred the already fuzzy edges of reality. His cake tasted like the party she'd given him, like chocolate cake and cherry Kool-Aid and bubble gum. The innocence of the flavors and the experience of the kisser confused her, and confusion made her respond more than she should, share more than wisdom demanded.

Only when he began to unbutton her vest, with a touch here and a touch there for emphasis, did she drag herself back from the brink.

Reid didn't seem surprised that she had regained her sense. He held her until her knees stopped wobbling, then he flashed a grin and ran up the stairs two at a time, a spring in his step.

When Margaret recovered enough to walk, she turned and ran smack into Chantal.

"Who are you trying to kid?" Chantal's eyes were big and round, and her feet seemed to have rooted themselves to the floor.

Margaret tried twice before she could speak. "What do you mean?"

"Any man who kisses a woman like that is worth hand-to-hand combat. You don't pass him on to me without a qualm." Chantal was indignant on Reid's behalf, then said sensibly, "Besides, he doesn't want me."

"What?" Margaret shook her head as if she'd been hit. "What?"

"He doesn't want me," Chantal enunciated.

"Did he say that?"

"Dear girl, he didn't have to. He was very pleasant, very nice, and with no hesitation introduced me to his delightful friend from France."

"I hoped he was kidding." Margaret's sense of imbalance, so typical when Reid was around, had disappeared, and she imagined and discarded options with lightning speed. She snapped her fingers and suggested, "Maybe we could—"

"No."

"You haven't even heard—"

"I don't need to. Margaret." Chantal wrapped her hands around

Margaret's jaw. "Listen to me. The man is nuts about you. He gives off an aura of desire so strong, I breathe it in when I stand close to him. I could hear the hum clear across the room with the music playing. Loudly."

"Maybe he should bathe," Margaret mumbled.

Chantal ignored her and continued with her litany. "He watches you across the room. He admires you with his eyes. He listens for your voice. He threatens other men verbally when they get too close to you."

"It's only unrequited lust," Margaret said.

"If I could find a man who'd lust after me like that, he'd never escape my clutches. Reid Donovan is not going to let you go." Chantal released Margaret's jaw and took her by the shoulders. Punctuating each word with a shake, she said, "So you might as well enjoy the ride."

Eighteen

"She's a fine-looking woman." Pierre waggled his eyebrows in exaggerated continental flare.

Reid looked up from his plate of scrambled eggs to see Margaret coming through the door of the dining room, two plates of Abigail's steaming, fluffy biscuits in her hands. "Shut up and eat your Eggos, Pierre."

Pierre, of course, paid no attention. Since their fraternity days, Reid had been issuing orders and Pierre had been ignoring them, and Reid would have been surprised to see the handsome Frenchman listen for once. Instead Pierre said, "I've always been a sucker for women in uniform. Those prim outfits make a man wonder how she looks beneath."

Reid glared at his friend—who was rapidly becoming his former friend. "She's not as good-looking as you think."

"Ah?"

"Yes, there's a reason you never see her with her collar unbuttoned." He leaned toward Pierre and bared his teeth. "She's hairy all over, like a bear."

"But only during the full moon, right?" Pierre laughed aloud, and the other guests turned from their conversations and stared at the two men huddled at the head of the table. Lowering his voice, he suggested, "Maybe she'll eat me up."

"Only if all her taste is in her mouth," Reid snapped.

Pierre opened his lips to speak.

Reid cut him off. "Which it isn't, so don't even try."

Pierre grinned and stuffed another bite of waffles into his mouth, and groaned with pleasure. "You Americans eat the most wonderful things."

"Homemade biscuits, bacon, Cajun sausage, scrambled eggs, fresh grapefruit halves from the valley, all prepared by Abigail's loving hands—and you eat frozen waffles. How did Frenchmen ever get the reputation for being gourmets?"

Waving his fork in a dripping syrup circle over his place mat, Pierre proclaimed, "Our lovemaking addles a woman's brain and makes her susceptible to suggestion. We make love to them, then we tell them we're gourmets."

"What a plan," Reid said. "Maybe I should make love to Margaret and then tell her she loves me."

"You *are* glum this morning. Didn't you get the birthday present she was promising last night when she danced with you?"

"*Non.*" With that one word, Reid exhausted half of his repertoire of French. "She wants me, but she doesn't want to want me."

"Maybe she needs another man to open the blossom of her womanhood." Pierre kissed his fingers with Gallic fervor.

"Maybe you'd leave in a body bag if you tried."

"Oh, ho! *Mon ami* sees the green monster of jealousy." Pierre lifted one of Reid's eyelids and peered beneath. "Oh, ho! *Mon ami* has been stricken with ze *amour.*"

"Knock it off with the Maurice Chevalier imitations."

"Who better?"

Good point. "Never mind about my love life. Tell me what you think of Martin Security."

Pierre dropped the accent, and the guise of French rake, and became what he was—an *agent de police.* "My professional opinion, you mean?"

"Yeah."

"I can only tell you what I was told." He held up a fist and lifted one finger. "One. The Houston Police are almost fanatically certain that this firm is stable." Another finger. "Two. Your dear Uncle Manuel insists Martin Security is solid." Another finger. "Three. Cliff Martin checks out with every source I could find in the States."

"Damn."

Pierre folded his fingers into a fist. "Why are you worried?"

"I have this niggling feeling—"

"—That something's not right?"

Reid nodded. "With Martin."

Examining his friend thoughtfully, Pierre said, "As a colleague, I have great respect for your instincts. As a policeman…pfft. Instincts are nothing but the uneasy feeling you get when you're in a situation and tension is building."

"That's what I'm afraid of."

"Nevertheless…" Pierre visibly debated with himself, then made the decision to speak. "Corruption is a European problem. A Latin American problem. In Europe and Latin America, it's well known that the police can be bribed. Here in America, that's not a problem. Usually." He lifted his eyebrows. "Is it?"

"Not usually." Thinking hard, Reid fiddled with his napkin. "Of course, any time you put people in a position of power, there are those few who abuse it."

"But it's not just a few. It seems as if, well… Usually, you understand, as a foreign *agent de police,* I am shown almost anything I ask to see. You Americans, you are so proud of your computers, your programs, your apps, your organization. You think that we in France are in the Stone Age of police enforcement, so you brag. This time, when I made a few casual inquiries about this case, the police shut me down as if I were a common nosy citizen. And from what you've told me, they've been criminally reluctant to give even you information."

"That's true, but I've never been involved with the police before. I thought they were always so—"

"*Non,* not to the family involved. I tell you, I've been trained to observe, to tell if a man is lying by the way he stands, by the way he moves his hands, and *mon ami*"—Pierre placed his hand on Reid's shoulder—"I think the whole Houston Police Department is lying through their teeth."

"The Houston Police—"

Pierre hushed him.

Reid lowered his voice. "—Have been lying to you?"

"And you."

"My God. Why?"

"If this were Europe or Latin America, I would know why. It's not, so I'm lost."

Still incredulous, Reid insisted, "The Houston Police are corrupt?"

"No. Yes. I honestly don't know. Almost, I said nothing, for I'm not sure…" Pierre rubbed his chin with his hand. "I can only say—do not totally depend on their resources. Maintain your own resources, too."

"I thought I was. What about Uncle Manuel?"

Pierre started eating again. "He has been lying, too, but he's an old man, and so proud of his falsehoods. Perhaps he's in with the police and their scheme, but more likely he has perhaps slipped a bit and the police are manipulating him. It's your grandfather I don't understand."

"That's nothing." Reid poured syrup on his bacon and used his biscuit to sop it up. "I've never understood Granddad."

"I think you understand him very well. I think you two are as alike as two peas in a pod." Pierre observed Reid, then crumpled bacon on his waffle, slid a soft fried egg off the platter onto the top of the bacon and waffle, then anointed the stack with half a pitcher of maple syrup. "And don't you think the way your grandfather seems almost anxious to be kidnapped is odd?"

"Anxious? He's not anxious."

Leaning closer, speaking softly, Pierre said, "Your grandfather relies totally on his servants—traditionally the originators of extortion schemes—and he forbids excess security men. He ignores your warnings about Martin Security, when it wouldn't—shouldn't—matter to him who the security firm is."

"He's a cantankerous old man," Reid protested. But Pierre had planted doubts, and he wondered if that was the whole truth.

"Yes, but…You're right, I suppose." Pierre shrugged. "It's all probably my imagination. Or mostly my imagination. You know, you're in charge here. Why don't *you* change the security firm?"

"Where did you ever get the idea I was in charge?"

Pierre protested. "A man's home—"

"This is my grandfather's home."

"Will you live here after you marry her?"

"No, I'm taking her house-shopping to find another place here in Houston—" Reid stopped, realizing what he'd admitted.

Pierre threw back his head and laughed out loud.

Heads turned.

Margaret stared.

Reid shushed him.

In a well-oiled maneuver from their college days, Pierre dropped his fork and Reid dropped his napkin, and they both leaned under the table.

"Marriage," Pierre said. "At last!"

"Don't rub it in."

"This woman—"

"Her name is Margaret," Reid said sternly.

"Of course, forgive me. This Margaret has tightened the noose around the neck of the most notorious flirt on six continents?"

"There are seven continents."

Pierre's eyebrows shot up. "You've *been* to Antarctica?"

"No, I haven't, and I'm not as bad as all that. You know I reached the age of good sense a damn sight earlier than you."

"Then all those stories I hear about you—"

"I've been celibate for longer than I want to discuss." The corners of Reid's mouth turned down. "I've been involved with two women since I was thirty. Two. Long-term relationships."

"*Non?*"

"*Non.* They never felt right." Reid raised his hands helplessly and dropped them. "I didn't know what was missing—until Margaret."

"Lucky Margaret, I'd say."

"I agree with you. Now, if only I can convince her..."

Beneath their noses, a fork appeared. Slowly, like little boys caught in a misdemeanor, they raised their joined heads.

Margaret knelt beside them, dangling silverware and napkin.

They both turned red.

Without a word, she pressed the necessary accouterments into their hands and disappeared.

With as much mutual dignity as they could summon, they sat up in their chairs to see everyone staring at them.

"How much do you think she heard?" Reid asked out of the corner of his mouth.

Pierre refused to speculate, using only a shrug to express himself and moving on to a subject of intense interest to him. "Does this mean I can make a move on that little redhead who flirted with you so determinedly last night?"

Reid recognized opportunity when he saw it. "Take her. With my blessing. In fact, if you could get her to France with you for a couple of weeks, I'd appreciate it. I'm tired of the distractions Margaret sticks under my nose with the assumption I'll snap at them like a weak-minded fool."

"Weak-minded? Hmm." Pierre scratched his chin. "I wouldn't call you weak-minded. Nor even weak-willed. Perhaps you should press your suit with a little more strength."

"Sweep her off her feet? Don't you think I want to? I'm so frustrated I'm jealous of my own grandfather. Besides"—Reid snorted—"she's had enough defense training, she's liable to sweep me off my feet, and the landing would not be soft."

"I'll hear the landing all the way to France."

Reid watched Margaret as she moved through the dining room, coordinating the service, speaking to the guests. "I suppose you will."

Nineteen

The door closed with a bang. *"What* are you doing?"

Margaret jumped, knocking her head against the frame of Reid's bed. "Ouch." She rubbed the spot ruefully. "Did you have to sneak up on me like that?"

"Next time I enter my bedroom," Reid said, "I'll make a lot of noise in case you're crawling around on the floor...doing *what?*"

Sitting with her back against the bed, she explained, "Mr. Jim and Amy are at Manuel's, playing pool and eating his wife's tamales. Nagumbi has disappeared—"

"He's doing some snooping for me."

"Of course he is. And Abigail has the day off. Everyone's out of the way, so I thought I'd come in here and have a look around." Possibly she had phrased that badly.

But as Reid leaned against the closed door of his bedroom, he seemed to be merely an illusion. He wore a black work-out suit that faded into the dark wood, making him a still and ghostly face and hands. Only the ruddy highlights of his hair glowed with life.

Yet for an illusion, he was solid, focused, and she...she too clearly remembered those dances in his arms. That had been a week ago. A whole seven days had passed, filled with work, worry about Mr. Jim, helping with Amy's homework, but at the most random times, she would recall Reid's heat, his strength, his incredible concentration...on her.

How seductive was that? To have a man who ignored everyone else...for her. Who made her feel fascinating, young, attractive...it had been far too many years since she'd been anything but a butler, a mother, and a widow.

Now she felt warm, flushed and desirable, and that created an intoxicating cocktail.

"Find anything interesting?" he drawled.

She needed to snap herself out of her daze. And him, too. "You are interesting, yes, and gorgeous, too—but you know that. On the other hand, I can clearly see problems—"

"I meant *in my room.* Did you find anything interesting in my room?"

"Oh." Time to cover up a very embarrassing gaffe, and fast. She stood, brushed off her black skirt with brisk motions, and made a mental note to talk to the cleaning team about dusting under the beds. "I should have asked if you minded. I'm just so used to going in and out of the rooms as I please, it never occurred to me. But this was your friend's suggestion."

"What friend?" Reid snapped.

"Your French friend. Pierre." She couldn't restrain the smile that curved her mouth. "Now that's an interesting man."

"Is he?"

"You know he is."

"Some women might think so."

"Most women do think so," she corrected, thinking of the way Chantal had fallen. "Those continental manners, the kiss on the hand, his accent—"

Reid stepped away from the door. "That *bastard.*"

Startled, she said, "He's nice!"

Reid's eyes glowed with an angry, unholy light. "He's worthless."

"He is not!" She almost sputtered in indignation. "We had a long talk about your grandfather and these kidnapping threats, and he gave me more suggestions than I've received from Martin Security and the entire Houston Police Force put together."

"Suggestions," Reid sneered.

"Yes, suggestions," she repeated. "He *suggested* I search for listening devices in *your* room and *your* study, because—"

Reid grabbed her hand and jerked her into his bathroom. "Hush." Reaching into his deluxe shower stall with its pulsating shower head and its built-in seat and its array of soaps, he twisted the knobs until the water gushed out full blast.

Pitching her voice above the roar, she asked, "What was that about?"

"*If* my room is bugged, we don't need to tell any listeners that you're on to them."

"Oh." She pushed up her sleeves to combat the increasingly steamy atmosphere. It was the steam from the shower that was making her warm, not Reid's proximity. "You're right, of course. I'll go back in and search, and we'll remain silent."

He blocked her path with one arm across the door. "Running away again?"

"Running away?" She pretended that she didn't know what he was talking about, and stepped back. "No, I'm merely doing my job."

"Your job description does not include treating *the master's* grandson like he has a terminal case of cooties."

She sputtered a weak laugh. "Cooties?"

His grim mouth never wavered. "Cooties. In fact, it's been a week since my party, and during that time you have rejected me and everything about me. I try to talk to you, to get to know you, and you flee as if the devil is on your heels. I send you flowers; you decorate Granddad's study with them. I send candy; it ends up in Abigail's kitchen. I arrange to take Amy to the zoo; your daughter and I go alone while you go off to lunch. The only time I see you unaccompanied by your various guardians is if you're in a room and I trap you there."

"Like now?"

Abrupt and precise, he removed the bar of his arm. "Go."

Perversely, his permission made her stay. Speaking slowly and carefully, like a trainer to her new tiger, she said, "I don't understand what you expect of me."

He crossed his arms over his chest, and he seemed taller than he really was—and that was too tall. "It's what I *don't* expect of you. I *don't* expect you to act as if I'm about to jump your bones, when all I've been trying to do is *ease* you into a normal relationship."

"Normal?"

"You know. Conversation, teasing, hand-holding, walks in the sunshine. The things that men and women do when they're approaching a merger."

"I don't want a merger…with you." She shouldn't have said it like that. But better to be blunt than to give him encouragement. Right?

"Call it a hostile merger." He sounded pleasant, almost happy, but he wore his barracuda smile. "It happens all the time. A big, bad corporation gobbles up a tiny little company, and together they cause a growth explosion."

Now she tried to slip past him.

But she'd missed her chance.

His hands grasped her waist and lifted her onto the counter with one easy motion.

She lifted her knee slightly in warning.

He flinched—he was a guy, flinching was required—and moved to one side. He leaned one hip against the counter. "I just want to kiss you, darlin'. Would you incapacitate me for one little kiss?"

"Why shouldn't I?" If this was a hostile merger, then hostility was her due.

"For one little kiss?" He sounded incredulous. "Do you really think one little kiss will be that earthshaking?"

"No…" No, of course it wouldn't, and she had things to prove to him. If he wanted to kiss her, she'd let him. She'd provide proof of her own indifference to him. And prove to herself he wasn't the spectacular lover her unruly body expected.

He leaned forward, slowly and carefully, giving her time to withdraw if she wished. He stroked his closed lips on her closed lips, a dry kiss of mutual exploration.

His touch woke nerve endings she'd decided were atrophied.

Atrophied nerve endings kept her safe. Awake nerve endings could cause trouble. *Would* cause trouble. And that wouldn't prove anything to him or her except that she was…susceptible. So maybe experimenting wasn't such a good idea, after all.

"Okay. You've had your kiss." She tried to slide off the counter.

He held her in place. "You call that a kiss?"

"What would you call it?"

"A preliminary." He did look surprisingly unmoved.

The jerk.

"Let's do this right," he said. "Okay?"

She could remain unmoved, and sound indifferent, too. And she did, when she said, "I suppose."

Making a yummy sound, half growl, half moan, he slid his fingers up the length of her leg to her knee. His other hand reached out and flexed around her other knee. "You're so sweet." He spoke fervently and stepped between her legs, catching her by surprise.

By surprise! She had been out of the game for far, far too long.

Come to think of it, she'd never been that good at the game in the first place.

He pulled her close against him.

Her skirt rode up. The tile was cool and smooth beneath her thighs, contrasting with the heat of Reid close between her legs.

He fit them together.

She looked down at them, where they were joined but for the insignificant pieces of clothing, then up at him.

His sherry eyes gleamed fire and pleasure…and challenge.

Surely she could retain her composure; surely she could.

But her brain functioned at a subnormal level, clogged by the riotous tide of hormones. She felt dependent, vulnerable, and she shivered as one hand slid under her skirt and all the way up to her hips.

He wrapped his big hand around the nape of her neck. "I've waited for you forever—and I didn't even know what I was waiting for." With his thumb, he lifted her chin. His lips sipped at her mouth like a connoisseur tasting a well-loved wine.

She opened her lips a little, wanting a taste of him, forbidden though it might be.

He encouraged her, subtly coaxing until her tongue was in his mouth and she was on the offensive. Her hands tugged at his hair. Her arms pulled him into her chest.

He was warm and muscular. He smelled…good, like soap and water and sizzling hot sex. He was everything she had unwillingly imagined, and she moved against him as if he was a familiar and cherished lover.

To hell with the rules.

He held her tightly, and groaned as if luxuriating in her aggression.

The sounds of his pleasure woke her from her exploration.

How did he so cunningly make her want what he wanted? How did he shut off the well-primed defenses that had historically kept her from disaster?

She pulled back, retreating from a precipice over which she could not afford to plunge.

He softly tsked, and tilted her, arching her back over his arm and taking command of the kiss.

In one easy movement, he rendered her off balance in body and spirit, and her squirming accomplished nothing but to make her aware—more aware—of his erection. She fought to keep her eyes open—a distraction to the most accomplished of kissers—but found her lids kept drooping. The most revealing of tiny moans vibrated at the back of her throat.

His hand found the arch of her neck and rested there, as if he were reveling in the sounds.

When he pulled back and looked at her, draped across his arm and stunned with pleasure, a peculiar expression crossed his face.

In any other man, she would have called it love. That tender quirk of pride and delight alarmed her more than any other manifestation of desire, and like a rabbit burrowing from trouble, she ducked her head into his chest.

His voice was a rumble, an earthshaking event that she could feel as much as hear. "You're the woman for me, and I'll convince you of it with all the bricks and blocks and mortar at my disposal. I'll build an edifice of knowing in you that you'll never destroy with your fears and your skepticism."

Twenty

"Oh, no, you won't." Margaret pulled away from the false comfort of Reid's arms. His hands tangled in her hair, and she could hear the "ting, ting" of her pins as they struck the tile. "No edifices for me."

His hand went to her cheek, and he stroked it. "Wouldn't you like to come with me and discover my secrets? I'm only a man, after all, and you might find what's between us isn't as cataclysmic as you fear."

He might be a man, but he wasn't *only* a man. And the cataclysm she feared shook her even now, after only a kiss. His face was a course in salesmanship, but she was steadfast. "I'm refusing you."

He stared, eyes stunned, then shot back across the bathroom as if she'd burned his fingers. With a wealth of bitterness, he accused, "You'd care for a rabid dog and destroy a lover who's had all his shots." Reaching into the shower again, he adjusted the temperature.

"I have the right to refuse you," she said, sliding off the counter.

"Yes, you do. And I have the right to take a cold shower." He walked into the shower, slapping the door shut behind him.

"Don't be foolish." She reached down and caught her skirt as it sagged around her waist.

When had his nimble fingers undone the fastenings at the back?

She swung the frosted glass door wide. "Your clothes…"

His work-out outfit sopped up water. His sweatshirt stretched. The elastic in his pants strained under the weight. Water turned his hair black and ran in rivulets off his face. He glared. "Run away while you can, little girl."

She felt foolish and quite unlike the rational butler she knew herself to be. She found herself wringing her hands. "You can't expect me to leave when so much is unsettled."

He gestured grandly. "Then come in. Perhaps this cold water will thaw a little of that frozen interior."

That made her mad, as mad as he seemed to be. "I must be frigid," she mocked, stepping in and up to him. Cold water pelted her, spraying off his shoulders and around his face. "That's the *only* reason any woman could resist you."

"How true that is." He pulled his sweat shirt off and flung it through the open shower door at the mirror where it splatted water all over the glass, the sinks, the tile.

A tantrum. He was throwing a tantrum.

"Now look what you did," she said. "I'll have to send one of the maids in to clean up the—" She turned back to face him. She faltered.

The sunshine filtering through the window flattered him. She'd seen it all before. Shouldn't she be inoculated against the stroke of light and shadow over his skin? Shouldn't she know that strength was merely an illusion and that her belief that he could hold her, protect her, keep her from loneliness was nothing more than a wistful fantasy?

Yet her hands tingled, wanting to stroke him.

She bent down, pulled off her one wet, black leather heel and tossed it after the sweat shirt.

"Now look what you've done." He imitated her in high falsetto. "I'll have to call one of the maids to clean up."

"God, you're a jackass."

He laughed with deliberate insolence. "God, you're a tease."

"I'm not!"

He laughed again, and she followed his gaze down to herself. Her unfastened skirt hung on the curve of her hips. Her jacket sagged about her shoulders, baring her bosom where the clinging white of a silk button-up shirt hid nothing. Her black vest framed her breasts for emphasis. Her bra was obviously unruly, for one chilled nipple thrust itself above the cup and dared him to take notice.

He noticed.

He burned like an oil fire with no way to extinguish it. Yet he controlled the flame with a mighty stillness, and his lips scarcely moved as he warned, "Run. Away. Now."

The only sound in the bathroom was the rush of water and her own harsh breathing. She couldn't stop looking at his face, at the tense muscles and hot eyes. She couldn't stop looking at his body, lean and hungry for her.

Their chemistry exploded when put in contact, but still he denied himself what he could have so easily. He was impatient, but not unselfish…and something in her ignited.

The something seemed to be in her heart. She might not want this fire, but it existed. The flames urged her, cajoled her, dared her to reveal a little bit of herself. An unimportant part of herself. For if she touched him, joined with him, surely that wouldn't mean she liked him…loved him.

He said again, "Go."

"No."

The word dropped into the stillness between them, breaking it like a stone breaks the ice on a puddle.

He moved on her with savage intent. He crowded her against the copper tile wall. He plastered his body against hers and kissed her with the finesse of a liberty-bound sailor.

And she kissed him back.

"God," he breathed into her mouth. "Give me all of you."

His exhilaration poured more fuel on her flames. She tried to wrap one leg around his hips, but her skirt was too tight.

He tried to unzip her shirt, but the thin silk was wet and unwieldy. His hands flashed to her neck, and the material ripped with ease. A few buttons clinked on the floor, but most hung intact on the torn blouse.

Her excitement raced to meet his. "You dare," she breathed, and in a grand gesture, she flung off her jacket and shirt.

As with all grand gestures, it went awry.

Her hands caught in the tight cuffs, but Reid jerked both buttons free for her, then stopped to stare at her breast. "Like a puppy's nose peeking out, begging me to pet it," he said.

She tried to chuckle insouciantly, but as he touched one trembling finger to that impudent nipple, her breath caught in her throat.

He looked at his finger as if he'd touched a light socket and been zapped. "I can't wait." His palms spanned her waist and stroked the skirt all the way down her long, long legs. He slid back up her body and placed a lingering kiss on her plain white cotton underwear. He tossed her clothes over the top of the door, and as he looked at her, as his gaze absorbed her, he groaned. Groping behind him, he adjusted the water, bringing it to a comfortable temperature.

She was committed now. Committed to this act of love. She corrected herself. To this act of *lust*.

There was no turning back.

And she couldn't lie to herself. She didn't want to turn back. Aware of her power over him, she pulled her headband off and shook out her hair with a challenging smile. Ducking beneath the water, she let it run over her until she was soaked, until the scraps of material she still wore revealed everything…but hid too much.

Reid's expression challenged her in return, but without a smile. Taking up the shampoo, he measured the creamy liquid into the palm of his hand.

She watched curiously as he spread it between his hands and reached for her. He slid his fingers into her blond hair, and massaged her, and rich, white, lather sprang to life.

Uncertain, she tried to take over from him.

He brushed her hands aside. "Relax," he whispered. "Feel this."

Sensuality, he forced her to realize, was not confined to the accepted erogenous zones. His fingertips fed magic through the nerves in her scalp, strong and firm massaging her neck, then the kiss of a butterfly's wing around the shells of her ears. His gaze followed a blob of shampoo as it drifted down the side of her neck, down her chest and then lingered on the edge of her lacy bra.

Each breath she took incited him.

Each breath he took made her aware of his size, his strength, his fever.

His eyes met hers once more, filled with a mixture of desire and a hard possession. Plunging his hands into her hair again, he brought forth a renewed lather and muttered, "I thought I just liked the smell, but this shampoo is…erotic…"

"Yes." The motion of his fingers both relaxed her…and excited her. Never in her wildest sexual fantasies—and lately, she'd had quite a few—had she imagined anything like this. She didn't know where this would lead…but she followed eagerly, breathlessly.

Gathering drifts of fragrant woody-scented suds, he rubbed them on her neck, on her chest, on the one nipple that pebbled beneath his hand. The front clasp of her bra slipped open, seemingly by itself, and those torturing hands wandered to her stomach, down…

She caught his hand.

"Let me," he whispered. "Let me just…" He rubbed shampoo on his own chest. Linking their hands, palm to palm, he pulled their bodies together. And moved. Skin glided, flowed, in the most decadent sensation Margaret had ever experienced. It was like being massaged with mink or sable, but the masseur was alive and rippling with muscle. He groaned, a gut-wrenching expression of pleasure that brought her almost to the peak. Almost…

Too soon. Too embarrassing. Too needy. She caught herself, stopped herself.

With a boldness that stole her breath, he slid his hands under her bottom and picked her up. He pressed her against the wall and wrapped her legs around him.

She moaned, "Heavy…"

"No." He was guttural with need. "Saved myself…"

His hips undulated against her.

The sensation was too exquisite to endure.

She wanted him inside her. Now. Quickly. *Now.*

But damn it. He was still wearing his work-out pants.

She held onto his shoulders. Tried to hook her heels under the elastic at his waist. Stupid, futile move—and one he seemed to appreciate.

He put her legs down. Pushed her under the shower head. He scrubbed the soap from her hair, rubbed the lather from her body, took her panties from her hips and let them drop to the floor.

As he rinsed himself, she shrugged her shoulders, and the already unhooked bra slid away.

Wiping the water from her face, he stared seriously into her eyes. "If we do this now, will we be parents in nine months?"

Margaret covered her mouth in surprise.

She nodded.

How could she have forgotten?

Reid pulled her close and kissed her, a kiss of promise. "I'll take care of it." He peeled off his pants.

Erection. He had an erection. She had known he had an erection, but to see it, veined, strong and beautiful…

He aroused every single one of her senses. His kiss tasted of sensuality. The scent of his shampoo filled her head. The sight and sound and touch of him pleasured her. He was carnal satisfaction personified.

Then, like a magician, he produced a condom package out of his pocket and showed her.

Twenty-one

There was reality, like a lump of coal sitting in the middle of Reid's palm.

Aghast, Margaret asked, "Do you always keep them on you?"

"No, darlin'." Reid chuckled and eased her down on the cool tile seat. "Over time, body heat will destroy the latex. Didn't you know that?"

She shook her head.

"So I only carry one when I hope to hustle one sexy, overconfident little butler."

She should be insulted that he was so self-assured.

But mostly she was relieved.

She did *not* want to stop now.

He pushed her knees apart and knelt between her thighs. He touched her lightly, easing her open. He looked, and his eyes heated with molten desire. "God. Beautiful. You're so...beautiful."

His gaze made her feel beautiful. His gentle touch made her feel...

She whispered, "If you don't do this soon..."

A smile played at the edges of his mouth. "What will happen?"

She didn't know exactly how to say it. Finally she blurted, "What's the female equivalent of premature ejaculation?"

He leaned close. His lips brushed her ears, his breath whispered along her neck. "Decadence incarnate. The first of a multitude of orgasms."

She put her hands on his shoulders, kneaded them like a cat, and with each touch, she absorbed the intensity of him. "Please," she said. "Now."

"A little more." He leaned back again. "Let me prepare you a little more."

"You can't. There is no *more.*"

But he didn't believe her, because when he looked between her legs, he licked his lips as if he was s starving beast viewing a gourmet meal. His eyes narrowed, his breath grew deep. Always intense, he was now heated, focused, absorbed. His hands slid up her thighs, up until his thumbs touched her, opened her...

She knew what he wanted to do. Would do. And the mere realization made her want...

Want.

She thought perhaps she absorbed desire from him, for never had she suffered such a fever before. When he put his mouth on her...she leaned against the cool wall, tilted her head back, and knew nothing but lips sucking at her clit, his tongue sliding over her and in her, while his fingers rubbed her, thrust into her, deep into her.

For the first time in years, everything was about her.

And she convulsed in sweet agony.

He laughed. The sound wasn't threatening or humiliating, but pleased and excited. "Help me," he commanded, tearing the foil and pressing the condom into her palm.

Her hands shook as she stared at the roll, then at him. His face was rigid, waiting for her to decide, waiting for release.

"All *right.*" She gathered her nerve, and laid her hand on him.

Here was the source of his heat and his hurry. His erection strained and pulsated and transmitted to her his urgency. She rolled the condom along his length.

"Look at me, love." Reid's eyes flashed a message of enchantment. "Now." He entered her easily. As her flesh swallowed his, an indescribable savor relaxed her muscles.

Then they were off, galloping away with the pleasure.

He slowed for her when she shuddered, slowed when her toes pointed and her teeth clenched, slowed as climax after climax jolted her. Then he hurried off again, flying toward his satisfaction and never quite getting there.

His voice cajoled, tantalized, whispered suggestions that tickled her ear as they teased her mind. His hands stroked, caressed, propelled her head to his chest, urged her mouth to taste him.

His approval showered on her, like the water that splattered off his shoulders in a fine mist and ran in rivulets down his chest.

Their rhythm unbroken, he pulled her off the seat, sinking to rest on his bent knees. His hands steadied her spine as she took control, using her legs to drive the pulse of their lovemaking.

His mouth caught her nipple and suckled eagerly.

She slowed the demands of her body to savor it.

The tendons of his shoulders strained beneath her hands as he tensed to match their separate tempos, but at last he gasped, "No more." Holding her clamped to him, he swung her onto the floor of the shower and began to thrusts deeply, powerfully, gloriously.

Her back melted into the floor tiles, her feet clenched his spine. Spray drenched her. Rushing water surrounded her. The grandest climax of all burgeoned within her.

She couldn't contain it. It was too grand, too overwhelming to mandate. In one titanic surge, she clamped her arms around him, her legs around him, her body around him. Sounds broke from her, uncensored by art or prudence.

Sounds echoed in her ear as Reid groaned and gasped.

For both of them, every muscle was devoted to their flowering. Every movement amplified their elation. It was earthy sorcery, magic carnality, and for a moment they were lost in the mist of victory together.

Then the pace slowed. Stopped.

Breathless with triumph, she released him, arms and legs falling away to rest on the tiles.

He sank atop her. Tiny aftershocks jarred her, and he encouraged them with subtle meanderings of his fingers, with deft rocking of his hips.

She came to rest at last. Opening her eyes, she saw his shoulder jutted up, protecting her from the spray. She saw the copper tile surrounding her, felt the discomfort of the ceramic floor, heard the clamor of the water as it cascaded down the walls.

Reid leaned to one side and caressed the sun of her hair where it joined her face. "Next time," he said, "we'll use the trapeze."

Twenty-two

Reid's voice reverberated through his chest, through Margaret where they joined.

She blinked.

"It's a good thing we have instant hot water." Elevating himself, he stared down at them, at her, as if he savored the closeness.

She flushed with a sudden glow. He looked at her as if she were the most gorgeous woman in the world. As if she were a goddess of ancient Greece, with arms and head attached. As if she were the first woman he had ever seen.

His voice rumbled with tenderness. "Next time—"

Her attention snapped into place. "Next time? What do you mean, next time?"

He raised his eyebrows. His eyes smiled. "Just what I said."

"No next time. No way."

"You're mighty bold for a woman in your position." He nodded at their twined bodies, at her lax ease.

Her legs snapped to attention. "Please."

"Get off? Of course." He slowly removed himself from her body.

The physical pang of regret shocked her. She felt empty, and wistful.

He pushed himself up, resting on his hands and knees above her. His posture showed his reluctance to leave her. His eyes devoured her as she slid away. Rising, he extended a hand to her. She gazed at the broad palm with indecision until he teased, "What are you afraid of? I've already done my worst." Reaching down, he grasped her wrist and hauled her up, and laughed indulgently. "Or my best."

"Yes. Yes. It was very nice."

"Wow. Please. Don't flatter me with such exorbitant praise. It'll go to my head." He reached for the bar of soap. "I've fallen in love with this scent. What do you think it is?"

"Some forest-like stuff…" He was distracting her. She planted her feet firmly. She wanted to gaze at him, to reason with him.

But he turned her to wash her back.

Speaking to the wall, she said, "You've had me now — "

"Amen to that." He rubbed her shoulders with soapy hands, rubbed her back, slid in twin circles on her buttocks.

"—And you've discovered I'm just a woman."

"Not just a woman," he corrected. "My woman."

Panic closed her throat. She turned to face him.

If he had been angry or cold, she could have handled it. But Reid was amused and lenient, willing to humor her and sure he would get his own way. He smiled and soaped his hands again.

She said, "I have a daughter, an impressionable child. You and I can't have sex whenever we—"

"Sex? That wasn't sex." He scrubbed soap down her arms, between her fingers, across the palm of her hand. "That, my unsophisticated darling, was the most magnificent mating since peanut butter and celery, Triscuits and Brie." Leaning down, he lightly bit her nipple. "Yum."

"Unusual combinations," she choked.

"Yes, we are. But perfect together."

Her traitorous body shifted toward him, eager to indulge itself even while she denied it. "I don't want to be one of your women. I can't come running for a quickie every time you whistle. I'm a butler, a mother—"

"My woman," he repeated. He transferred his attention to the other breast.

Spelling it out, she said, "I cannot fornicate with you every — "

He interrupted her. "Do you know who encouraged me to come after you?"

"Your grandfather, no doubt," she said bitterly.

"Oh, no, my fabulous darling. I've heard urging and suggesting and downright nagging this last week, and it all started at the zoo."

Margaret's mouth snapped closed and the last remnants of passion fled. Drawing herself up, she said, "That's a terrible thing to say."

Reid leaned back against the copper colored tile and folded his arms across his chest. "Take the bull by the horns, Amy said. No use waiting for Mom to change her mind, she said, because once it's set, only a federal amendment could sway it."

"You brought it up to her. You prompted her!" she cried.

His temper flared. He grabbed her arms and dragged her close, chest to chest. "I do not drag children into these kinds of battles."

But Margaret boldly searched his eyes. What she saw there relaxed her suspicions and made her sorry. He looked hurt; she had impugned his honor and doubted his affection for Amy. " I apologize." Still... "How did the subject come up?"

"You know your daughter; you know she's sharp as a tack and twice as bright about human relations as any psychotherapist. Is it any surprise that she's noticed what's happening between you and me?"

"Nothing's happening between..." She faltered; he looked so sardonic.

"This"—he gestured around the shower—"was a hell of a passionate nothing."

Twenty-three

Margaret sat on the balcony outside her bedroom and stared into the night. The planet Venus shone just above the trees, bright and unblinking, and she cursed it. "Goddess of Love, indeed. Are you responsible for my behavior today?"

Hm. Surprising. She got no response.

She had made a terrible, terrible mistake by opening the doors to her own sensuality. She'd put her body in the deep freeze for so long, she'd imagined she was frozen solid. Now life pulsed into the frostbitten parts, and it hurt. It stung, it throbbed, and she didn't want to have to deal with it.

Why did it have to be with Reid?

In some vague way, she'd imagined that someday she'd find another man and they'd marry. Her dreams had been of a mature love, gentle and kind and tender, without the peaks and valleys that characterized youthful passion. So what if she hardly qualified for the senior citizens' tour of Florida? At thirty-four, she felt as if she'd lived forever.

Luke had been sick for so long. So wretchedly sick, and each day had been filled with midnight, and each week had stretched eternally. The young woman she'd been before had vanished in the nights of illness. All her inner joy had faded; if it weren't for Amy's youthful exuberance, she thought she'd be terminally grim.

Now Margaret had made love with a man who acted as if he'd discovered sex. His eyes had glowed as he appreciated her body with hands and mouth. He'd made no secret of his heady arousal, yet combined his impatience with inventiveness and endurance.

He'd laughed when they made love. Laughed! As if sex was a joyful experience, as if he'd never been so happy.

Damn him, he'd driven her to impatience and inventiveness and rekindled the demands of her body—and, she feared, rekindled the demands of her own loving heart.

She groaned out loud.

From behind her Amy said, "Mom?"

Margaret jumped, half-afraid she'd been talking to herself. She turned to face her daughter. Her voice hit a high note. "Yes, dear?"

"Are you okay?"

"Fine, dear."

"You sounded sick."

Margaret hesitated. What could she say? "I sat on my foot wrong."

"Is it asleep?" Amy came onto the balcony. "Do you want me to massage it?"

Sticking out her stocking-clad foot, Margaret grinned through the darkness at her daughter. "Talked me into it. Shut the door behind you or you'll let bugs into the house." The screen bounced against the frame, and Margaret winced at her daughter's enthusiasm.

Amy pulled up a chair and took her mother's foot into her lap. "You always do this for me when I have growing pains."

"I had 'em when I was your age, too." Margaret couldn't resist. She stroked Amy's blond hair with a loving hand.

They kept the porch light off to discourage the insects, yet the city surrounded the estate, and glowed constantly. Margaret could dimly see Amy's animated face, her height, and her developing figure. Her daughter was growing up so quickly. Too quickly.

"Did you have two parents when you were my age?" The tone was innocent. The question was not.

Margaret considered carefully before answering. "No, actually, I didn't. My parents were divorced. They treated me like a hot potato. *You take her. No, you take her.* Getting stuck with the kid was punishment."

"I'll bet you missed having two parents."

Oh. That's where Amy was headed. "That's why I always adored your daddy's family so much. So close and loving."

"Yes, now I feel like I have two families. Daddy's family and Mr.

Jim's family."

The kid was not in the least subtle. But Margaret had a question she'd longed to ask, and the quiet and darkness around them made it easier. "Do you remember your daddy?"

"Sure." Amy sounded perky and certain. "He was funny."

"He was that. Do you remember what he looked like?"

"Yes." Amy didn't seem to be so positive about that. "He was thin and his hands trembled when he held me."

Margaret was quiet, remembering those last days filled with pain and grief.

Amy's voice grew quieter, more subdued. "I've seen your wedding picture. He was good looking when he was young, wasn't he?"

He never had the chance to get old.

But if Margaret said that, what would that do but make Amy feel ignorant and uncomfortable? A child of nine can accept what her mother struggled with, and Margaret didn't want to destroy that acceptance. This was better for Amy. The girl's fading memory left her with no bitterness and an eager resolution to find another father.

"Do your feet feel better, Mama?"

Margaret leaned over and patted her hand. "Yes, thank you. That felt so good, I drifted off for a moment. Aren't you supposed to be in bed now?"

"I had to massage my mother's feet first."

"I knew I kept you around for something."

Amy laughed, but didn't move from her perch on the chair.

Uh-oh. When her daughter sat still, trouble was brewing. Maybe the dark made it easier for Amy to confess something, too. Maybe she hadn't come out simply to urge marriage on her mother. "What is it, honey?"

Amy squirmed. "I've been wanting to tell you this for a while."

Margaret grew concerned, and in her most soothing tone, she said, "You can tell me anything, dear."

"I know I can." Amy sounded strained. "But you're going to be mad about this one."

"I promise not to get mad."

"Promise?"

"Promise."

"Sir Gramps has left me his horse ranch in east Texas."

"What?" Margaret shouted, surging to her feet.

"You *promised*," Amy reminded.

Margaret just stood there. She knew her mouth was hanging open. She knew she'd failed to live up to her daughter's expectations of a fair hearing. But never in her life had she imagined... "Tell me about it," she whispered.

Amy's voice squeaked. "Are you mad?"

"No, I'm not mad." Margaret took a deep breath and subsided into her chair. "Not much, anyway. Not at you, anyway. *How* did this happen?"

"Well, remember when I went to the stud farm last spring break?"

"Yes."

"I came back and told Sir Gramps how much I loved it and I wanted my own horse and all that stuff, and you told me to stop telling him or we'd have a horse grazing on the lawn, and it was against the law inside Houston."

"Right."

"Remember how Sir Gramps laughed and said if you spread a little money around, nobody cares how much manure's in the grass?"

"Except he didn't say manure. I remember." Margaret reached up and massaged her own neck. She could see where this was going, and she wondered how she could have missed it before.

"Well, when I came back from California, Sir Gramps told me he wanted to give me a gift. So he gave me the stud farm."

"And you said...?"

"Thank you," Amy said proudly.

Margaret began to chuckle. It was too much to suppose a nine-year old would have the phrase, *This is too much,* in her vocabulary. "Dear girl," she tried to say, but the laughter kept coming. "Dear girl," she tried again. "We can't afford to have him give you a stud farm."

"Why not?" Amy sounded indignant.

"We can't afford to feed the horses. We can't afford to pay the taxes. We can't afford any of it. A stud farm is a rich man's toy."

"It's okay," Amy answered, very sure of herself. "Sir Gramps left me the money to pay for all that stuff."

Abruptly Margaret's laughter stopped. "What do you mean, he left you the money to pay for it? How much money?"

"I don't know, I didn't ask him. I was just so happy." Amy

squirmed some more. "But then I started thinking…maybe you wouldn't like it."

"An understatement if ever I've heard one."

"I'm sorry," Amy said, misery in her tone.

Margaret held out her arms.

Amy moved into her lap and put her head on Margaret's shoulder.

"Don't be sorry, honey. It's Mr. Jim all the way." She rubbed Amy's back. "You're going to have to hold me if you grow much more."

"I *am* getting big, aren't I?" Amy asked proudly.

"You sure are. Whatever happened to that little baby I rocked?"

Amy laid back against the crook of Margaret's arm and looked up at her. "I'm still here."

Squeezing her tight, Margaret patted her daughter until she was sure Amy no longer worried about the *gift*. Casually she asked, "When did Mr. Jim say you would get this gift?"

"After he died. He said he wanted to give it to me, but he was…"

"Was what?"

"He said something really weird. I think he said he was baiting a hook with his will." Amy was puzzled.

Margaret was not. "That damned old—"

"Mah-om!"

"Never mind. I'll take care of it," Margaret assured her.

"Do I have to give it back?"

"You haven't got it yet. But yes, you'll have to give it back. At least now I know why Reid was so angry when he heard about that will." She pushed Amy to her feet and swatted her behind. "Bedtime."

Amy kissed Margaret. "Mom, we need to go get me some school supplies for my science project."

"Okay, honey. We'll go this weekend."

"Mom, I need to get started," Amy nagged.

Margaret sighed. "Is it going to be as messy as last year? I'll tell you right now, I'm putting my foot down when it comes to living plants."

"Okay," Amy said brightly.

"And no animals of either amphibious or reptilian extraction."

"Okay." The child's chipper enthusiasm dipped.

Margaret hugged her with all her might. "Call me when you're in bed and I'll tuck you in."

Amy made it through the door, and then she stuck her head back out. "If I had another father, he could tuck me in sometimes."

She slammed the door before Margaret could reply.

Margaret clasped her head in her hands. Who remembered the handsome, vibrant man she married?

Other people did have their memories.

His father remembered his son, Lucius.

His colleagues remembered their friend, Dr. Guarneri.

Only she remembered him as her husband, Luke: talking with her, fighting with her, loving her. Those memories were fading, and she fiercely resented it.

She resented Reid.

She'd satisfied her curiosity about Reid, and she'd never let him take her again.

But she was haunted by one question. She watched Venus set behind the trees and asked that heartless goddess, "How can I handle the fact *I* want to take him?"

Twenty-four

The next morning, someone knocked at the open library door.

Reid lifted his gaze from the pile of work on his desk to see Cliff Martin hovering just inside.

"Mr. Donovan," Martin said, "can I speak to you for a minute?"

"Of course. Come in." Reid watched with a cynical amusement as Martin sneaked through the study door like a substandard James Bond and with exaggerated care, eased it shut behind him.

"I hate to bother you when you're working."

"It's all right." Rubbing his neck beneath the casual open-necked tennis shirt, Reid gestured the security man into a chair. "My eyes are exhausted, anyway. Where's your cohort?"

"What?"

"Nolan Salas. Where is he?"

"He had work to do on our computer. He's smart, you know. I guess that's why my father sent him..." Cliff frowned and rubbed his nose.

Reid leaned back in his executive chair and studied Cliff. The man was wearing the same brown pin-striped suit he'd worn the first time they'd met, and it looked as if he'd slept in it every night since. The bags under his faithful hound-dog eyes were more pronounced. The smell of cigars hung heavy around him and telltale yellow stained his fingers.

But Reid couldn't ignore the taut shrewdness of the mouth, nor could he ignore Pierre's suggestion of corruption, so he said gently, "I make my living with these computers."

"Oh, yeah."

Reid idly scribbled Salas's name on a notepad, and underlined it firmly. Time to check out his background. "Do you think Salas is smarter than me?"

"No. I mean, he's not rich or anything." Cliff fumbled in his pocket and pulled out the half-smoked stub of a cigar.

"Not in here."

"What?" Cliff raised the wounded, infuriated, innocent face of a nicotine addict.

"You can't smoke in here."

Cliff's eyes slid to the smelly ashtray.

"Uncle Manuel and his pipe. Unfortunately, I don't have enough seniority to forbid him his pipe." Reid's words hovered unspoken in the air—*But I do have enough seniority over you.*

Dropping the cigar back into his coat pocket, Cliff dusted his fingers. "I'm quitting anyway."

"Good idea," Reid said. "What have you uncovered about the extortionists?"

"Me? Nothing. The police here don't take kindly to folks sticking their noses into official investigations. My job is just security; making sure they don't snatch your grandfather."

"What has Salas found out?"

"I don't know."

"If he's good with computers, surely you had him hack into the police mainframe."

"No. No! I mean… Well. Yes. He tried." Cliff fumbled at his pocket, saw the way Reid looked at him, and took his hand away. "He wasn't successful."

"Are you sure?"

"Yes. He wouldn't lie to me."

"Hm." Reid tapped his fingers together. "Where were you when my grandfather was snatched?"

"Busy trusting the wrong people, I can tell you. I should never have taken that time off to go to my uncle's funeral." Cliff clucked his tongue mournfully. "I mean, I leave town for one day, and see what happens? This kidnapper's definitely an insider." He tapped his forehead. "Knows too much."

"I'm afraid I have to agree." But was it Cliff? Or Salas? Or one of the other staff? "Have you found any incriminating evidence about the, er, insiders?"

"Everybody has some *thing* that makes them a suspect. That footman, Simon, needs the money. He's going to school and working and sending home money to his mother. Abigail's in love with that Nagumbi fellow—maybe she's doing it to get his attention. Nagumbi —" Cliff rolled his eyes. "That guy is strange."

"He's beyond suspicion," Reid said firmly.

Cliff snapped to attention. "Of course. But it would certainly make my work a lot easier if we could put more men inside. Having one guy standing around dressed like one of the queen's guard might be entertaining for old—for Mr. Donovan, but it's tough getting good men who are willing to do it."

"Money is a mighty incentive."

"I know, but don't you think we could get a few more people in the house?"

Reid shook his head.

Cliff persisted. "Just a few more people to beef up security? With only one guy inside and a couple lurking outside, I'll tell you the truth, I can't guarantee we'll always be able to keep tabs on your grandpop."

"Mr. Donovan"—Reid stressed the name—"doesn't like the feeling of being trapped in his own home, and if we tried to bring *more* people in, he'd have *all* of them thrown out."

"Can't you use your influence?"

My God, the guy was a whiner. "I'm combat-trained," Reid said. "So is Ms. Guarneri. You'll have to depend on us."

"You, yes." Cliff wagged a finger. "I don't know about Ms. Guarneri. She's actually what brings me here."

Reid raised a questioning eyebrow.

Cliff drew it out. "Are you ready?"

"Yes," Reid said.

Cliff delved into his suit coat again, this time pulling a plain gold envelope from the inside pocket. In contrast to the rest of his person, this envelope was unmarked, uncreased, and clean. Pulling his chair closer to the desk, he opened it and pulled out several photographs. Half standing, he spread them out, one at a time, before Reid.

Reid had no more time for speculation about Cliff.

In the pictures before him, Margaret sat in various poses. Worried, smiling, serious, concerned, all her expressions were caught by the camera…as were the expressions of the two men with whom she visited.

Good looking guys, one with a hawk nose, the other with a scar and nineteen-eighties Fabio hair.

Masking his shock—but not soon enough, he feared—Reid studied the snapshots with strained nonchalance. "Who are these guys?"

They both looked dangerous.

Women liked dangerous.

"I dunno, but I thought this was something you should see," Cliff said. "Our Little Miss Margaret seems to have more going on than she tells us."

Reid gestured to him to continue.

"She's been meeting these guys frequently for lunch."

"Only for lunch?" Reid asked, remembering the afternoon Margaret had taken off to go get Amy. Surely she wouldn't involve her daughter with these…strangers.

"Yeah, only for lunch. I talked to the owner of the café. Margaret used to meet them about once a week. She's kicked it up to two, three days a week."

"Who are the men?" Frost touched Reid's face, his words.

"Can't say. Swarthy buggers, though, aren't they?"

Reid leaned over the pictures again, picking them up one at a time. "Yes, they are."

"Terrorists or Mafiosi," Cliff suggested.

"Or…foreign dignitaries." Hey. Reid was trying to be fair.

"Yeah. Foreigners. You know how they are. Always organizing into gangs and blowing each other's heads off, when they're not kidnapping helpless old men."

"Do you have any evidence for what you're saying?" Reid looked up at Cliff.

"Nope. That's why I brought this to you. Usually I can find information on anybody if I try. Hell, I can tell you which breakfast cereal our Miss Margaret preferred when she was eight. But these guys are a total mystery, and that's not normal. They don't seem to have a job. I followed them. Don't seem to have a past." Cliff subsided into his chair. "As good-looking as those two are, I couldn't help but wonder if our Miss Margaret's had her head turned."

Reid picked up one snapshot and studied Hawk Nose's profile: tanned skin, flashing white teeth, dark hair falling gracefully across his forehead. "I don't see what's so attractive about *him*."

"Neither do I," Cliff agreed. "I can't see what's so attractive about his brother, either, but there's no accounting for women's taste. Every damn time our Miss Margaret left the café, those two guys had to fight off the females." Digging in his pocket, he pulled out the half-smoked cigar. "Couple of damn Roman gods."

"His brother?" Reid stared at the photo, at Margaret, seated at the table, smiling at the guys without a wary tremble to her lips. Reid would give half his fortune to have her look at him like that, and here she was, smiling at a couple of hoodlums…a couple of Roman god hoodlums. Absorbed in his agonizing appraisal, Reid never noticed as Cliff struck a match and puffed until the cigar glowed. "How do you know those are brothers?"

"Look at them." Cliff stood up and shuffled through the photographs until he found what he sought. His stubby finger pointed at the two male faces. "If those two aren't related, I'm not Cliff Martin."

Reid looked up.

What an interesting thought.

Maybe this *wasn't* Cliff Martin. Maybe that was what made all his instincts jangle. He'd have Nagumbi check it out.

Cliff stood, his stogie smoking between his fingers, and looked at his employer. But he couldn't keep eye contact. He shuffled his feet. He stubbed out his cigar in Manuel's ashtray.

Reid shook his head. It was hard to believe this fool was anything but what he said.

Nevertheless, he would have Nagumbi look into Cliff's background, and into computer wizard Nolan Salas. The results might be interesting. And enlightening.

Returning to the matter at hand, Reid snapped, "Have you brought this to the attention of the police?"

"No, sir." Cliff leaned over to gather up the photographs.

"I'll keep these, if you don't mind."

"Sure. Keep 'em." Cliff began to back toward the door. "Got 'em backed up on my hard drive."

"Why haven't you gone to the police?" Reid asked.

Cliff's retreat accelerated. "There's nothing incriminating here, just suspicious. It'd take more than this to interest the police. I just thought *you'd* be curious."

"I find it all very curious."

"Yes. This will give you something to think about as you shower."

Twenty-five

Hands in pockets, Reid watched silently as Nagumbi scanned his bedroom and bathroom with some rented electronic device that picked up on electronic devices.

Finally, Nagumbi turned off his machine and shook his head. "There are no listening devices installed in the area. Which is not to say they haven't been removed."

"Or Cliff Martin made a random comment."

Nagumbi raised his eyebrows. "About…?"

"Nothing that was any of his business. Or yours. But Martin hit too close to home for comfort." One day, Reid and Margaret had their moment in the shower. The next morning, Martin had brought his suspicions to Reid, and said, *This will give you something to think about as you shower.* And today, here he was with Nagumbi, scanning his bedroom for bugs.

That pissed Reid off. And worried him. But really, it pissed him off.

That memory, of his time in the shower with Margaret, was private, a treasure to be recalled in detail, a pleasure to be relived in private moments…a hope for the future.

Nagumbi continued, "Cliff Martin's identity checked out. He's son of the Kentucky security magnate. Of course, whether or not he's Cliff Martin is immaterial. He could still be our suspect."

"Social media?"

"Indeed. According to his own social media, he is the foremost bodyguard and security expert in the United States, and indeed, the world." Nagumbi pulled his iPad from his jacket pocket. He tapped the screen, and never changed expression as he read, "According to a disgruntled girlfriend, *Cliff Martin couldn't find my clit when I drew him a map, and any loser who owned an Indiana Jones hat could beat him up.*"

"Oo. Scathing." But Reid couldn't help but grin.

"Yes." Nagumbi worked his iPad. "Nolan Salas was harder to trace. He's an immigrant from Guatemala, now an American citizen, in the United States legally, but his origins are cloudy at best. The senior Mr. Martin thinks highly of him, citing especially his computer skills."

Reid thought about the small, thin, unobtrusive man who was so easily overlooked. "I like him for our villain."

Nagumbi tapped his iPad. "His social media appears to be quite open. He has a girlfriend who is an engineer and as unremarkable-looking as he is. He collects coins. He visited his parents last year in Guatemala and posted pictures of them. Everything seems to be above board."

"As far as I can tell, Cliff pays no attention to him. Salas could be doing anything, especially if he knows how to hack into a computer."

"Very true. A person who successfully manipulates a computer should never be underestimated." Nagumbi tapped his iPad again. "You asked me to investigate Margaret Guarneri."

Reid tensed.

"She's a widow with a daughter, a butler with a degree in English literature."

"Social media?"

"Absolute none. She is as discreet a servant as you or your grandfather could ask."

Reid respected Nagumbi's opinion, so he had to ask. "Do you think she's trying to blackmail me and my grandfather?"

"No."

"Good. I don't either. But I'm…involved, and not seeing clearly."

"Yet you have the good sense to recognize your own vulnerability." With his typical economy of movement, Nagumbi put his electronics away in the box. "Tonight, when it's quiet, I'll scan the library and the kitchen, and I am one by one checking the backgrounds of all of the staff."

"Good. Thank you." Reid watched Nagumbi leave, and thanked God and his grandfather for giving him the one person he could trust above all others.

Nagumbi spoke with an economy of words, moved with poetic care, and understood security in a way Reid thought nothing short of amazing. If he had one failing, it was that he didn't comprehend the messy complications created by the softer human emotions. Greed, cruelty and revenge he understood. Love, jealousy and a need for approval were beyond his comprehension. Although Reid thought that Abigail had begun to chip away at Nagumbi's stoic exterior and perhaps, just perhaps, she would find a beating heart at his center.

Reid headed downstairs to the library, and found Margaret with his grandfather, both laughing about the papers Jim had dropped.

Only Margaret had the ability to joke with Jim about his unsteady grip, and take care of him, and make him like it.

She glanced up at Reid, smiled as if she couldn't help herself, then nervously slid back into the persona of butler.

What did that mean? What did she have to be nervous about? Why did she persist on sliding out of the room every time he came in?

Man, she annoyed him.

He made his way to his desk and sank down in his chair, and watched her.

The woman looked nothing like a criminal. Rather, she looked like the love of his life.

Yet why would she be meeting strangers on the sly?

After speaking with Cliff, Reid had cross-examined her about her lunchtime activities. She met friends, she admitted. When pressed, she said their names were Dommy and Jules—two androgynous names if he'd ever heard them. And when he pressed too hard, the woman felt no qualms about telling him to mind his own business.

Reid wished he could ask her about Cliff's parting remark. What did Cliff mean, *Something to think about as you shower*? Had it been a random remark signifying nothing. Had one of the staff seen Margaret leaving his bedroom? Or had Margaret acknowledged their relationship to Abigail, perhaps? Bragged about shampoo as an aphrodisiac?

For more than one reason, Reid hoped so. He hoped she was reaching that moment when she realized that what existed between them was real, permanent, passionate, and meaningful.

Instead, resistance seemed to be her mantra, and if she hadn't told Abigail about their adventure in the shower, she would flip out. In fact,

Reid was pretty sure she would flip out at the mere hint that Cliff knew anything about their private activities, especially if Cliff had heard it through the grapevine.

The lack of answers left Reid with his instincts. He felt no suspicion of Margaret. True, his instincts clamored when he looked at her, but the clamor sounded like wedding bells.

That might be the problem. Maybe, just maybe, he couldn't see the warning signs for the stars in his eyes.

Jim pounded on the arm of his wheelchair. "Reid. Reid!"

Reid switched his gaze to his grandfather.

"Nice to have your attention at last, boy." Jim was looking annoyed. "Would you stop glaring at Margaret long enough to let her finish helping me clean off my desk? She's as jumpy as a grasshopper in a prairie fire. Turn those brooding orbs of yours to your work."

"All right." Reid stared at his computer screen.

A spreadsheet. He liked spreadsheets, especially spreadsheets that showed a healthy increase in his bank account.

But not right now.

He looked back at Margaret.

Damn, she was a fine-looking woman. Clad in that black and white butler's suit, she set his heart to thumping. But if it were up to him, he'd put her in pure teal blue, or perhaps in that marvelous African violet purple.

It bothered him that he daydreamed about her wardrobe. He was a guy with a guy's typical distaste for shopping, but for Margaret he'd traipse through every store in the Galleria with an open wallet… Perhaps she had reason to meet these men, and perhaps that reason had nothing to do with extortion. Perhaps the loving in the shower yesterday couldn't keep her satisfied. Perhaps… Reid shook his head and muttered, "No." Without self-flattery, he knew that the steam in that bathroom hadn't all been from hot water.

Out of the blue, he said, "Maybe the extortionists have given up."

Two heads, one white and balding, one silver as moonshine, lifted from their labors. Two pairs of blue eyes stared at him as if he were mad.

"Wouldn't that just take the cake," Jim said.

Reid looked at him sharply. It sounded—it *looked* as if the old man was disgusted.

"We can only hope," Margaret answered.

"Since I've been home, no more notes," Reid observed.

"True. We haven't heard a word from the bastards." Jim rubbed his spotted hands as if they ached. "Maybe we could let up on the vigilance a bit."

"No." Both Margaret and Reid said it at once.

Their eyes locked.

Reid drew a breath. "No, it's not hurting us to keep our ears to the ground." Uncoiling himself from his chair, he said, "Come on, Margaret."

"What?" Margaret stared as he loomed over her. "What?" she asked again, as he grasped her by the wrist and drew her toward the door. Flinging a hand back, she said, "Mr. Jim!"

"The boy's mad," Jim advised her. "Better do what he wants."

"In a pig's eye." Those two men made her so cranky. They were autocratic, scheming, cantankerous men.

She prepared to dig in her heels if Reid pulled her up the stairs, but he confounded her and dragged her down the hall to the kitchen instead.

She said, "I've got a luncheon date that I need to keep."

"With Dommy and Jules?" Reid asked.

"Yes! Yes, with Dommy and Jules. They're going to meet me out front and we're going to—"

Reid had no patience with this. "Too bad."

She tugged back on her wrist.

Reid yanked her closer to him. "You'll hurt yourself," he warned.

They hurried through the kitchen.

"Where are you two going so fast?" Abigail asked.

To Margaret, her friend was only a blur of green and pink feathers. "I don't know."

"To West University," Reid answered.

Before Margaret caught her breath, she was belted into his BMW 328i sedan. "Why are we going to West U?"

He adjusted the air conditioning so it blew on her. "Remember our martial arts bout in the gym? Remember what you promised afterwards?"

Yes, she remembered. She remembered promising all kinds of things with clinging hands and open mouth, and she'd delivered on every promise.

"It's time to pay up," Reid said.

"I—"

"We're going to look at a house."

"At a…" She grimaced. "Yes. I knew that."

"Oh, Margaret. The things you imagine," he teased.

She flounced around to stare out the window.

In Houston, summer always took up residence in early March, and now, in September, as the heat dragged on, the lawns and leaves were a tired green, the flowers drooped, and every living thing waited for that first cool front to sweep through and bring relief from the unrelenting sun.

Reid handed her a pair of sunglasses.

She slid them on her nose and looked to see if she could spot her lunch dates. They weren't visible, but she wondered if they lurked nearby.

Her conscience twitched.

She needed to speak to Reid. She didn't want to, God knew, but she had to *explain* stuff to him. Turning her head in slow increments, she studied Reid's profile. He looked rugged. Damn. He looked scary. He looked as if he could make the kind of scene she dreaded. And enjoy it, too.

She turned her head back, then peeked around at him again.

She opened her mouth, then shut it.

She didn't *want* to explain stuff.

He'd want to know why she hadn't said something sooner, and she'd have to explain she'd sort of been enjoying his frustration, and he'd want her to explain why…

It was just messy.

Maybe she would explain something *else*. In a hurry, she said, "I've been meaning to talk to you."

"Okay."

She stared at him, speechless.

Glancing at her, he smiled briefly. "I'm ready."

"I doubt it," she whispered. Aloud, "It's about your grandfather's will."

He grunted, although whether in response to her statement or as a reaction to the pothole he swerved to miss, she couldn't tell.

"It seems that Mr. Jim left Amy a considerably bigger bequest than he had told me." Margaret noticed her leg was jiggling up and down, and she laid her palm flat against it to calm herself.

"Oh, that." He sounded totally uninterested. "Yeah, I know."

Her voice got loud and shrill. "You know he left her the stud farm?"

"Yeah. His lawyer felt it behooved him to tell me about the bequest to A. M. Guarneri." Reid's mouth quirked. "He was working on Granddad's orders, of course. I should have realized it sooner."

"Why?" she asked, fascinated.

"No lawyer of my grandfather's would ever release that kind of confidential information unless he wanted his license revoked and his reputation destroyed. Granddad would have him run out of town on a rail."

Margaret covered her mouth and thought stuff through. When she had it, when she understood, she said, "So Mr. Jim's lawyer hasn't really been fired."

"Yeah, he's been fired. I fired him. It's too damned bad nobody was listening except me." The wry twist of Reid's mouth told her he was laughing at himself.

"You fired him, and your grandfather rehired him."

"I fired him, but he doesn't work for me, so he didn't listen. He only pretended to. The whole bequest-thing was nothing more than bait to bring me here to meet you."

Margaret gaped. "You knew that?"

"It didn't take long to figure."

"Then Amy's bequest is a joke?"

"Not at all. Granddad *has* left her the stud farm."

"You'll stop him?"

"Me?" Reid swerved again, this time in amazement. "Me? You think I can do something to change Granddad's mind? You think *I* want to be run out of town on a rail?"

"But that farm's got to be worth—" Her imagination failed her.

"A lot," he agreed succinctly.

"Amy said he left her money, too."

"Oh, that." He watched her from the corner of his eye. "Only a couple of million. Depends on the horses."

Margaret felt as if she'd had the breath knocked out of her. She audibly dragged in oxygen. "A couple of million?" she croaked.

"Dollars?"

"That's the way money is generally figured."

She was not amused. "Two million dollars? He can't go around leaving people two million dollars. He'll go broke."

"That's true." Reid nodded. "If he went around giving out two million dollars once a month, he'd be penniless in about twenty years."

"Oh, my God." Her hands curled in her lap.

"That's if he didn't earn any interest on his money, of course."

"Oh, my God." She could hardly breathe from dismay.

"That stud farm could lose a million every year for the next few years…if we have a bad run of luck." Reid was spectacularly unimpressed. "The money my grandfather left Amy will get her on her feet with the business. If she decides she doesn't like it, I can buy it back."

"Oh, my God."

Reid patted Margaret's bouncing knee. "You lost the bet with me. Amy has to get to Harvard somehow."

"Merit?"

"That's a strong possibility, too. Don't worry about it."

"But — "

"It'll all work out."

"Yes. It will. Just FYI, I have to be back at Mr. Jim's before Amy gets home from her sleepover."

"A sleepover?"

"Her best friend's birthday party…five girls…they went to the movies, then went swimming, then…I imagine they giggled until five in the morning." Margaret shook her head. "Those poor parents."

He chuckled. "How much time do we have?"

She glanced at her plain, black leather band watch. "She's supposed to be back after lunch. So…about two hours."

"We can do that. Now look." He pointed. "Look at what I brought you to see."

West University was a cool, quiet, trendy little area close into the city where doctors, lawyers and professors made their homes.

Reid and Margaret pulled up in front of a new Georgian two-story with a red brick exterior and a large front porch. The lot was wooded, and the house fit in among the trees as if it had been designed to do so.

Margaret wanted to protest, to hash this inheritance out, but Reid had dismissed it as unimportant. She swallowed her words and stared at the house, not because she was overwhelmed—for how could one be overwhelmed while living in a River Oaks mansion?—but because Reid seemed to expect it.

"How do you like the shutters?" Reid asked with apparent concern. "I had the builder paint them forest green."

Margaret turned her head and studied him. In faded jeans, a white t-shirt, and white running shoes, he was the epitome of casual. Yet to the discerning eye—and Margaret's eye was very discerning—this stuff was expensive. She guessed the t-shirt and jeans had been hand-sewn by an Italian grandmother who made a fortune catering to rich Americans, and the shoes' leather had been chewed to their current supple softness by trained llamas.

Worse, Reid didn't know the prices, or care. When some buyer at Nordstrom had brought him selections to choose from, all he had done was frown or nod. And he looked great. As in everything he wore was a showcase for his well-toned body, and every inch of his body made her itch to touch him. "The color adds distinction. To the, er, shutters. Did you say you were buying this as an investment?"

"I'm buying it, for sure. Nice neighborhood, huh?"

"It certainly is." The narrow street was lined with a grand mixture of houses. Big, new homes—like the one they sat in front of—rubbed elbows with homes from the forties. Trees shaded the sidewalk; hedges were mature and thick. A girl whizzed past on her skateboard, shouting rude comments to a boy in his swim trucks.

"A family place. My dog will have a great time in this yard," Reid said with pleasure.

"I didn't know you had a dog."

"I haven't yet, but I've always wanted one. Come on." Reid opened his door and stepped out.

Margaret flung herself out of the car. How could any man be so stupid? How could he be talking about a dog he didn't even own?

"You're too independent." Reid took her hand and led her up the walk.

Margaret sniffed. "Thank you for your critique."

"You're too thin-skinned, too."

"Am not," she muttered.

"There are many, many things I like about you. Do you want me to name them?"

"Good Lord, no. There are children present."

He opened the door with a tagged key from his pocket. "I like to talk about your wonderful qualities, especially the ones that attract me."

"No."

"Spoilsport."

They stepped inside.

Air conditioning created a haven from the heat.

He shut the door behind them, and locked it.

The smell of sawn wood, mortar and Sheetrock dust identified the house as new construction. The entry and living room were tall, with vaulted ceilings to draw up the heat of a Texas day. The light filtered through a skylight in the roof, through undraped windows and down the stairs from the second story. Rolls of carpet and pad lay about, waiting to be installed.

Their shoes made tapping noises on the concrete floor.

"Come and look at the kitchen," Reid held Margaret's hand, but his desire to drag her from place to place seemed to have diminished. Instead he let her lead, directing her with nudges and encouragement.

The kitchen was big. Very big.

"Good layout," Margaret approved, frankly bewildered but willing to play the game. "I like the cooking island."

"I do, too. The cabinets are birds-eye maple with African blackwood trim."

"Spectacular." She touched the wood. It felt like satin.

"Because the wood has so much movement, I thought a stainless steel countertop."

"No, that wouldn't be right. Maybe a dark basalt?"

Reid lifted her hand and kissed it. "My decorator predicted you would say that."

Hastily Margaret said, "It's your choice, of course."

"I could do my famous pasta primavera in here."

She couldn't believe it. "You *are* going to buy it, then."

"I said so." He watched her with a half-smile, a close-trimmed lock of cinnamon-colored hair falling over his forehead. "There aren't any listening devices here."

"Um… That's good. I mean…makes sense. Why would there be?" She blushed and tried to stumble her way back to a normal conversation. "Did you find any listening devices in the mansion?"

"Not a one. Our extortionist missed his chance there. Come upstairs and look at the bedrooms."

He tugged.

She followed him up the stairs. Like she had a choice.

No listening devices. She had never needed to be in his bedroom. That whole incident in the shower need never have happened.

Yet try as she might, she couldn't suppress her thrill at the memory of that shower.

"There are five bedrooms up here," Reid said. "Do you like it so far?"

"Nice." God, he confused her. So he wanted her professional opinion. He was buying this house. To live here?

Well, why not? He was a big boy, old enough to live alone while in Houston. She would have expected him to buy something a little more upscale—this house was mere upper middle class than high end.

Actually, she would have expected him to buy a condo. This house required yard work and didn't have room for a maid. His midnight orgies would be interrupted by the security police, and the neighborhood kids would scrape their bikes on the paint job of his car.

Now, more than ever, she realized she didn't understand the workings of his mind.

They made a flying tour of bedroom one, bedroom two, bathroom one, rec room, bedroom three, bedroom four. There they stopped.

"Here's where we'll put Amy." He waved his arm around the charming, rose-painted room. "Won't she love it? It has its own bath. There's a tree outside her window, and if she's careful, she can climb right out into its arms. I'll build a tree house." He considered. "I'll have a tree house built."

Twenty-six

Covering her throat with her hand, Margaret tried to subdue the choking noise that climbed from the pit of her stomach.

"Did you eat something that didn't agree with you?"

Her voice wasn't strong, but it was definite. "I'm having trouble swallowing."

Acting concerned—and he had to be acting, she thought hysterically—he stepped to her side and wrapped his arm around her waist. "What's the matter?"

"*What's the matter?*" Unexpectedly the question came out in a shriek.

He jumped back.

Moderating her tone—a little—she repeated, "What's the matter? You're talking about living together, and you ask, *What's the matter?*"

"What did you think I was talking about in that shower?" He had the guts to sound reasonable.

She raised her hands in incredulity. "Sex?"

"Damn it, Margaret—"

"All right, *good* sex. I don't understand you. I don't understand you at all. Why are you acting like this? I'm your grandfather's *butler.*"

He pointed his finger close to her face. "If you call me *sir* right now, I'll put you across my knee."

"Why shouldn't I call you *sir*? You can't move me in here like the …the mistress of a Regency rake." She stuttered in her excitement. "Tucked in a little hideaway for your entertainment, not daring to poke my nose out—"

A spark of anger leapt to his eyes, then died. He laughed a little. "I would have never suspected it. You really have a vivid imagination, haven't you?"

She glared at him. And burst into tears.

In a flash, he enfolded her in his arms.

She didn't want to pull away. It felt comfortable here and she relaxed; relaxed enough to sob, "That's what Luke used to say."

"Your husband?" Alert, Reid stroked her head.

"He used to say if we could harness my imagination we could light the whole west side of Houston." The storm of tears was passing already.

With his arm on her shoulder, he turned her and led her toward the master bedroom. "What did Luke think of your plunge into the stuffy world of butlers?"

"I did that after…after the funeral." She sniffed and wiped at her face. "I wanted a quiet job, routine and simple. The kind of job where I could raise Amy in comfort and stability."

There it was again; that word. Stability.

"I wanted to get away. After I paid medical bills, there wasn't any money left from the life insurance, so I borrowed from my father-in-law and moved to England and enrolled in Ivor Spencer's school."

He smiled. "I bet Amy loved England."

"This is a nice room." She pointed to the windows set high in the wall, close to the cathedral ceiling. "Those should have stained glass."

"I'll make a note of it."

She ignored him, wandering into the sitting area and then into the bathroom. "Hey, you could play basketball in here." She stuck her head out the door and grinned at him. "It's almost as big as yours at Donovan's Castle."

Her nose was red, her eyes were puffy, her cheeks were tearstained. It brought such a welling of tenderness in him, he told her, "You're beautiful when you cry."

She ducked back in the bathroom, and called, "That's not what that mirror in here says."

"Didn't Amy love England?" He heard the sound of toilet paper unrolling and a nose being indelicately blown.

"No."

Margaret didn't reappear, and he stepped over a roll of carpet and one of carpet pad to reach the bathroom door. "I can't imagine Amy not enjoying England."

"It was a hard time for her." She tested the faucet; the water was hooked up. She leaned over the sink and sluiced her face until the worst of the redness was gone.

When she raised her head, Reid stood behind her. Their eyes met in the mirror. He smiled at her, and she sighed with resignation. "No towel," she complained, and he pulled the handkerchief from his pocket and offered it. Dabbing at her face, she escaped the confines of the bathroom.

Reid followed close on her heels. "What happened, Margaret? What happened to Amy?"

She poked at a roll of carpet with her toe, and when she was satisfied no critters would run out, she seated herself on the end. She sat erect, knees together, skirt twitched down.

He watched and analyzed. She didn't want to talk about it, nor did she want to attach too great an importance to it by refusing. So she sat like the perfect lady, all prissy and sweet, hoping the cracks in her composure wouldn't show.

Her voice almost didn't cooperate. It quavered for a minute, swooping low and then high. "Luke and I had done everything to prepare her for his death, and she saw a lot of death in the hospital around her. So when he actually dropped his form—"

"What?"

A tiny smile lifted her lips, but she didn't meet his gaze. "That's what Luke told her he was doing. He was dropping his human form for another. So she comprehended her father's death only too well. So well, in fact, that she understood mortality at an age when most children still believe they can stop a moving car with their bodies."

"She was afraid she would die?"

"No." She raised one hand out of her lap and rubbed her temple. "She was afraid I would."

Reid watched the betraying movement.

This part of her story she didn't want him to hear. Perhaps she didn't want to hear it herself. But more than that, she feared the growing destruction of the walls around her.

He was breaching all her defenses. He sympathized, he really did, and if it were anyone else, he'd wait for the natural sharing that he knew would come.

But with Margaret, such friendship was an impossibility.

For how could he allow her walls to remain when his own were in shambles?

He sat down next to her, close enough so she could feel his warmth yet not touching—fostering, he hoped, the illusion of freedom. "What did you do?"

"It got so that I couldn't leave her with the sitter, couldn't go anywhere without her." She fell silent, remembering.

"You had difficulties, too," he guessed. "You had to put aside all your own grief to tend to hers." Subtly, she shifted away from him, and he was surprised. He searched her face for clues; why should the mention of her own sorrow distress her so?

Yet she gave him no time to analyze, rushing on with her story. "At last, I did what I should have done originally. I sent for my father-in-law." A slight, fond smile crossed her face, smoothing the lines of strain.

"Is that the grandfather she visited this summer?" he asked, deliberately defusing her wariness. "The one with the shaving cream Twinkies?"

She laughed with pleasure and, it seemed to him, relief. "The very one. He's a wonderful man. He kept her busy. They went all over London together, visiting the places he'd seen when he was in the military and dropping their calling cards at Buckingham Palace. I still don't know what he said to her, but when he left, she was at peace."

"And you?" Shrewdly he checked her cautious face. "When did you stomp your feet and scream at fate?"

The edges of her glossy composure crumpled just a little. "Hmm?"

"When did you cry and mourn? You'd lost your husband, and you were at least fond of him—"

"I loved him." Her quiet sincerity spoke for itself.

"You loved him. He died after an illness…" He fished, wanting her to tell him about it.

She dropped her eyes to her lap, adjusted her fingers, ignored him.

He waited, but she never looked up, and so he pushed on. "He died and left you all alone with a child and no viable means of support and a huge medical bill. There must have been a time, in the wee hours of the morning, when you cried."

"Of course there was." She said it too quickly, almost guiltily.

With a gentle finger, he lifted her chin and stared into her eyes.

"Have you never taken the time to finish the grieving process?"

Her arms crossed over her chest and she hugged them to her to shut him out. "I have grieved for Luke every day since he left us."

But, ruthless opponent that he was, Reid ignored the unspoken and dealt with the actual words. "But that anguish should have eased by now. There are certain steps you must take to heal, to prepare to face life again. Are you telling me you haven't been angry at Luke for leaving you? That you haven't screamed at fate for the rotten deal it tossed you? That you haven't begged God to change what can't be changed?"

"I'm not trying to tell you anything." She enunciated clearly, clipped off each word with her teeth. "It's none of your business."

"I made it my business in my shower." Swinging one leg over the roll of carpet, he straddled it and placed his hands on her shoulders. He cupped them and rubbed them as if she were a horse and he the stable master. "Our relationship can't develop if you're stuck in the past. The time to free yourself from your unhappiness is now and—"

Her hands flashed up and broke his hold on her shoulders. Her gaze, before so timid, sought his in a fine fury. "I'm not unhappy!"

He fell back a little.

She followed. "I'm not unhappy. I'm not stuck in the past. And I sure as hell don't care what's healthy for our relationship."

"Now, dear." He sounded like an accountant placating his tyrannical wife.

But she never noticed. "You sit there, so complacent, a little rich boy who's never been unhappy his whole life long, and you dare judge me and my *grieving process* as insufficient." Her finger tapped his chest, her nose bobbed so close to his, he could feel her heated breath. "You damned idiot."

Then she surprised him. He'd drawn her as he wanted, tapped into her pain and anger and released them. But the scene didn't continue as he'd envisioned. Like a growling cat, she reached over and grabbed his shirt at the tails, yanked on it, and tried to take it off over his head. She wanted it *off*.

He did not want it off, not until he figured out what was going on. He struggled, but awkwardly, feebly—and he had not taken into account that she was a mother.

"In my time," she panted, rising onto her knees on the rolled carpet, "I've wrestled a two-year-old for possession of a shirt, and you don't stand a chance."

Being compared to a two-year-old surprised Reid enough to allow her to pull the whole thing over his head.

She tossed it down and went for his belt.

He grabbed her wrists. "What are you doing?"

He wavered between patience and amazement when she snapped his hold and jerked his belt open. "You figure it out."

"Margaret…" His voice trailed off. Her fingers wrestled with the button front of his jeans, and that caused a most miraculous change to come over his body.

Okay, it was just the normal change that occurred when he was around her, but he was a guy. If he wanted to call it a miracle, he could.

She looked up in triumph. "Ha!"

He eased himself back on his elbows, trying to relieve the unexpected pressure. "What does that mean?"

"It means…" She opened the final button and inched her slender fingers inside his fly. "It means you're going to get what you have coming to you."

Twenty-seven

"That sounds like a threat." Actually, Reid thought it sounded like a great idea.

"Don't you want to initiate your new house?" Her smile wasn't kind or generous or feminine.

In fact, he decided, it looked downright predatory. "Our house," he insisted.

But she reached inside his underwear to cup his balls.

And he forgot what it was he wanted to say. He fell all the way back, so the carpet supported his back, and his arms dangled off the sides.

She chuckled.

He decided that this kind of forceful sexual conquest was not politically correct. They would have to have a serious talk about it...later.

Those magic hands of her massaged his groin with a firm and gentle pressure, and when she urged his pants down, he cooperated. Fully. Eagerly.

She took his jeans and underwear down to his ankles, and there they stuck on his tennis shoes. She would have left everything where it was.

But he said, "No," and pushed his shoes off one by one.

Immediately she stripped him of the last of his clothes and flung them aside. Crawling up between his legs, she smoothed her palms up the inside of his thighs. Leaning forward, she kissed his hard-on. "This is very impressive," she whispered.

"Thank you." Stupid response, but the best he could do when all the blood in his body had left his brain for areas south.

She licked him, a long, slow, warm, wet savory tasting.

"Thank you," he said again. Just as stupid, but a lot more fervent.

She took him in her mouth.

No more stupidity. He couldn't speak at all. He managed to groan, deeply and pitifully, as the gentle suction of her mouth made him crazy with need. He was on the verge…

And she released him. She looked him in the eyes and smiled as ruthlessly as Cruella Deville before once more starting the long trek up his body, up his stomach, up his chest, kissing and tasting all the way. He moaned at the fire she left behind, and when she laid her full weight on him he thought he'd found heaven. Sweetness above, rough weave below; the scent of woman and paint and newness; the rustle of leaves against the window and the rustle of clothing against his skin.

Dipping her head, she murmured against his lips, "Do you like this?"

Her voice was husky and amused and acted like a prod to his masculine pride. He wrapped his arms around her, prepared to roll off and land with her on the tail of carpet that flopped off the side of the roll.

He made a mistake and looked into her face. Satisfaction strengthened the smile on lips with a tendency to tremble. Vulnerability and success chased each other through her shadowed eyes. While one hand pinched his ear to hold him still, the other stroked through his hair as if she found comfort there. What could he do? He supposed he could handle being mauled by a woman—her mouth sank into his with a steady, delicate pressure—just this once.

God, her tongue drove him wild with its exploratory fervor. When she came up for breath and nibbled at his ear, then soothed the sting with that same tongue, he discovered his hand was under her skirt. He didn't remember putting it there, but when he stroked her, she moaned and thrust her hips against his…and he couldn't help but take that as encouragement.

She tugged imperiously at his hair, wordlessly urging him to turn his head. She tasted the cord of his neck, and hummed as if she found him delicious.

Her appetite made him hungry…for her.

She settled herself more firmly on top of him. Lightly she scraped his nipple with her fingernails. "It's hard," she whispered. "Are you cold?"

He groaned. Finding the edge of her panties, he skimmed his hand inside. Down the cleft, down until he could slip one finger inside her. "You're wet," he whispered back. "Are you on fire?"

She didn't say anything. She couldn't. Her head was tossed back, her teeth bit into her lower lip, and sweet pain and pleasure possessed her.

"So soon?" But he barely breathed the words, unwilling to break the spell. His thumb pressed against her clit, and like a firecracker in his arms, she exploded. He pushed her to her limits, judging when to release, when to resume, prolonging her climax for her rapture—and his own.

When at last she came to rest, he could wait no longer. "Help me," he instructed, sliding the underwear down her legs. She roused enough to help rid herself of the essentials, but not enough to deal with the intricacies of buttons on vest and blouse and skirt.

Reid struggled for a moment alone, then muttered, "To hell with it." Lifting her, he settled them together, his erection pressing against her, her dampness hot against him.

What necessity couldn't do, the touch of bare flesh accomplished.

Galvanized, she struggled to set her feet on the floor, one on either side of him. She lifted herself.

He could see the renewed sparkle in her eyes. He groaned when she took him in her hands and fit them together.

But she'd lost the edge of command, and as she struggled to take him into her, he raised his hips beneath her and thrust inside.

She gasped. Her eyes half closed.

He wanted to find the heart of her, push her to another cataclysm of joy, but the fierce stillness of her body worried him. "Did I hurt you?"

Wordless, she shook her head.

"Do you want me to continue?"

Her lids slowly lifted, and she stared at him as she slowly shook her head again. Then, she lifted herself up, right to the point of despair, and drove herself down, bringing them back to heaven.

Good. God. Almighty.

She smiled.

He looked at her face in the dusty sunlight filtered by the leaves outside. He scrutinized the structure of bone and expression that he loved. He examined her body, encased in tie, shirt, vest, coat. He looked at her skirt, at her strong, bare thighs. His hands went to her bare hips. He hiked her skirt to her waist, and he held her tightly as she came off him again, and back down.

He wanted to explode into action. He wanted to explode...period.

But as she moved up and down to a slow and steady rhythm, he kept his hands on her, and when she tried to accelerate, his hands held her to a crawl.

She resisted, a little at first, then more and more frantically.

But he merely smiled—or snarled. "No," he said. "No. Torment should be a mutual pleasure."

She called him a name that was no endearment.

He laughed, a gasping, startled laugh. "Sweet talker," he said, and sucked in his breath as she reached behind her to prowl with her fingers between his legs.

The way she touched him loosened his grip on both her hips and his sanity.

Suddenly *she* controlled the pace.

The torment did indeed grow into a mutual pleasure. He knew nothing else but Margaret, and more Margaret. Her scent, her strength, her heat...Margaret like sunlight in his soul.

Twenty-eight

For Margaret, the blotting of thought lasted only as long as her hormones danced in her veins.

She tried to prolong the ecstasy, to hold it close and cherish every moment.

But inevitably, reluctantly, she returned to the reality of Reid beneath her, a large and open room around her, and a most embarrassing reflection of herself in the mirrored wardrobe doors.

She gaped, horrified; she was half-dressed with her skirt around her waist and Reid still buried deep inside her.

She met Reid's eyes in the glass, and she was even more horrified. His slow smile burned the heat into her skin, and she couldn't tear her gaze away.

Then the room tipped.

The floor rushed up.

She landed with a padded thump.

Reid tucked her into the corner between his body and the carpet roll.

It was then she realized she'd gained herself a temporary respite, at best.

He smoothed the loose strands of hair out of her eyes. "How long has it been for you? Three years?"

"Not even a week."

"Ah, you remember." He sounded so satisfied.

She grimaced. "I wasn't ever going to let you do this with me again, you know."

"Did I miss something? Did you *let* me do this with you?" His sarcasm was heavy and sure. "I thought you *demanded* that I do this with you. I could have sworn you ripped my clothes off and tossed me down, regardless of my wishes, and took your wanton pleasure—"

"Oh, shut up. My wanton pleasure seemed to coincide with your wanton pleasure, you know."

"I know." She waited for him to say more.

Wisely he didn't.

This was a conversation she was unlikely to win. She nibbled her lip, wanting to clarify to him that she wasn't always so wanton. "You're right. It's been almost three years since my husband died." Her thoughts arched back into the past, and she explained, "But it's been longer than that since I slept with a man."

"Is that what you call this?" His mouth curled tenderly. "Sleeping?"

"You know what I mean." Observing the pride that puffed him up like a peacock, she decided he didn't need to know too much. Her desire to avoid embarrassment seemed to bring with it unwanted side effects. She could have kept her resolution, too, if her traitor eyes hadn't filled with tears and the dastardly man hadn't pulled her into his chest. Her words were muffled and unstoppable. "The last six months Luke was alive, he couldn't function. I think that killed him as rapidly as anything. He loved sex. With him it was a joy to be shared, and when we couldn't share anymore...God, he shriveled up and died."

Reid warmed away her tears and her chill. His arms wrapped her body, his hands stroked her back.

Margaret sniffled and rubbed her eyes across his shoulders. "I guess you can tell I'm new at this." She looked at him. "I shouldn't be reminiscing about my last lover with my new lover."

Reid smiled using all his teeth.

Margaret wondered if she had annoyed him.

But he corrected her firmly. "Luke is a part of you, a most important part. You don't live eight years with a man and not have memories and love to remember. I'm no fool. I'll never be jealous of a dead man, I'll only be jealous if you keep all those memories so tightly locked up I feel they're a treasure I'm not allowed to sully with my mortal mind."

"Sometimes..." She hesitated, but it had to be said. "Sometimes, I almost like you."

"Well, we can't have that, now." He rolled back and held up one leg. A white sock still wrapped around his foot, and he pointed with mock disappointment. "Look at that. You didn't even knock my socks off."

Unwillingly amused, she smacked his shoulder and sat up. "I'll knock something else off if you don't watch your tongue." Glancing about, she located her panties. Too aware of his charming assessment, she shimmied into them, tucked in her shirt, found her shoes, and turned back to him, still on the floor. "Are you going to lie around buck naked all day?"

"Come here." He crooked an enticing finger.

"Absolutely not." She laughed, but warily. "We can't hang around in an empty house."

He was still waggling that finger at her. "Why not?"

"You'll have rug burn on your rear." A reasonable point.

"Not if we follow my plan," he crooned, with his innocent shark-tooth smile. "Come here."

"We have to go back."

"Come here. I won't do anything."

"What kind of fool do you take me for?"

"A hundred kinds of a fool if you think you'll go back without coming here."

"I'll go back without you," she warned, sidling toward his pants—the pants that held the keys.

He smiled and waited until she reached down to pick them up.

Then she was tumbling through the air.

He landed on top of her.

She should give him one good chop across the Adam's apple. But he smiled with such almighty delight, she didn't have the heart. "Now what, you big jerk?"

"Now I'll give to you a little of what you gave to me." He nuzzled her neck. "It's been too long. I want to see those breasts."

"They look the same as last time." She wriggled beneath him as he tugged at her bow tie. "Kind of round with nipples."

"One can't be too sure."

His breath fogged her ear, and she began to lose her sense of direction. "We need to go back. Your grandfather—"

"Will be pleased as hell to know what we're doing."

"How's he going to find out?"

"Granddad?" He raised his head incredulously. "Sharp shooter Donovan? You think he won't *know*?" He raised his head further, his body still. "Listen."

She heard it, too. The scrape of the key in the lock downstairs.

"Mr. Donovan?" A man's voice floated up the stairs, booted footsteps echoed through the empty living room. "Mr. Donovan?"

"It's the builder," Reid said. He steadied her as she rose and straightened her clothes with rapid, precise gestures.

"Want me to go stall him?" she sassed.

"Wicked wench." He stood up and stretched, and displayed muscles that rippled and lengthened. He watched her watching him, and chuckled. "Who do you think would be the most embarrassed if he found us here, and me without a stitch of clothing?"

"I'll go and stall him."

Twenty-nine

Reid took Margaret's arm as they went down the walk.

Angrily, she shook it off. "Did you *have* to give me back my bow tie when you came downstairs?"

"How was I to know he'd wink like that?"

"I am mortified."

He pulled her around to face him. "I'm sorry. It's just that...I'm so conceited about you, about us, I want to shout it to the world."

She didn't seem to be at all touched by his declaration. "Try to refrain." She strode to the car and stood tapping her foot, waiting for him to open her door.

With a sigh, he turned to look at the house. Proposing to her there had seemed like such a marvelous idea, but she'd taken it all wrong.

She thought he was propositioning her.

Before he could clear it up, she'd distracted him with her memories, then with her body. At the time, her rather forcible seduction of him had seemed like a good omen. Not just a good omen. An incredibly good omen. A wonderful, miraculous, life-altering omen.

Now he wasn't so sure. As a release for her anger, it had worked.

As a diversion from his questions, it had worked better—and who was in charge here?

How had she muddled his normally clear thinking by offering the rewards of her body? No other woman had ever so affected him. It was that empathy between them, the empathy he'd used to tantalize her. Now he discovered it could be turned against him, and he wanted to curse and to cheer, both at the same time.

She was steering clear of any emotional breakdown. She was too relieved to be away from the crying and too glad to chuckle about her father-in-law.

The upshot was, she'd never grieved for her husband. Amy's problems had overshadowed her own while the sorrow flowed naturally. Once Amy was healed, Margaret had her feelings firmly locked inside.

Something needed to be done.

"I want to be there when Amy gets home. So, Mr. Donovan, are we going?" Margaret tapped her finger on her watch.

Something would have to be done, but in its own time.

"Sure are, sweet thing." Reid strode down the walk and around the front of the car.

He stopped in astonishment.

Etched on the hood was a long gouge in the paint. "What the hell?" He rubbed his finger on it.

Margaret smirked at him. "It looks similar to the time Amy scraped the handle bars of her bike along Mr. Jim's limo," she informed him. "That's the chance you take when you're around children."

Back at the house, Margaret got out of the car and headed for her cottage.

Reid watched, and sighed.

The woman was a trial—and well worth it.

Good thing, because he was anticipating a whole life spent loving her.

He went into the house and into the library.

It was after lunch, and he assumed, that as usual, his grandfather was taking a nap. Probably a good thing since Reid had to deal with some matters of interest. Picking up the phone, he summoned Nagumbi, then settled down to do some research.

When Nagumbi came through the door, Reid looked up from his desk. "Nagumbi, I have a job for you."

Nagumbi seated himself with the care that characterized all his movements.

Tossing the packet of photographs at him, Reid ordered, "I want to know who those guys are."

"Where did you get the pictures?" Nagumbi asked, placing them one by one in a line of the desk.

"Cliff Martin. According to him, Margaret has lunch with these creeps a couple times a week."

Nagumbi assessed the photographic evidence before his eyes. "Is that a reason for concern?"

"I don't know." Reid leaned back in his chair and rubbed his eyes. "I don't trust Martin, and as you've taught me, I never trust the information if given from an unreliable source. But something happened today that made me wonder."

Nagumbi raised one brow.

Reid nodded, familiar with his friend's method of conversation. "I took Margaret to the place in West U and showed her around. When we left, I checked the rearview mirror and there were these two guys"—he waved a hand at the photographs—"standing on the corner watching us drive away. Or watching me drive away with Margaret. They glared at me like I was a pervert."

"Did they follow you?"

"Not the way I drive."

"Did Ms. Guarneri see them?"

"I'd swear she didn't."

Nagumbi leaned back in his chair and steepled his fingers. "Unless she's a better actress than you give her credit for."

"I've thought of that." Reid shook his head. She'd been horrified, mortified, aghast, by the million-dollar inheritance for her daughter. If she was an actress, she was wasting herself in Houston—she belonged in Hollywood.

"I will check into this, as you require. In all actuality, this coincides with my own investigation."

"Of what?"

"After the return of your grandfather from the kidnapping attempt, I found the police report inadequate."

Reid found himself not at all surprised. "Pierre warned me. Have you unearthed any little discrepancies?"

"Quite a few. When I have a report which satisfies me, I will come to you." Nagumbi pulled his iPad out of his jacket pocket, tapped the screen, read it and shook his head. "At the moment, I must satisfy myself with what is public record." He nodded with cold pride. "Of course, I am also maintaining an extra watch on the elder Mr. Donovan as my time permits."

"Which activity do you believe will reap the most benefit?"

"Public record, when used by officials correctly, is nothing more than another bureaucratic tool of confusion. I believe, knowing Mr. Donovan's propensity to do as he pleases, that an extra vigil over his movements would not come amiss." Nagumbi slid the iPad back into his pocket.

Without hesitation, Reid ordered, "Do it."

"I'll seek him out at once. I still believe you should be aware that Ms. Guarneri may not be what she seems. Women," Nagumbi intoned, "are the bane of mankind."

Reid looked at him sharply. "Abigail giving you trouble?"

"Such a little woman could hardly give me trouble." Nagumbi's expression never changed. "She is more of a nuisance. A flea with one dog."

Reid wiped his grin away. "What's the problem?"

"She seems to feel that the two of us could..." Nagumbi squinted in pained remembrance. "...could *make beautiful music together*."

"Perhaps you could."

"She is too young and too flamboyant. I'd soon bore her."

"She's old enough to know what she wants, and her flamboyance is expressed only in her clothes and her cooking. Abigail's as solid as a rock." Reid swayed his chair back and forth and examined his friend. "She's wanted you for quite a few years. You could do worse."

Nagumbi's eyebrows lifted in a slow and dignified manner. "You seem to have given it some thought."

"I'd like to see you happy."

"Happiness is nothing more than a state of mind. I am content."

"No, I want you *happy*."

Nagumbi's face never twitched. "Ms. Guarneri seems to be involved with you in the manner in which you wish me to be involved with Abigail. Are you happy?"

Reid laughed softly. "I'm happy, frustrated, amazed, impatient."

"Wary."

"That, too."

"Shouldn't this love you tout so unsparingly defeat all suspicion?"

"Is that what love is? Sometimes I think it's a magnetism."

"Between two people?"

"Yeah. You know, it draws us, fighting, into this whirlpool—"

"Very attractive," Nagumbi said with calm distaste.

"Once we're in there, the colors and feelings flash around and confuse." Reid sighed.

He'd wanted to propose to Margaret at the house in West University; now he was glad he hadn't. This struggle between his emotions and his suspicions ripped at his heart, disturbed his mind.

Was he thinking clearly? For the first time in his life, he doubted it. "I can't let love blind me to the possibilities. There's too much at stake here."

"I'm glad you still realize that." Nagumbi picked up the pictures. "You have no information on these gentlemen?"

"None. You'll have to start from scratch."

"And you believe I should give Abigail's claim on my attention credence?"

"Absolutely."

Nagumbi inclined his head. "Fascinating."

Thirty

Margaret brushed at her fresh, newly-pressed, newly-starched and newly-donned butler uniform, straightened her jacket, lifted her chin, and opened the door to the library. She stepped inside—and there he was, Reid Donovan, at his desk, his sharp brown eyes fixed on her… knowingly.

Well, why not? After their interlude this morning at his new house, he knew almost everything there was to know about her, including a lot more than she wanted him to know. But she had a problem. A potentially ugly problem. And she needed his help. "Do you know where your grandfather is?" she asked.

Reid glanced at his watch. "Napping, I suppose. Doesn't he lie down this time of the afternoon?"

"Yes. Usually." She swallowed. "But he's not there. I checked."

"Is there a reason for concern?" Reid smiled as if he didn't quite believe her. As if she came in simply to see him.

Nothing could be farther from the truth. If it was up to her, she would avoid him until he forgot it all, however long that took. But… "I can't find Amy, either."

Right away, he got the seriousness of the situation. "When did you miss her?"

"A few moments ago." Margaret wrung her hands. "She isn't where I thought…I mean, she spent the night with a girlfriend, and I called to see when they were sending her home."

Slowly he stood. "And?"

"And they said they had done so three hours ago."

"While we were at the house?"

She wanted to cringe at the reminder. Not only had they made more than a casual tour of the house, but during that time her daughter had been unattended, and a mother's guilt knew no rest. "Apparently."

"Are these people reliable?"

"Of course." She knew she sounded huffy, but the fine edge of panic had begun to gnaw at her.

"All right," he said soothingly. "Did she come back here?"

"Abigail says Amy ate lunch with Mr. Jim."

"Then?"

"Then nothing. No one has seen them since."

Reid glanced out the window. "Have you checked the pool? Amy's a water baby, and you know Granddad likes to paddle around the shallow end."

"They're not there." She followed his gaze out the window. It was so green out there, and sunny and bright. It didn't seem fair. But she knew from experience how unfair the world could be, when everything and everybody went on with life and she was cold and afraid. "Maybe I'm being silly, but it seems so *strange*. With Mr. Jim's kidnapping, I just…I'm so…Mr. Jim wouldn't have sneaked out with Amy, would he?"

"Why do you say that?"

"You know how he chafes at the restraint this whole situation has laid on him. He wants to go where he wants to, when he wants to. And Amy"—Margaret wrung her hands —"Amy could tease him into doing anything."

"I don't believe she'd ask Granddad to take her out when she understands the danger." Reid turned and alertly examined Margaret. "She does understand the danger, right?"

"I never exactly told her what is going on. All these kidnapping threats started after she left for the summer, and I didn't want to worry her. She loves Mr. Jim, and she's had too much worry in her life." And because Margaret had wanted to protect her daughter, she had potentially put her in danger.

"I understand," Reid said. "Why would Jim and Amy go out together?"

"Amy's been nagging me to get school supplies for her science project. I've been busy." Busy having sex.

"Steady," Reid said. "Once we find them, we can both have a guilt fest."

He understood. Thank God, he understood. "Do you suppose she'd ask Mr. Jim to go with her? Of course she would. I've been a fool."

"Have you checked to see if all the cars are in the garage? If the chauffeur is on the grounds?"

Slowly, steadily she nodded. "That's really why I came in to see you. One car—and the new chauffeur—are gone, and no one is answering their phones."

"What do you mean, no one?"

"Not Amy. Not Mr. Jim. Not the chauffeur. No one." Margaret spoke slowly, as if Reid needed help comprehending. "And Amy has instructions to always answer when I call."

Reid pulled his cell phone from his pocket and came around the desk. "Damn that old man's hide. What do you suppose he's done now?"

"I don't know." She crossed her arms in front of her, re-crossed them, dropped them to her sides.

"I'll call Cliff Martin; he assures me he's always available." Reid punched the automatic dialer. "I'm sure this is all much ado about nothing." He didn't sound as if he believed himself.

She didn't believe him, either, but she said, "You're probably right. I'm just being fussy." An indefinable relief hit her as she put the responsibility in Reid's capable hands. He would handle this. He had a toughness to him, a confidence that reassured her.

He spoke into the phone. "Cliff Martin, please. This is Reid Donovan." He winked at her.

She weakly smiled back.

She smiled until he said, "I really don't appreciate being kept on hold this long." Tapping his foot, his expression changed from pleasant reassurance to impatience and then hostility. "What do you mean he's out of the office? Locate him for me. This is Reid Donovan. No, you don't seem to understand. I'm his primary client."

Drawn by uneasiness, she moved close to his side and put her hand on his arm.

He nodded at her, his attention still on the conversation.

The muscles beneath her hand tensed. He braced his feet and said in a low menacing tone, "Out of town? How could he have gone out of town? Last time he left town, my grandfather was kidnapped. Who is it this time? His mother? Well, his relatives are certainly dying in droves, aren't they? Let me speak to Nolan Salas. *Now.*" His face grew still, and he barely moved his lips when he said, "How inconvenient that the two men handling our case are both unavailable at the same time. Where is Mr. Salas?"

Margaret felt breathless, terrified, and she massaged her neck as if that would ease the constriction.

Reid listened. "I see. If he comes in, please have him call me at this number." He hung up. "Cell phones next."

He made two more calls.

The first, to Cliff Martin, went right to voicemail.

Reid left a terse message.

The second, to Nolan Salas, rang five times before going to voicemail.

Another terse message.

Reid turned a grim face on Margaret. "Did you check with Nagumbi?"

"He isn't on the grounds."

"Did you call him?"

"He didn't pick up."

"Let me try." Reid dialed, listened and hung up. "Huh."

She didn't like the tone of that, *Huh.* "What's wrong?"

"I don't know yet. I talked to Nagumbi not two hours ago," he told her. "He wasn't happy with the police reports, so he was off somewhere, investigating."

"Do you think he's in trouble?"

"Nagumbi doesn't get in trouble." Reid sounded very sure about that. "If he's not picking up, there's a damned good reason. Where is everyone? Do they know something we don't?"

"I'm so afraid they do." She shivered and crept closer. "I'm afraid they do."

"Let me call Uncle Manuel." Hooking an arm around her waist, Reid sank down in the chair and took her with him.

She didn't struggle; she wanted to be close. A cold emanated from the pit of her stomach, a twist of pain and fear. She leaned against him, seeking warmth.

He pulled her even closer, used the telephone with one hand and rubbed the other up her arm. As soon as the phone was answered, he dropped into Spanish. *"Hola, Tía Dela. Como esta usted? Sí, bien, pero donde esta Tío Manuel?"* He put his hand over the mouthpiece. "Aunt Dela has a soft spot for me."

Margaret remembered the petite, smiling Hispanic woman from Reid's party, and relaxed a little. Because both Manuel and Dela did indeed have a soft spot for Reid. Margaret could hear a flood of Spanish coming across the wires.

Reid frowned. His Spanish got more insistent. He switched to English and then back to Spanish. He hung up the phone and stared at it.

"What is it?" Margaret asked.

His gaze shifted to hers. "Suddenly, after years of communication, Aunt Dela is having trouble understanding my Spanish, and she's conveniently lost any ability to speak English."

"Why?" Margaret whispered.

"I suspect she doesn't want to talk to me. She said she'd have Uncle Manuel call me. He got a phone call and he went out."

"Out where?"

"She didn't know, or wouldn't say."

"Will he call you?"

"Yes, she was positive he would." Reid wrapped his other arm around her. "It would seem you were right. Something stinks here."

She strained back against his hold. "We've got to do something."

"I'm not going to call the cops, if that's what you're going to suggest. Nagumbi doesn't trust the cops, and I trust Nagumbi."

Right now, Margaret didn't trust the cops, either, and for reasons she should have explained much, much sooner. But it was too late now, and so she kept her mouth shut and nodded.

Reid continued, "Someone will call us back, so while we wait for the phone call, let me get ahold of my tech guy at Donovan headquarters. As long as these cell phones are on, he can trace the GPSs."

"Yes! Their cell phones. Their GPSs." She felt so foolish. "Why didn't I think of that right away?"

"Because you didn't know for sure anything was wrong."

"We still don't know, do we?"

"We know everyone's dodging our calls or unable to answer. Investigators call that a preponderance of evidence." Reid sounded so sensible. "Now try to relax while I get these numbers to my tech guy."

She listened as Reid spoke to Booker—apparently was his tech guy's name—and in short, clipped sentences gave him his instructions and the phone numbers. When he hung up, he said to her, "He's sending me information as he gets it. In the meantime, let's wait for a phone call from Uncle Manuel. I'm sure there'll be one. And relax. Whatever is going on here, we both need to be clear-minded."

She didn't want to relax. She wanted to jump up and run around and be frantic. She wanted to fight or shout or...do anything. She'd been trained to handle situations like this, but she'd prayed it would never happen. Now a situation confronted her, and deep inside she wept.

Yet he was right. All they could do was sit and stare at the phone in silence.

Reluctantly she leaned back into him, her head beside his.

The silence fell between them like a stone. They wandered alone in their thoughts, unable to lie to each another, unable to comfort.

"It's not true, you know," he said abruptly.

"What?" She was bewildered.

"It's not true that I'm a spoiled rich kid who never knew a moment's sorrow."

Thirty-one

Lost, Margaret cast about her mind until she remembered. Remembered what she'd said that very morning.

She had been in a rage because Reid was poking at a sore spot, trying to get her confess to unremitting sorrow, and she'd shouted at him.

Now she cringed. She remembered what Jim had said about Reid's parents. How could she have been so insensitive? How could she tell him she knew without him realizing how deeply Jim had confided in her?

"You think I'm crazy about my Granddad, and it's true." Reid looked out the window, and he picked his words carefully. "He took me in when the whole world fell on my head and around my shoulders."

She realized how uncomfortable he was, telling her this.

"I grew up in the Pacific Northwest. Did you know that?"

She nodded.

"Granddad told you?"

"A little."

"The Seattle area is a wonderful place. Mountains behind and the Pacific Ocean in front and hills and rain and fresh air. I love Houston. It's been good to me, but Seattle is a young boy's paradise. Camping, hiking, fishing. My dad and mom did everything with me." He drew a deep breath; it quivered. "They died when I was eight. But I wasn't like Amy. I wasn't prepared."

"Your grandfather took you in, though, right?" she prompted.

"Yes, but it was a tough few years. I resented him so much."

"Resented him?" Thinking of their current relationship, she was astonished. "Why?"

"My folks were unpretentious. My dad eschewed money and all it stood for and my mother simply wanted to educate the poor. I always knew my grandfather sort of...despised them." Now Reid's eyes met Margaret's, and a warm amused communication passed between them. "I don't know how my dad got to be like that, but I suspect he'd found that money couldn't buy his father's attention and turned away from all the, er, trappings of wealth. That's what Dad used to call it, with the emphasis on *trappings*."

"Then you got stuck with your grandfather."

"Yeah."

"What happened to your mother's family?"

"I wondered that for a long time after she died. I used to fantasize that Jim had used his influence to have them shipped to Siberia. When they escaped, they'd return and snatch me from this stifling life of luxury."

"Gee, you mean that wasn't the case?"

"Amazingly, no. My mother was an orphan. I guess marrying a woman with no family and no money was one of my father's rebellions that worked out."

"Did they love each other?" The nosy question slipped out.

Reid seemed to see nothing wrong. "God, yes. We were a family, a magic circle where others could come and go and no one could intrude. They understood each other without a word sometimes, and I'd wonder how they did it." He turned his head in to his shoulder and wiped a tear off his cheek with a shrug.

Margaret pretended she hadn't seen it.

"I missed them so much. I wanted my dad to toss me over his shoulder and fling me into bed, and I wanted my mother to tuck me in."

Reid was like a living cage of comfort, his body warm beneath her back and legs, his arms encircling her. The two of them faced a crisis. They were poised on the very brink of panic, waiting only the call to action. And he was telling her the only story that could have engaged her attention—his own. "When did you decide to give Mr. Jim a chance?" she asked.

"I never *decided*. But he transplanted me from a life of freedom in Seattle to a life of rich boy in Houston, and then did everything in his power to make me happy. I was such a snot about it." He grimaced. "I made him play G. I. Joe for two years. I loved watching his eyes glaze over with boredom, and then—" Reid poked her with his elbow—"he'd try and get up off the floor after his knees had been folded under him for hours."

"Reid!" She was laughing, half horrified.

He shrugged, clearly embarrassed at his younger self. "I told you I was a snot. I resented him for being alive when my parents weren't. I scared myself when I began to love him, and I was really scared when the memories of my folks began to fade."

"Was he kind and understanding?"

"Jim? Are you *mad?*"

She hid a grin.

Reid realized she was joking, and said, "Funny girl. He used to blow his top regularly and tell me to shape up, and then he'd go storming out. I'd wait to see if he'd abandoned me, but he always came back for more. After a while, I had to give up on my grudge. I took pity on him and paid attention to what interested him. I made him happy with my talk of oil stock and price per barrel."

"No more G. I. Joe?"

"I gave it up."

"Sounds to me like you grew up too fast."

"If life hands you lemons, make lemonade." With that phrase, he seemed to have summed up his life philosophy.

She sympathized. "Being a kid is demanding, isn't it?"

"Yeah, but it made me tough."

He didn't feel tough. He felt warm and safe and supportive.

Then he said, "Just like it's made Amy tough. How much tougher do you think she has to be?"

"What? What do you mean?" She twisted in his lap and stared at him.

He was serious, his eyes steady on hers, his mouth a firm, straight line. "It would be good for you and me to make a home where she could relax that eternal vigilance and loosen that stiff upper lip."

"What?" He was talking about the two of them making a home together? Absurd! He was talking about Amy…about Margaret's little Amy…being tough because she *had* to be? "You don't know my daughter!"

"Actually, I do. We've got a lot in common, Amy and I." Reid sounded both sensible and steady. "We both lost our support too soon, and we wander through life being strong. I'm strong because I'm a man, because I'm expected to be. She's strong because if she isn't, you'll feel like a failure."

Indignation and hurt blazed in Margaret's gut. "What? Did she tell you that?"

"No."

She stood and looked down on him. "Then how do you know?"

"There are some things about Amy I recognize. At my party, she was unofficial hostess. For my grandfather, she's his support and companion. She told me about how pleased you were with her progress in the martial arts."

To Margaret, every word sounded like a critique. "So? Every woman needs to know how to defend herself."

"I'm not arguing about any of it. Don't get me wrong, you've done a wonderful job. She's a very self-assured young lady. But she found out that being self-assured relieves your worry, and now she's a little more of *everything* when she's with you."

The hostility bubbled up again. "You think *you* can help?"

"I think that she and I need a home, somewhere we can go where we can shiver if we're frightened and cry if we're hurt and gather fortitude to face the world."

"I'm supposed to do all this for you?"

"No." A tiny smile tilted one side of his lips, and she knew he had her where he wanted her. "Amy and I will do that for each other, and in the process, do it for you."

How dare he? How *dare* he? "I can take care of myself."

"Of course you can." He sounded as if he didn't believe her.

And when she thought about it, when she thought about everything he had said, she could not believe what a diabolical man he was. "You. You're putting a guilt trip on me. You're saying if I don't move in with you, it'll be bad for my daughter. Where did you learn that? That's blackmail."

Reid put his hand on the small of her back, and stroked his palm down to her bottom. "Hey, anything that works."

She slapped his hand away.

He let her go.

She paced, her mind twisted, confused, angry—and hurt. He

presumed to tell her what was good for Amy. He thought she was oblivious to Amy's needs.

Oh, God. Was he correct?

And would she ever see her daughter again to hold her in her arms and make everything right?

"All right, here we go." Reid stared at his computer screen. "Cliff Martin's cell phone is off. Nolan Salas is east of downtown, moving at walking pace. Uncle Manuel's phone is at the police department. Good goddamn thing. He'd better be on the case. It looks like Nagumbi is…nowhere."

"His phone is off. It shouldn't be. Why would he turn it off?"

"There's always the chance he forgot to charge it."

"Nagumbi?" Reid released a dry cracked laugh. "Nagumbi forgets nothing."

Margaret wiped her fingers across her trembling lips. "What about Mr. Jim's and Amy's phones?"

"They're off."

"No. No." She put her hands on the arm of Reid's chair and looked into his eyes. "No."

"Excuse me." Simon spoke from the door.

Margaret whirled around to face him.

Reid rose, his eyes fixed on Simon with fierce intensity.

Simon walked toward them and held out a large, flat envelope; his hand trembled. "It's for you, sir. I think this is important."

Margaret snatched the envelope and scanned the front. "This is it," she said. She held it out to Reid, still sealed. "I know this is it."

Thirty-two

Margaret spoke with such confidence. So, so very much confidence. Confidence she didn't want to have…but she'd been here before, handled this situation before.

Never removing his eyes from her, Reid took the brown envelope without touching her fingers. In a guttural voice, deep with agony, he asked, "*What* is this, Margaret?"

"A note." Wringing her hands, she stared at the envelope, waiting…waiting for him to tear it open.

He stood like a statue, holding the note, his hand outstretched.

So she explained impatiently, "From the kidnappers. Like the others."

His hand didn't draw back, but trembled slightly.

She looked up, desperate to know what the note said and not understanding his reluctance.

In an instant she realized he hadn't yet vanquished all his suspicions. He didn't like it—it gave him pain—but her lover distrusted her still.

She didn't have time for hurt, only a flash of anger and a hissed, "Bastard." Snatching the envelope from him, she tore it open.

She scanned the contents. She threw it on the floor. She twirled as if she would run out the door; she stopped as if she didn't know where to go.

Picking up the note, Reid read it, and with a well-restrained violence, shoved it in his shirt pocket. Picking up the phone, he punched the number for the Houston Police. He demanded to speak to Detective Morris, the police spokesman, and tapped his foot through several interdepartmental transfers before roaring, "Uncle Manuel? What the hell are you doing down there?"

His dear old retired uncle didn't sound feeble and out-of-touch. He sounded furious as he roared back, "I'm trying to get these yahoos in line. I leave the force and what happens? The whole damned place falls apart."

Like a ton of bricks falling on him, Reid realized what was going on, realized what he would have realized weeks ago if he hadn't been distracted by his rioting hormones. In a frozen calm, he asked, "What have you done?"

What he heard made him shout, made him pace, made him want to take his grandfather and lock the old man in a dungeon. "And you along with him," he told Manuel. "Your grand plan has netted the kidnappers two hostages, and by God, Granddad and Amy better both be home and in bed before night falls, or I'll put you through Tía Dela's meat grinder." He slammed the phone onto the desk, picked it up, and slammed it again for emphasis.

Margaret did not turn around.

He spoke to her back. "The kidnappers have both of them. *Both* of them. Got off with them while they were shopping. The police don't know where they were taken. After the rash of kidnapping threats, Granddad went to the cops and offered himself as bait, figuring that—" He stopped. "Margaret, turn around." His voice was stern, the voice he used when he commanded. That voice never failed him.

But she didn't turn, she didn't flinch.

He said, "Margaret, it's time for us to talk."

He heard her whisper, "I've been through this before. I can handle it. I know what to do."

He stared at her.

She stood poised on her toes, her back straight, her shoulders shrugged up. Tendons stood out on her neck. Her arms were thrust straight down; her hands were rigid, splayed starfish of tension. To all appearances, she appeared ready to start a race as soon as the gun went off.

He circled around her, observing her.

He saw desperation. He saw dread. He saw sorrow.

How foolish his brief paranoia had been. All of Margaret's world was bound up in Amy. All her love and her fear focused on her only child. This woman would never have sent her child into danger, not for money, not for any reason.

Afraid to touch her, afraid she would shatter, he said gently, "The police already know about Granddad and Amy. They're recovering them now."

Without turning her head, she looked at him. "I've been through it before," she said with feverish conviction. "I can handle it."

" I know you can," he soothed. "Let's sit down, shall we?"

She stared as if he were speaking Korean.

Moving with the slow patience of a wild bird trapper, he sidled up and put his arm around her. "Shall we sit down?"

"No." Her voice was expressionless, inanimate.

"Margaret, we can't just stand here."

"You sit down."

"No, that's all right. I'll be here with you." Glancing around the room, he tried to think of something, anything, that would ease her out of her self-inflicted rigidity.

Everything looked so normal. His computer hummed, his books lay scattered on his desk. Propped on his end table was a snapshot of his grandfather and Amy, taken at Reid's birthday party. In a neat stack in his organizer were the papers for the house in West University.

Nothing here that would ease her.

His instinct was to get her outside, out under the trees, out in the pool, out where the sunshine and heat would melt her. "Let's go for a walk," he murmured.

She wavered for a moment, still on her toes. "A walk? A walk?" The amazed inflections in her voice made it sound like a new language. "Fine."

She put her weight back on her heels. That made her the height he remembered. But nothing else about her seemed familiar.

She was in shock; trapped in terror.

Easing her forward, he saw Simon and Abigail in the doorway.

"What news?" Abigail asked.

Still moving forward, slowly and steadily, he informed her, "Granddad's been kidnapped, and Amy with him."

Abigail groaned and put her hand over her eyes.

But Reid couldn't allow anyone else to collapse. The household had to be up and running, and so he said, "Would you make something light for them to eat when they come in?"

She dragged her fingers from her face and stared at him.

"It'll have to be something that can be put back until they get here," he said.

She wet her lips. "Of course, Mr. Reid."

He suggested, "A soup or a salad, maybe?"

"I know how to cook for an uncertain dinner hour," Abigail said huffily. "I can take care of that."

"Thank you," Reid said. "That would be a load off my mind."

Abigail turned toward the kitchen, muttering, "We've got tomatoes. We've got basil. I'll get fresh mozzarella. I'll make caprese skewers and a simple pasta salad."

Reid pulled Margaret to a halt in the hallway. "Simon?"

"Sir?" Promptly, the footman came to his side.

"Ms. Guarneri and I are going outside. I need an extra battery pack for my cordless phone. I can't afford to lose power."

"Immediately, sir." But Simon didn't move. He stared intently at Margaret.

"Shock," Reid explained.

"Do you want a blanket? Shouldn't she lie down?"

"I can't even get her to *sit* down. The heat out there will warm her."

"Right." Simon disappeared, returning in a moment. He took Reid's phone and affixed the battery pack. "If land line rings, I'll get it. If it's someone about the kidnapping, I'll forward the call to you."

"Thank you. I know I can depend on you to keep it together." He patted Simon's shoulder and moved Margaret toward the front door.

Simon leaped to open it.

They passed out into the sunshine, into the still sweltering heat of September.

Reid passed a worried glance over Margaret, but she still seemed cold, frozen by possibilities. Unable to stand it, he stopped her on the porch.

She stared blankly while he untied her tie, unbuttoned her collar. She moved obediently forward when he urged.

Where should he take her? They couldn't wander without destination around the grounds, yet to sit her down seemed a cruelty. She needed a distraction—hell, *he* needed a distraction. As they rounded the corner of the house, inspiration visited him. "Come on," he murmured. "I've got something to show you."

She obviously didn't care where they were going, but he kept up a patter for the sake of normalcy. "This is not the way I'd planned to surprise you, but perhaps it's better. This is one of those things like a warm blankie or a favorite teddy bear." He opened the side door to the air-conditioned, five-car garage.

Cool air whooshed out.

Flicking on the lights, Reid led her back past the luxury cars and to the narrow door at the back wall. Moving with quiet care, he opened the door to the small storage room where cans of paste wax and tubes of lubricant filled the shelves.

The smell of wet cedar chips rushed out. Inside, a nightlight shone dimly.

Margaret crinkled her nose.

"Let me go in first," he instructed.

She waited docilely.

He checked on the residents of the room, then called, "Come in now."

Imitating him, she tiptoed inside. He watched her eyes widen, watched as her calm facade crumpled into delight.

"Puppies!" Her blue eyes shone, guileless with joy. "Where did you get them? Will mama dog let me touch them? How old are they?"

"The animal shelter; if you're gentle; and about four weeks."

Moving with caution, she knelt beside the basket. "They're precious, and all gold and auburn." She extended her hand to the mother and let her sniff it. "Are they golden retrievers?"

"Golden retriever, Irish setter, and then they ran out of room on the card."

She laughed, almost naturally. "Heinz fifty-seven," she crooned to the puppies tumbling about the basket.

Clean, bright, inquisitive, they climbed over the sides and fell on their faces in their rush to be first to greet their visitors. The mother sat erect on the padding, watching with anxious eyes as her babies sniffed and chewed, but she made no effort to restrain them.

Margaret seated herself on the concrete floor and immediately winced when one intrepid explorer bit her leg. Scooping him up, she held him up to her face. "Watch that." He bit at her nose, his teeth snapping in youthful vigor. "Oh, you're a stinker."

Another puppy climbed into her lap, snuggling into her skirt as if it were a hammock. A third pulled at her cuff.

"Aren't they sweet?" She took her cuff out of the little dog's mouth. "Are there five?"

"Yeah," Reid agreed absently, contending with his own two tiny visitors. "They were going to put them to sleep. I couldn't stand it, so I grabbed them all."

"What's your grandfather going to do with them?" She smoothed her hand over the soft and curly coat of the baby in her lap, accepted a nudge of the cool nose in her palm.

"Granddad? He's not going to do anything with them. I figured I needed a dog."

"*A* dog?"

"So I got a little carried away." He jerked his foot away from one little guy and told him, "Do you mind? That's my *shoe*." Reid crisscrossed his legs and rolled the puppy over in play. "I've got friends who have kids. When these little dickens are weaned, all my godchildren will be gifted with a puppy."

"How many godchildren do you have?"

"Four. That leaves Mama and one other for us." He checked her face. "Do you think Amy would want to pick out her favorite puppy?"

Margaret looked up at him, stricken.

"The dogs are for our house," he said. "*Our* house, the one I showed you today."

She still stared at him, her eyes sick and afraid.

He insisted, "You and me and Amy and our dogs."

"Dear God." Like the victim of a terrible flu, Margaret held her belly and leaned over until her forehead touched her knees. "I don't know if I can stand this."

Thirty-three

The puppy in Margaret's lap whined for escape and wiggled away. Reid scooted to her side.

"Margaret," he said hoarsely. "Sweetheart, it's going to be all right."

He leaned over her, wrapped one protective arm around her, and heard her moan, "I've been though it before. But this time I *can't* handle it."

The puppy who'd been in her lap and the one who'd snapped at her nose; they both whimpered. One licked frantically at the side of her face. One rubbed her arm with his head.

Reid dragged her into his lap. "You've got to have faith, darlin'. Keep a little faith."

"Faith!" Her head jerked up and smacked him under the chin, and her bitterness exploded like a supernova. "Faith. This is one of God's horrible ironies—again. Last time it was Luke. This time it's Amy. I marry a doctor who treats cancer, and he dies of cancer. I choose a career to keep my daughter secure, and she's kidnapped because of it." Her eyes blazed with a horrible light, so dry and wide, they looked as if they'd never shed a tear.

"Your husband—"

"Died of cancer. At the very hospital where he fought to save lives. The best treatments couldn't save him, couldn't save him from suffering. I loved him, and I watched him fade from two hundred pounds to one hundred twenty. I watched him lose his hair and his body control and saw him through heart failure and lung collapse. I watched him go into remission—twice. I listened to the doctors say they had it licked—twice—and he died anyway. It seems like I spent the whole three years standing in a hospital corridor waiting for the results of tests and surgeries and chemotherapies. Standing there with those damn fluorescent lights flickering. Looking up at those lights for all those hours while they took my blood and strained out the platelets and then passed it back to me. Sitting in a hard chair in the room and trying to pass strength through my touch to Luke. Seeing his face in that sickly white light and knowing finally it wasn't going to work." She raised her gaze to Reid's. "Nothing worked."

At last he had the explanation for her backward-stepping caution, for her suspicion of love and her dismay at intimacy. She'd gone every step of the way with her husband: bled for him, rejoiced for his remissions, held him in her arms when he died. She didn't know if her heart could take the grief of loving, and she couldn't remember the joy. Her needs must be rejected for fear of attainment; if she loved, wouldn't she also suffer?

As Reid watched, her bitterness dissipated. Her face softened. Her eyes filled with tears. A slow, soft pain bloomed and grew. Sobs shook her body long before they found an outlet in sound. Then she buried her face in his neck in convulsive agony. Her fingers clawed at his shoulders. "Now they've got my Amy. They've got my baby."

He said nothing. He offered no comfort but for the firm press of his arms around her.

This was what she'd been denying herself. This release of energy and grief would be a catharsis for her.

She hugged Reid's back, tried to pull away.

He held her more tightly. He cradled her.

When she gave up trying to spare him, her tears fell on his shoulder, his chest.

He dug out his handkerchief.

She soaked it with grief.

At last the dreadful weeping eased, the time between sobbing bouts became longer. When she'd stopped, completely stopped, she rested on him, limp with spent emotion.

Thank God. He didn't know if he could bear anymore…and yet, who was he to complain? He had wanted her to grieve…but never had he imagined she would also have to face the additional possibility of harm to her baby. To Amy.

For a long time, Margaret kept her face turned away from him, but finally she sat back into his arm and looked up at him. "You are the most patient man I have ever met."

He examined her tear-stained face. "You look like hell."

"Always a sweet-talker."

He was pleased to note that she didn't try to hide herself. She trusted him now, trusted him enough to let him see her when she'd been ravished by despair. She knew he wouldn't turn away. He added, "And you've scared the dogs."

She lifted her head and observed the puppies, huddled close to their mother in their basket. "Poor lambs."

His butt hurt from sitting on the concrete. One puppy had piddled on his ankle. The arm he held under Margaret's shoulder was asleep. The terror he felt for his grandfather and Amy lived like a coal burning in his gut. And yet...in some ways, he felt better. Oddly hopeful. "You realize this changes everything. I understand you now. Not all of you, but a lot more than I before."

She shifted as if that made her uncomfortable.

He continued, "And not nearly as much as I will know tomorrow, and the day after, and the day after that."

She felt well enough to snap, "Have all your nasty little suspicions been vanquished?"

His affinity for the fragile, indomitable woman in his lap amazed him. "There's still some explaining to be done, but yes. You've vanquished me."

"That was never my intent."

"I know. Damn it." He stroked the damp tendrils of hair away from her face.

"What did the police tell you?"

"It wasn't the police. It was Uncle Manuel."

Clearly, that was news to her. She hadn't heard a word in that office, hadn't noticed anything once she read the note. "He was at the police station? What was he doing there?" The words lagged as she thought, and she sat up slowly. "What have he and Mr. Jim cooked up between them?"

"There's been this extortionist around town, preying on the elderly relatives of wealthy folks—"

"I know that," she interrupted impatiently.

He put his finger across her lips. "—And the police know who it is.

Not that they would tell me. But they haven't been able to pin any evidence on him. Last time, he slipped through their fingers. But he's still operating, so they know he doesn't know that they—"

"—Know." She waved a hand impatiently. "I get the picture. Go on."

"So with the help of my dear Uncle Manuel, my grandfather was recruited to be the sitting duck in a trap."

"That idiot old man," she breathed. "I should have realized he'd have his fingers in the pie. Wait until I get my hands on him."

"Granddad and Uncle Manuel have been throwing you at me, and me at you, as a blind to cover their activities."

"It's worked only too well." She bunched her hand into a fist.

"If it's any consolation, Uncle Manuel apologized for Amy. They never meant for her to be taken. They thought with the head honcho out of town, nothing would happen."

"Out of town?"

They stared at each other.

Then Margaret reached into Reid's soaked t-shirt pocket and pulled out the creased, tearstained note. She held it to his face. "I could smell it when I cried."

He sniffed, and crinkled his nose in disgust. "A cigar. A cheap cigar. Cliff Martin is our man."

Thirty-four

Looking as if she had bitten the worm in the apple, Margaret said, "I was right, all the time."

"As was I. Every time I looked in Cliff Martin's eyes, I was sure someone much smarter was driving that bus." Reid swore, angry but in control. "My instincts shouted at me, Pierre tried to warn me, but—"

"Mr. Jim, Manuel, the police—even my connections were lying to me." She scooted out of Reid's lap and stood, straightening her skirt.

"Your connections?"

"I kept checking with the detectives who had been assigned to the original case because I thought something emitted a foul odor, and those trustworthy gentlemen assured me… Wait until I get my hands on them." Her fingers curled in anticipation. "They'll wish they'd never been born. I'll tell their father what happened, and he'll string them up on the clothesline."

So those guys she was meeting were detectives on the police force?

They didn't look like detectives. They looked like hoodlums. Really handsome hoodlums.

And why did she tell him those guys were none of his business? Why didn't she want him meeting them?

None of that made sense.

Reid got slowly to his feet, easing the kinks out of his knees, hoping that someday he would get feeling back in his butt. "There'll be a lot of people dangling from that clothesline."

"Of course"—her face clouded—"if anything happens to Amy, they'll string themselves up."

"She'll be fine. By God, she'll be fine." Reid plucked the note from her and opened it again. Aloud, he read, "*What we have here is a failure to communicate. I want money for dear old Granddaddy, but I got the little girl, too. That should up the ante. And up your ante if you don't come through. I'll be calling you with instructions…* Look. This time, the note was not printed on Granddad's printer."

"What a relief." She was sarcastic.

He was good with that. "Cliff Martin has never actually kidnapped anyone before."

"What?" She snapped to attention. "Really?"

Reid raised his head. "He's into extortion. He threatens, they pay. He's never had to take someone."

"So he's an amateur." She put her hand on Reid's wrist and squeezed. "He'll be easy to take on."

Reid shook his head. "He's an amateur, and nervous. The charges would have been extortion before. Now they'll be kidnapping with intent of bodily harm."

Her hand fell away. Her expression was stricken. "If he fails, he's got nothing to lose."

"Now that he's up to his ass in alligators, let's hope he remembers his goal is to drain the swamp."

She flung out an arm, knocked over a plastic box full of clean rags, and caught it before it hit the ground. Carefully she returned it to its place. "How could the police have messed up twice in a row?"

"How could Cliff Martin have disarmed us enough that we didn't pursue our suspicions?" Reid went to the door. "He's sly and clever. Out of town, indeed."

"You didn't tell the police we got a note, did you?" Thoughtfully, she drew out the words.

"Why do you think that?"

"Because they haven't arrived to examine it."

"Give that girl a lollipop." Reid folded the note and put it back in his pocket. "The police would do nothing but put it in their files—while it gave us the clue we needed."

With a snap that surprised him, she said, "This means that the chauffeur isn't really dead."

"What chauffeur?" he asked.

"Remember? The unreliable chauffeur I hired? He was put in place to protect your grandfather. After that first kidnapping, the police didn't want you questioning him, so they said he was dead. He's not dead."

Reid opened the door. "He would have been if I'd gotten hold of him."

"Exactly. But it relieves my mind that nobody died for my mistake." Leaning down, she gave the dogs one last pat.

They moved out into the garage. The line of expensive cars was missing only one—the Bentley that had taken Jim and Amy to their kidnapping.

Dry-eyed, she stared at the empty space. "What do we do now?"

"Nothing, much as it rasps me." He longingly touched the speedy BMW roadster. "If we had an inkling as to where Cliff was holding Granddad and Amy, we'd go after them."

Margaret's voice rose hopefully. "*We'd* go after them?"

"Pierre said that the whole police force was lying. He asked about corruption, insinuated somebody on the inside was making money on this deal."

"You don't trust them even yet."

"Do you?"

"Well, I…yes!" She floundered. "They're the police! Private citizens can't go around trying to rescue people. Someone who doesn't know what they're doing might—"

"Mess it up?" He captured her gaze, reminding her without words of the colossal muddle the police had made of this whole situation. "Even if someone in the police force is not deliberately undermining the case, they're doing a shoddy job of capturing Martin in the act."

"Yes, but you and I—"

"You and I are trained in physical defense, and we have a stake in this kidnapping that the police can't imagine."

"When civilians get involved in cases like these, their emotions trip them up," she answered, telling him something she'd heard one hundred times. Her guilt appeased, she added, "On the other hand, we might be able to sneak in and take care of things without guns—and when the police get involved, I'm afraid my baby will get caught in the cross fire."

"We'll have Simon call the cops in"—Reid consulted his watch—"an hour."

"All right." She nodded tightly. "I'm with you. I'll go. All we need is a place to start. And on that note, I must ask—is Salas involved?"

"Salas? Nolan Salas? In cahoots with Martin, you mean?" A place to start, indeed. Reid looked at Margaret, red-eyed and disheveled — and brilliant.

"Yes, he could be in cahoots with Martin, or he could be spying on him for the FBI or …I don't know. Spying on him to steal the money." Margaret lifted her furious, intelligent gaze to his. "Either way, you said Salas's GPS placed him east of downtown. East of downtown is a tough part of town. At a time like this when everyone is looking for him, what's he doing *there* and why isn't he answering his phone?"

"Because he's tracking Cliff Martin. Or he's Martin's partner." Hope and excitement rose in Reid like bubbles in champagne. "Margaret…that's a long shot. And…you are a clever, clever girl."

She smiled tightly.

"East of downtown." Reid took his hand off the classic Beemer. "We're going to need the cheapest vehicle possible to get us there, because it's probably going to get stripped."

"We'll take mine. After this, Mr. Jim will be forced to buy me a new car." She started toward the door.

Reid's cell phone rang.

They stopped in midstep.

Reid pulled it out, looked at the number and shrugged. "I don't know who it is, but it's a local number." He put it on speaker and nodded to Margaret.

She answered, "Donovan residence."

The voice they heard was the last they expected. "Mama?"

"Amy?"

"Mama, listen—"

"Amy, are you all right?" Frantically, Margaret tried to take the phone out of Reid's grasp. "Speak up, I can hardly hear you."

He held it out of her reach. "Amy, it's Reid. Where are you?"

"In a hotel room, downtown. I can see the big buildings from the windows. The street sign says Mount Phegley, and the cross street is Schmidt. He's got us on the third floor on the alley—"

Good information. Reid was proud of the child. "Who's got you?"

"That big, fat Mr. Martin." Amy sounded furious.

"That's what we thought, honey. Go on, tell us everything you know about your location."

"There's a fire escape right outside the window—that's how I got out. I ran down the steps and found an open window and crawled into this groaty room. There's a land line. I'm using it." Amy spoke urgently, quietly.

"Is he following you?" Reid asked.

"Not yet. He didn't see me go. Nagumbi broke through the door. I went out the window. I heard a shot." Amy's voice rose to a wail.

Margaret said, "Steady, girl."

"Who shot who?" Reid queried.

"I don't know," Amy said miserably. "I'm afraid Nagumbi was hurt. Cliff had the gun."

Margaret covered her mouth.

Reid rubbed his temples. "Nagumbi never carries one. I warned him—Go on, Amy."

"You've got to come and get Sir Gramps, and bring his pills. He's wheezing and he looks white, and that fat *bastard* keeps telling him he'll shoot him if he dies."

Margaret started to chide her daughter for her language, thought better of it and shut her mouth.

"We'll be there as fast as we can," Reid promised. "Amy? Can you do something very hard for me?"

She didn't hesitate. "Yes."

"Go back upstairs to the floor where Cliff was holding you. Run down the hallway, make a lot of noise. See if you can get Cliff Martin to capture you again."

"No!" Margaret shrieked.

Reid ignored her. "If Nagumbi's alive, he'll get to you. If Cliff Martin's alive…just don't tell Cliff Martin you called us. Don't tell him, or he'll move you and Granddad, and it will take us longer to find you again."

Amy sounded faint and faraway. "All right." Then her voice grew stronger. "I'll do it. I can't abandon Sir Gramps, anyway."

"Maybe we got lucky." Reid crossed his fingers as if Amy could see him. "Maybe Nagumbi is waiting for you up there now."

"I hope so," Amy said.

"Go on, now, run," Reid urged. "We love you."

"I love you, too."

The line went dead.

"Come *on.*" Margaret headed out.

He followed, and vowed, "We'll get them. This time it's our turn."

Thirty-five

Margaret discovered that her pure English stood out among the babble of different languages and accents. Her height made her extraordinary.

But in the east side of downtown Houston, dressing like a ninja and skulking in the shadows attracted no attention. No one cared what they did. No one stared at them. And only one person spoke to them, a gaunt man who offered them a good buy on weed—or anything else they wanted.

Reid looked at him, eyes cold and hostile.

The drug dealer faded into the shadows.

Margaret was glad a black cap covered her blond hair, even though its enveloping cotton made sweat trickle down her back. She wished she'd taken Reid's advice and smeared combat camouflage on her face. In the dim, narrow alley, thick with garbage and dark with smoke, her pale skin shone like a betrayal.

She coughed and whispered, "It smells like someone's cooking fish heads in motor oil."

"Probably." He leaned back against the dumpster and studied the building that rose in the twilight. "What do you think? Do you think that's the one?"

"I told you what I thought. Amy might be wrong about the floor she's on, but she'll never be wrong about the streets. That kid has a sense of direction, and she can read." Margaret looked up at the few unboarded windows on the fire escape. "I don't imagine she saw where she was going when Cliff Martin shoved her up the stairs inside. She went running down the fire escape in a panic—she could have counted wrong. After all, there are two sets of stairs to get to the fourth floor because the bottom floor of the fire escape doesn't have stairs. You have to lower the last set of stairs from above."

"Right. We'll climb up to the fourth floor, but quietly." He smiled at her, a mere twist of his mouth.

His smile made her feel better.

This whole thing was making her feel better. At least they were doing *something*.

Her heart pounded. Her breath came in little gasps. She was sick from the threat to her child, but action stirred her blood, and the faith she felt in her partner was like a shot of caffeine. This was what she needed: not fear-filled hours waiting for a call from the police department that had failed her so far, but her own personal chance to slap the shit out of Cliff Martin.

The cops would say she was taking chances with her life and her daughter's. But Cliff Martin had a gun. The police had their weapons. And she was haunted by the specter of Amy's death by friendly fire...or from a traitor within the department.

No. They were doing the right thing. Better her and Reid dealing with Martin, talking him down, keeping the situation low-key, than taking chances that Martin would get nervous and try to shoot his way out...or make an example of one of his hostages.

She knew she was skilled in defense; she knew Reid's training surpassed her own. She knew they were prepared to die for Jim and Amy. Jim and Amy were kin, their flesh and blood. Maybe this wasn't the right thing to do, but when she weighed the odds, they had a better chance of success than the cops.

"Come on." Reid touched her arm.

She followed him to stand below the fire escape beside a boarded-up window.

"Up you go." He boosted her up onto the metal lid of the dumpster and climbed up after her.

The fire escape still hung beyond their reach.

He made a saddle of his hands. "Put your foot here."

Laying her palms against the aging brick, she did as instructed and with a grunt, he hoisted her above his head. She grabbed the iron platform above.

He took his hands away.

In a low voice filled with revulsion, she said, "I grabbed somebody's chewing gum."

He kept his voice low and unsympathetic. "Good. You won't slip."

She walked her hands down to the corner where no railing would stop her and swung herself up onto the discolored woven-metal platform covered with…

Don't look. Don't think about it.

She lowered the stairway. It creaked and moaned in rusty distress.

"Quiet," he said.

"Not possible. Damn." She jerked her hand back. "I pinched it."

"Bleeding?"

She shuddered. "Gangrene's a possibility." She shook the scarlet drops away, and leaned into her job again. "A real possibility," she muttered.

Above her, she heard a noise.

Reid gestured once, emphatically. "Get back." He leaned out of the light.

She put her spine against the building, kept her head down. Above her, a window opened in jerks, the painted wood swollen with humidity. She could hear a plaintive child's voice—*her* child's voice.

"I'm hot," Amy said peevishly.

Cliff Martin's voice, low and threatening. "I opened the window, kid. But if you try to escape again…"

"Have the cops arrived yet?" Amy's clear voice floated out into the evening air. "It's eight-thirty. They'll be here soon."

"Did you set up a timetable?" Cliff sneered.

"No, but a stupid kidnapper like you could hardly have fooled them for long." She sounded calm and logical, not at all frightened.

"Your confidence in me is overwhelming." Cliff's voice grew fainter; he'd turned away from the window.

But Margaret could still hear Amy. "A smart kidnapper would have brought Sir Gramps's pills. A dead corpse won't do you a lot of good."

From deeper in the room a voice quavered, "*Dead corpse* is redundant, Amy. All corpses are dead."

Margaret straightened. Mr. Jim was still alive, and Amy was not terrified…if only she'd stop needling Cliff Martin.

Margaret looked down at Reid, and silent urgent communication passed between them.

Her baby was right here. She could almost touch her.

His grandfather was right here. He needed Reid.

Margaret grasped the stairs again, lifting them with newfound strength. Only a few screeches of distressed metal disturbed the evening. The sounds were absorbed in the constant tumult of the city: the sounds of the freeway passing close by, the shouts of gangs as they patrolled their streets.

The steps settled into place.

Reid climbed up to join her. "This is it."

She looked down at her grimy, bloody hands. Her fingers trembled.

Reid, too, stared at her hands. Picking them up, he found the place where her skin had been pinched open and blood still oozed. He brushed it lightly with his finger, then raised it to his mouth. He sealed the area with his lips and sucked hard.

Tears sprang to her eyes and she tried to jerk away, silence accentuating her pain.

He kept a steady pressure until he lifted his mouth and spit the blood to the street below. "No gangrene," he whispered, folding her palm tight together.

It sounded like an order.

"Let's go," she said softly, and took the first step, then the second. Climbing the stairs with stealth and an ever-increasing speed, she fed her excitement with outrage. She focused on that window on the fire escape, her thoughts primitive, vengeful.

Reid climbed half a step behind her. She never looked back at him, yet she never forgot he was there. He was her accomplice. He had her back.

The fire escape outside the open window was as flat and dirty as the rest of the building.

She waited there, back pressed to the wall, eyes gleaming.

Reid joined her.

This was the tough part—getting in.

Inside the room, it was dark…and silent.

Why? Why wasn't Amy talking?

Had Cliff got sick of her taunting, and hurt her? Hit her? Killed her?

Reid made a move.

Margaret pushed him aside and dove through the window.

She landed on her feet. She dropped into an attack stance.

Thirty-six

Inside, Cliff Martin stood with his back against the far wall, holding a pistol to Jim's head. He held Amy pulled tightly against him, a hand over her mouth.

Amy's eyes were wide and terrified.

Cliff recognized Margaret, and looked relieved. "Well, if it isn't Albert the Butler." Raising his voice, he called, "Come in, Mr. Donovan. I know she didn't come alone." Cliff's hand shook, and as Reid climbed through the window, it shook harder.

Now Margaret truly understood Reid's comment about untested kidnappers. It didn't matter if the gun discharged beneath a shaking finger; Mr. Jim would be just as dead.

And as she watched, Cliff Martin slid his palm off Amy's mouth and tightly gripped her throat.

Another threat. He could break her neck before Margaret could reach them.

Reid put his hand on Margaret's shoulder as if stopping her lunging.

Never would she be so reckless. Already she'd come through the window to face a hopeless situation. She wouldn't jeopardize Mr. Jim and her daughter any further.

"Hi, Mom." Amy sounded matter-of-fact and unafraid. "I like the ninja costume."

Margaret's eyes narrowed.

Amy was, as Reid had pointed out, brave and self-assured. But her lower lip quivered and she chewed it with her teeth.

Margaret ached to hold her and hug her and tell her it was all right.

She ached in a different way, too. Anger bubbled in her, an anger to match the sorrow of the morning, to match the passion of the week.

She wanted to smash Cliff Martin.

She wanted to see his face bruise beneath her fist.

She wanted to see the police taking what was left of his battered corpse away.

She couldn't do any of that. She had to contain herself, and that made her even angrier. She settled for a tight smile. "Thanks, honey. I'm grateful for the chance to wear it before Halloween."

"Are you here to rescue us before the cockroaches eat my shoes?" Amy asked brightly.

"Are they huge?"

Amy indicated with her hands the length of the roaches, then tilted her head toward the man in the wheelchair. "Did you bring Mr. Jim's pills? Mr. Jim really needs his pills."

Margaret looked at Jim, slumped in his wheelchair, and her fury burned hotter.

An unhealthy sweat dotted his forehead and plastered his thin hair into a wispy gray paste. His hands were in his lap, clenched and shaking. The man for whom dressing was an effort found it a strain to be kidnapped.

Beside her, Reid held up a prescription bottle and took a step forward. "Here they are, Granddad. Let me give you—"

"Don't move again," Cliff ordered.

Reid froze.

Everyone froze.

Margaret stared at the gun pressed against Mr. Jim's temple.

If only Jim could reach up and bat it away.

But no. He was doing all he could just to sit up.

In slow motion, Reid took his step back. "Next time you decide to be the bait in a trap, Granddad, make sure you take these pills along for the ride."

Reid's face was impassive, his voice smooth. But Margaret recognized the signs in him.

Anger. An anger to match hers.

Mr. Jim laughed, and coughed. "Figured it out, did you?"

"None too soon," Reid agreed. "The cops closed in too quickly last time."

"Last time," Jim said, "I wore a homing device."

Cliff jumped and barked, *"What?"*

"Didn't your hired gunmen tell you?" Jim looked past the pistol and up at Cliff. "Or were they so busy running they didn't stop until they crossed the Mexican border?"

"So that's why they didn't finish the job," Cliff said.

"I hope you didn't pay them ahead of time," Reid said.

Cliff scowled. "Only half."

"But you learned your lesson. If you want something done right, you have to do it yourself, right, Martin?" Jim turned back to Reid and Margaret. "When the two hired hands ripped my shirt looking for money, they realized I was a live microphone. Now matter how convincing I was, they would *not* believe it was an external pacemaker."

Funny. Margaret almost laughed.

Jim pointed a trembling finger at her. "Remember how you questioned me? About my torn shirt? About the wires dangling from the wheelchair? You gave me a bad turn when you insisted on sending the wheelchair to be fixed. Good thing you two were so involved with each other."

"Lucky break for you, Granddad," Reid said.

"Lucky break, indeed." He took a rasping breath. "I planned every bit of it. I took one look at Margaret and I knew she was the woman for you, and I knew you'd give me a lot of entertainment before it was over."

"Always ready to please." An unwilling admiration swelled in Reid. His grandfather was obviously suffering, yet still feisty enough to needle his kidnapper—and scare Reid to death. "So you refused to wear a homing device anymore?"

"Right." Jim's voice faded, his energy exhausted. "Those idiot cops couldn't be trusted—"

"Not to move in too soon," Reid guessed. "So it wasn't sabotage. They were just too anxious to rescue you."

"They can come *now*," Jim said.

"You scared them, Granddad. And you scared me, so I didn't deliver the latest note to them. Not that I know what good that would have done, considering what a lousy job they've done with this case so far."

Jim still spoke clearly, but he kept his eyes closed. "Manuel told me that Cliff's seeming incompetence disarmed them. He's smarter than he looks."

Reid said to Cliff, "The man needs his pills."

"The man can die for all I care." Cliff's hand shook harder beneath Reid's hard stare. "He's the bait in a trap? A trap to catch me? Well, you haven't caught me yet, and I'll bet you didn't bring the money."

"You're right. I didn't bring the money." Reid's voice smoothed and urged, "But Cliff, think about the difference between being arrested for extortion and being arrested for murder. You don't want to shoot my grandfather."

"Don't I?" Cliff twisted the gun toward Amy. "Maybe I want to shoot them both."

Thirty-seven

Margaret looked at Cliff. Locked gazes and looked.

What Cliff saw must have scared the hell out of him. He cocked the pistol.

Time stopped. Breath stopped.

Then a sharp rap of knuckles on wood made them all jump.

Everyone stared at the door, wavering in the grip of uncertainty.

Reid glanced around at the filthy floor, the peeling paint. "Did you order room service?" he asked sarcastically.

Cliff glared. A second knock sent his gun to swinging in a wide arc.

"It can't be the cops," Reid wanted Cliff to be afraid, but not panicked. Panicked he was an even greater danger to them all. "They wouldn't knock."

But the visitors had lost their patience. One kick, and the feeble door flew open.

Two men in black leather jackets slumped on the threshold, looking like bored tourists, barely twitching.

Margaret said, "Thank God."

Amy pumped her fist and said, "Yes!"

Reid's first thought was, *Drug dealers. We're dead.* His second was, *I recognize these guys.*

Cliff recognized them, too. "The lunch crowd," he said.

The men from Cliff's photographs stepped into the room.

"Who the hell are you guys?" Reid asked.

"I'm asking the questions!" Cliff snapped, then repeated, "Who the hell are you guys?"

One man pulled the toothpick from his mouth and tossed it down.

The other stuck his hands into his pockets and answered laconically, "We're special forces for the Houston Police Department."

Cliff didn't seem to understand.

Reid did.

These *were* Margaret's contacts on the police force.

"You know," the guy said to Cliff, "we're undercover cops."

"Detectives?" Cliff squealed.

Everything happened at once.

Cliff touched the gun to Jim's head and shouted, "I'm going to blow him to bits."

One detective pulled his service pistol.

Margaret and the other detective leaped toward Amy.

Crazed with fear, Reid ran toward his grandfather.

And in a blur of motion, Amy arched off the floor. The edge of her foot jerked up in a slicing kick. She landed a solid blow right to Cliff's groin.

Cliff grabbed himself, discharging the gun into his own thigh. He screamed and dropped like a rock.

One of the detectives snatched Amy to safety.

The other slammed Cliff to the floor and handcuffed him.

Reid reached his grandfather's side and handed him the pills.

Jim wrapped an arm around Reid's neck and hugged him.

Granddad was alive. Thank God. He was alive.

Still fighting, Cliff rose to his knees—and met Margaret's fist coming in hard and fast.

Cliff fell backward, blood gushing from his nose.

Yeah. Reid nodded. *Don't screw with his woman and her child.*

"You bastard," Margaret shouted, and went in for another shot.

One of the cops grabbed her arm from behind and held her while she struggled.

Reid figured this was his only chance. Picking Cliff up by his collar, he held him and stared into close to his face. "Listen to me," he said loud and clear. "The justice system is too lenient, we all know that. But I've got money, I've got influence, I've got favors I can call in. I'm going to make sure you stay behind bars forever. I'm going to know you're dating the biggest bully in the prison."

Cliff wasn't finished yet. He lifted his head. "My father's got money, too. You can't keep me in prison."

From the doorway, a man's firm voice said, "Um, actually, your father won't do anything to help you." Nolan Salas stepped into the room.

Every head turned toward him.

He looked, as always, neat, tidy, and unobtrusive. "Your father sent me to Houston specifically because he suspected you, his only child, of embezzlement, and he did not, and does not, wish your activities to taint his reputation."

Everyone gaped.

Salas continued, "I have of course managed to track down the amounts of money you have acquired, and what you didn't spend has been returned to the families."

"No! I had to show him." Cliff gasped out the words. "He owned half of Kentucky by the time he was thirty—I'm going to own half of Texas."

"I don't think so, son," Mr. Jim said.

Cliff gave a sob.

Reid dropped him, wiping his hands on his pants as if he'd been holding a slug. He looked up from the bloody, whimpering Cliff to see his grandfather trying to smile at him.

"Pills?" the old man said.

"I gave them to you."

Jim showed Reid his empty, shaking hands. "Dropped them," he whispered.

Reid looked around.

Serious-looking men and women in blue uniforms crowded into the room, taking notes, putting up crime scene tape, and hustling Cliff out the door.

Salas was talking to one of the officers, who was taking notes.

Margaret huddled over Amy as the two hugged and cried.

The two tough-looking undercover policemen stood over the top of them, making comforting noises.

In the distance, Reid heard the wail of sirens.

In here, the uproar was incredible, and growing.

Reid hollered to the room, "Stop!"

The swirl of movement halted.

The noise in the room died.

The wail of sirens grew louder.

"We need to find Granddad's pills," Reid said. "They are somewhere on the floor and he needs them *now*."

The police all lifted their feet, one at a time, and shook their heads.

One of the black-jacketed detectives dropped to his knees beside the bed and shined his light beneath. "Here," he called. He waved his hand in the air and someone put a nightstick in it. He rolled the brown bottle out and gingerly picked it up. Dust fell in coils as he wiped it off with his handkerchief, and his mouth twisted as if he tasted something nasty.

"Make sure it has the right name on it," he advised as he passed it to Reid. "It could be anybody's."

Reid took it between two fingers. "It's Granddad's," he confirmed. "Can we get an ambulance? Granddad needs to go to the medical center."

One of the uniformed police assured him, "Ambulance is on its way."

Margaret handed Reid an unopened bottle of water.

He hurried to his grandfather's side.

Jim had Amy wrapped in one arm, and in his weak, old voice he scolded, "If you ever scare me like that again, you'll find out what spankings are for."

Amy promised, "Next time I'll let him shoot you."

"She's got you there, Granddad." Reid shook out two pills and held the bottle while Jim drank. Then he enveloped Jim and Amy in a hug. "I'm glad you're both safe."

Amy wrapped her arms around his neck and squeezed hard. "Me, too."

"Where'd you learn that kick?" Reid queried.

"I learned the kick at my class." She grinned. "I learned *where* to kick from my mom."

"I'll watch myself," Reid promised.

A somber Margaret joined them. "Nagumbi's out in the hall. He's unconscious, but the police are working on him. They say...they say there's a lot of blood loss."

Jim said nothing, and Reid checked him with sharp eyes. The old man's eyes were closed and his chin rested on his chest. Reid wrapped a supporting arm around him. "Do you want to lie down on the bed while you wait for an ambulance?"

Reid was able to gauge how bad Jim felt by the fact he didn't object to an ambulance. But he murmured, "On *that* bed? They'd have to delouse me at the hospital."

Reid turned to Margaret and in a quiet voice he said, "If Granddad or Nagumbi dies, I will take out Cliff Martin myself."

Margaret rubbed her bloodied knuckles as if they hurt, and nodded.

Yeah, at least she'd gotten in one good punch.

Two teams of EMTs arrived. One team loaded Jim up immediately, and assured Reid he would be fine.

The second team worked on Nagumbi for ten minutes, getting him ready for transport, and when Reid saw him, his friend was conscious and swearing about the pain in plain, precise English.

Reid thanked him for all he'd done.

Margaret gave Nagumbi a kiss on the cheek and repeated everything Reid said.

Amy thanked him for saving her life.

The police questioned Reid, Margaret, and Amy briefly, then the three of them found themselves on the street. Night had fallen, but the neighborhood was alive with floodlights, police cars, and curiosity seekers.

The undercover policemen strolled up.

One had a new toothpick stuck in his mouth.

The other slouched, yet when he looked up his eyes were piercing. Pulling his hand out of his jacket pocket, he offered it to Reid. "Dom Guarneri, at your service."

"Guarneri?" Reid repeated.

"And this is my brother, Julian."

"Guarneri." Reid couldn't believe it. "Margaret's brothers-in-law?"

"They're my uncles," Amy said proudly.

Reid caught Dom's hand and pumped it. "You don't know how happy I am to meet you." He grabbed Julian's hand and shook it, too, although it had never been offered.

The brothers exchanged glances.

Dom agreed with patent disbelief, "Yeah. We thought maybe you'd want to ride with us to the station and fill us in on the events of the day."

"I'd be glad to. Glad to." Margaret's family. Reid was meeting Margaret's family. He turned back to tell Margaret where he'd be, and bumped into her standing directly behind him. "Margaret, I'm going—"

"I heard." She stared hard at the Guarneri brothers. "I imagine you'll be wanting *my* testimony, too?"

"Not right now, Margaret." Dom hugged her. "You go take care of Amy."

She stumbled, obviously annoyed with his affectionate display. "You need Amy's testimony, too."

Amy piped up, "I like to give testimony."

"Later, sweetheart," Dom said. "Right now you two should go home."

Margaret broke away from him and stared right into his eyes. "According to police procedure, you'll need to question us right away. In depth."

"According to police procedure," Dom answered right back, "you were supposed to call us as soon as you found out where they were keeping Amy."

"We didn't trust you," she snapped.

Reid didn't like the way this conversation was going. Antagonizing cops, even if they were relatives, seemed like a bad idea. "I wouldn't say that, exactly."

She whipped around and glared at him.

"Don't, baby." Julian put his hand on his chest. "You'll break my heart."

Dom asked, "What's Pop going to say when he finds out you tried to take on a criminal without notifying the police?"

"Didn't Simon call with the message?" Margaret asked.

Dom pointed a finger. "Yes. But that's not going to get you off the hook, Margaret. We've told you a hundred times, when civilians get involved, they do stupid things. And you did, didn't you?"

She pointed a finger right back. "No. We had no choice. There was only one way in, and I took it." She was going chest to chest with this guy.

Amy observed, head turning from one to the other as if she was watching a Ping-Pong match.

Reid found himself doing the same.

"You'd think anyone who'd been in our family as long as you would have better sense." Dom backed off.

Margaret had made tough-guy Dom back off.

But he continued, "So we're taking Mr. Donovan to talk to him a little bit."

"You can't fool me. I *know* what you're doing," Margaret declared.

Which was more than Reid did.

"We're *talking*," Dom said. "Talking like civilized people. We've been wondering about Mr. Reid Donovan ever since you stood us up to go look at that house in West U."

Margaret blushed.

Julian spit the toothpick on the sidewalk. "Don't worry. We'll take good care of your boyfriend."

"Boys," Margaret warned. "I will tell your father on you."

"First you'll have to tell him you withheld information about that last note." Dom hooked an arm through Reid's.

Margaret put herself between them and the car. "Damn you, what would Pop have done?"

"Don't swear. It's not attractive in a lady." Julian wrapped his arm around her neck. "Besides, what the old man would do has nothing to do with it. He's retired cop, and you know what he thinks of a woman doing a man's job."

"Chauvinists," she snarled.

Julian knuckled her head and released her. "Hey, who do you suppose taught us how to behave? We'll catch you later, sis."

They walked away from the still-sputtering Margaret toward a black Ford 150 supercrew pickup.

Julian got in the driver's seat.

Dom pushed Reid into the middle of the front seat, and followed him in.

Julian drove off with a squeal.

"Do you think she'll chase us down?" Reid asked with interest.

"She's a determined woman." Dom twisted to look behind them. "She'll do what she wants." He twisted back and stared at Reid. "But not before we ask—what are your intentions with our sister-in-law? And don't make us beat the right answer out of you."

Reid was beginning to understand why Margaret hadn't wanted to tell him about her brothers-in-law.

He'd fallen in with the Guarneri Mafia.

Thirty-eight

Margaret paced the entryway. She'd reassured Simon and Abigail and the rest of the help, telling them an abbreviated version of the fight and rescue. She'd helped her daughter prepare for bed and tucked her in with the heartfelt gratitude of a mother who'd almost lost her finest treasure. She'd called the hospital and received a reassuring report on Mr. Jim.

She'd showered, washing the reminders of the day off her hands and her body. She'd bandaged her hand. She'd changed into a soft pair of jeans and a casual pink t-shirt. And now she paced.

Reid should have been home hours ago.

What had the Guarneri brothers done to him? Visions of Reid walking back to Houston on a dark and lonely road haunted her. She knew the Guarneri boys, had known them for more than twelve years. They loved her, and she loved them. She'd been the sister they'd never had. They'd moved to Houston to be with Luke during his illness, and to protect her from the vicissitudes of life. And when they'd encouraged her move to London, she had known she had only to call to bring them running.

The sons of an Italian immigrant policeman, Dom and Jules had been raised to be tough and resourceful. Their old-world values would hardly condone the cohabitation of their treasured sister with any man, and they had a distinct lack of reverence for money and the power it could bestow.

So as the clock crept toward midnight, she paced, and worried.

When the intercom buzzed and the security man at the gate announced their arrival, she flew out the front door and waited on the front step. As the black pickup pulled up, her anxiety made her shiver and rub her arms.

From the driver's seat stepped a stranger, a policeman in partial uniform. He tipped his hat. "Off-duty, ma'am," he said, as if that explained everything.

From the far side of the backseat stepped Julian. He was smiling, a rare and foolish grin.

From the near side stepped Dom, cackling like an old hen.

Margaret squatted down and squinted through the open doors of the car, trying to confirm her suspicion of foul play. When she couldn't see Reid in the feeble light of the overhead, she accused, "You dropped him, didn't you?"

"Wha…?" Dom seemed to notice her for the first time.

"Where did you put Reid?" She advanced on Dom, her fists clenched.

"Oh, hi, sis." Dom threw his affectionate arm around her shoulders and made kissing noises in the vicinity of her ear. "How are you?"

Even before the smell of his breath struck her, his boisterous affection let her know what had happened. "Whew." She fanned her hand in front of her nostrils. "How much did you guys drink?"

That seemed to bring out the hysteria in the Guarneris. They laughed and laughed. Julian stumbled around the car, hanging on the fenders, and repeated her question to his brother, and that set them off again.

Margaret tapped her toe and waited for the hilarity to die down. "What…did…you…do…with…Reid?" She emphasized each word, and quickly thrust her fist in their faces. "If you start laughing again, I'll show you how good I've gotten in my self-defense classes." She glanced up at the driver.

He shook his head. "They called me to drive, not defend them. Ma'am, you can do whatever you want."

Julian held his hand over his mouth and snorted.

Dom collected himself enough to say, "Reid? Reid's right in there." His unsteady finger pointed in the general direction of the pickup.

"Where?"

"There," Dom insisted. "On the floor in the back seat."

"Did you beat him up?" she cried, horror-struck.

"Naw." He waved his hands in wild negation. "Come on, Jules. Let's get our sister's boyfriend out of the car. She's worried about him."

Like little boys, they made smoochy noises in the air.

She growled.

Together they lunged at the door of the backseat.

From inside, Margaret heard, "You'll have to carry me inside. My feet are no longer connected to my body."

Compared to the mumbles of the Guarneris, the voice was clear and strong and articulate. Yet she could hardly believe that the Reid she knew could say something so stupid.

The Guarneri brothers giggled as they pulled at Reid.

First Reid's feet, then his hands flopped out. He was bent like the scarecrow from Oz. He lifted his head from his knees and smiled at her. "Hi, Margaret. I bet you'd like an explanation."

First the relief hit her.

He wasn't hitching a ride with the leader of the chainsaw massacres. He wasn't in a boxcar heading for Mexico. He wasn't in an emergency room having them set his bones.

He was safe.

Well, hallelujah.

Then the outrage hit her. She'd been home, worrying her keister off, and he'd been out cruising the bars with her hard-drinking brothers-in-law.

That son of a bitch.

Frigidly she replied, "I'd say I know exactly what happened."

Dom and Julian tugged at Reid's hands until he tumbled out of the truck. They caught him before his face hit the ground and hoisted his arms around their shoulders.

His feet did a little dance; his knees gave way one at a time. His resemblance to the scarecrow increased with every step he couldn't take. But his voice was still clear and pure. "Now, Margaret, I know what you're thinking, and it isn't true."

Dom added his earnest agreement. "No, it's not. Come on, Julian, let's get him up the steps."

Reid continued, "They suggested we go talk it over at a bar, and I agreed."

"Upsy-daisy," Julian said. "Lift those legs. Hey, Web, give us a hand here."

The driver came to push from behind.

Still talking, Reid began the slow ballet up the steps. "I told them I don't drink, but they insisted on buying me a beer."

"Have you ever heard of a Texan who doesn't drink?" Dom asked

Julian shook his head in wonder.

Reid continued, "I didn't want to make them mad, so I drank it."

"One little, teeny beer." Dom raised his fingers to show her how little and teeny it had been.

Reid slid back a step. "The reason I don't drink, see, is because I can't tolerate liquor in any form."

"Right." Margaret opened the double door to allow the procession in.

"Don't be that way," Reid begged. "Have you ever seen me take a drink?"

She thought back over the time she'd known him. Then she thought again. "Well...no."

"There's a good reason for that," Reid said. "At our dinner parties, water flows like wine. You'll notice my grandfather never drinks, either."

"No kidding," she scoffed. "The doctors are hardly going to allow that."

"He *never* drank. Found out he couldn't hold his liquor the hard way, on an oil rig. He decided to ride that sucker. You'll have to ask him to tell you that story someday." Reid laughed. "It's a corker."

"Sounds like it. How many beers did you have altogether?"

Dom answered, clearly unbelieving. "Two beers."

This time it was Julian who held up his fingers, indicating two. "*Two* beers. And he talks like this. His brain works fine. His body"—he sliced his hand across his own throat—"kaput."

"We had a marvelous conversation," Reid said. "My bedroom's up the stairs."

The group stopped and gaped at the winding stairway.

"No."

"Forget it."

"No way."

"We'll put him in Mr. Jim's room," Margaret said. "It's on the ground floor. This way."

She led them, switching on lights as she went, but the procession halted before the Mickey-and-Reid portrait hung with pride in the main foyer.

"Hey." Dom jiggled Reid in delight. "I never realized you knew Mickey Mouse personally."

Reid raised his bleary eyes to the painting. "Doesn't everyone?"

They stumbled down the hall, bumping the Ming vases and joggling the tapestries. When they reached Jim's room, she flung the comforter down to the foot of the bed. "Put him there," she ordered.

The three men picked Reid up and bodily tossed him onto the mattress.

"Fabulous." Margaret surveyed the disheveled marvel of a man. "Reid, do you want me to undress you?"

Reid lifted his head and smiled widely.

Dom and Julian's veto was swift and sure. "No, no." "I don't think so."

In unison, they climbed on the bed and began to tug at Reid's clothing.

Reid moaned at their less than gentle ministrations. "If my body wasn't numb from the neck down, I'd be horribly upset about this."

"If we believed your body was numb from the neck down," Julian retorted, "we'd let Margaret undress you."

Margaret leaned on the bedpost and laughed.

"I'm glad someone thinks it's amusing," Reid huffed.

Dom jerked at Reid's shirt. "We've had a long talk with this feller here. Questioned him about his intentions, found out his plans. Our father will be proud of us."

"Be sure you go home and call him," Reid ordered. "You promised you would."

"You want them to call my father-in-law?" Margaret said. "He's liable to come out here and clean your clock."

"Naw." Dom hopped off the bed. "Pop'll be relieved to hear you've got a man. He worries about you, you know."

"We're happy for you." Julian said. "This guy will take care of you for the rest of your life."

"No. No!" Margaret had agreed to no such thing.

As they left the room, Dom flipped off the light. "Come on, Julian. The evening's young. Let's go find us some babes who don't think so much."

Sputtering, Margaret followed them out to the front steps.

They patted her back and kissed her good-bye.

Their driver opened the door for them, and with a flourish, they leaped in and rode away.

"I don't need Reid Donovan." She shouted after them, and went in the house and slammed the door. "He's the man I'm sleeping with, that's all." She crept down the hallway and stuck her head in Jim's room.

Reid's breathing sounded soft and even.

She sneaked up on the side of the bed. In the light from the hall, she could see him.

He lay on his back, his arms thrown out, still in the same angle they'd left him.

She frowned. That spread-eagle position couldn't be comfortable. Moving slowly so as not to disturb him, she brought his arms into his chest and his legs together. She eased him onto his side and smiled fondly as he sighed and snuggled into the pillow.

What a beautiful man he was. She hesitated to cover him for the pleasure of gazing on his body. His legs were corded, powerful from exercise. She knew what the boxer shorts concealed, and the memory made her tingly. His chest tempted her with its rippling muscle and smooth skin. His face pleased her with its authoritarian angles and dark-bearded shadow at the chin.

Her fingers couldn't resist. She stroked the rough bristle. She caressed his sharp cheekbone, slid a fingertip across his eyelid. Brushing his short bangs away from his forehead, she whispered, "We're just using each other, aren't we? I don't know how the boys got the idea that you were a permanent kind of man, but you really have them fooled." She chuckled and pulled the covers over his legs. "I don't need you, and you don't need me, and that's the way I like it." She tucked the blankets up to his chin and went to the door. Adjusting the rheostat so the ceiling fan barely circled, she crooned, "You won't hurt me the way Luke did."

From out of the darkness, Reid spoke. "You mean," he asked, "if I were ill, you would abandon me?"

Margaret froze.

But he said nothing else.

And she shut the door behind her.

But she couldn't shut out the question. Nor could she shut out the pain in her heart when she thought of vital, dynamic Reid Donovan struck by sickness.

If he was ill, would she abandon him then?

Oh, God, she didn't want to think about it. She didn't want to know.

Thirty-nine

Margaret leaned her elbows on the kitchen counter. The seat of her stool swung back and forth, back and forth. Propelled by her hips, the rhythmic sway denoted the restlessness that had plagued her since the tumultuous events two weeks before. "What do you think the world would be like without men?" she asked Abigail.

The cook squirted dough onto the cookie sheet. "No crime. No crooked politicians. Just a lot of fat, happy women."

"Now that's not *all* true." Margaret slid forward until her chin rested on the cool tile. "There would probably still be a little crime."

"What set you to wondering?" Abigail asked.

"I was thinking that men are only good for one thing."

Abigail laughed. "You talk like a husband."

"I suppose." Margaret sounded wistful. "Isn't it fair to just want a guy for his body? Just once in my life?"

Abigail peeked up from her work. "I can't see that Mr. Reid would object to being hungered after."

Margaret snorted. The swing of her chair grew wider, and her lower lip stuck out like a sulky child's.

Abigail put down her cookie press and put her hand on her hip. "Does he?"

"Reid Donovan is a jerk."

"That's what you said the first time you met him. You mean you haven't changed your opinion?"

"He's a jerk for different reasons now."

"How can you say that? He's been dancing with you every night. He takes you to the ballet, he takes you to Oxheart to dine with the celebrities, he's kissing you in the corner every time I turn around. He and your kid are absolutely nuts about those damned mutts, and they spend hours together. Those Guarneri men are hanging around all the time with their feet on the furniture, eating us out of house and home. Come on," Abigail coaxed. "Tell Aunt Abigail the problem. You should have the glow of a woman in love, and instead you're moping around here. What else do you want?"

"He wants to get married."

"Sounds like a good idea to me, seeing as how you act like an old married woman who's had a fight with her man. But what can he do to you if you don't want to get married? Torture you?"

Margaret rolled her eyes up, and the swing of her stool became more pronounced. "He has his methods."

"Like what? Thumbscrews? The rack? The worst he could do is—"

Margaret's shoulders slumped.

"The worst he could do is...oh, dear." Abigail put her flour-dusted hands to her cheeks and chuckled. "You poor thing. You poor, poor thing."

"What?" Margaret snapped. "You think you're so smart. What do you think he's doing?"

"I don't think, I know. I'm surprised I didn't think of it before. You think I don't recognize the signs of sexual frustration? These past few years, I've been there myself, and I didn't have a man chasing me into corners and raising my blood pressure. That Reid is crafty." Abigail shook her head in admiration. "He is crafty."

"I had decided to give him everything he wanted. I decided to sleep with him, take what he was offering with both hands—"

Abigail laughed. "It's so big it requires both hands, does it?"

Margaret continued, "—And enjoy myself. Now he's changing the rules."

"Maybe he's not changing the rules. Maybe you should have asked for the rules before you started playing the game."

"You sound like Reid. Everybody's against me," Margaret said. "Everyone's nagging me to give in to Reid. Even my own daughter's turned traitor."

"You're jealous because Amy has more money than you do."

"Damn." Margaret slapped her hand on the counter. "Does the whole world know about that legacy?"

"Certainly everybody knows who was standing within a half mile when you were yelling at poor, sick Mr. Jim about it," Abigail said reproachfully.

Margaret avoided Abigail's eyes. "For one thing, he paid his lawyer to call Reid and tell him about it."

"Why would he do that?"

"Because that crafty old—"

Abigail cleared her throat.

"—Man knew Reid would come running to find out who was taking money from his grandfather. He knew Reid would assume I was A. M. Guarneri in the will. He knew I'd be the one who got the brunt of Reid's attention. And you know what I think?"

"What?"

"I think he hired me with this whole setup in mind."

"Girl, you have a persecution complex," Abigail chided.

"No, listen," Margaret said. "He said he wanted a great-grandchild. I think he was looking around, checking the possibilities, and here I came, all innocent—"

Abigail shook her head with sad resignation. "You have gone over the edge."

"Maybe," Margaret said grudgingly. "All I know is that the lawyer who set up the will is working for Mr. Jim again. I went by the study and I heard the lawyer and Jim and Reid laughing, those smug masculine laughs, and the lawyer said, *I needed the vacation.*"

"You had your ear pressed to the door?" Abigail asked, her fist resting on her hip.

"No, they didn't even *shut* the door." Margaret's voice rose. "They didn't even care if I heard them. They saw me walk past and laughed even harder."

"Don't you shout at me. I'm not old and sick like Mr. Jim, and I'll shout right back," Abigail told her with fire in her eye.

Subsiding sulkily, Margaret protested, "He shouldn't have left Amy so much more money than he told me."

Abigail waved one hand expansively. "It's peanuts to him. He loves that little girl, and his will is his own business. I don't see why you need to be sticking your nose—"

Margaret slashed her throat with her finger. "So sue me. I shouldn't have hollered at Mr. Jim. Even my brothers-in-law tell me to mind my own business. Even *they* think Amy's mature enough to handle a fortune."

"What do you think?"

Using her thumbnail, Margaret traced the grooves between the tiles on the counter.

"Hmm?" Abigail insisted.

Margaret mumbled, "I suppose that wealth won't spoil Amy."

"Because you raised her correctly. These days, everyone's noticed your daughter's more mature than you are."

Giving in to irresistible temptation, Margaret stuck out her tongue.

"See?" Abigail said. A bell chimed in the distance, and she wiped her hands on her apron. "There's Nagumbi, summoning me once again."

"It's five o'clock. Shall I send out for dinner, or will your master let you out of his room in time for you to fix it?" Margaret asked sarcastically.

"The man's been shot. Have some compassion," Abigail chided. But as she smiled, the dimples appeared and disappeared in her cheeks.

"Right. One crummy little bullet hole in the shoulder and he spends all his time in his room with the cook."

"I'm feeding him healthy foods."

"Is that why last week you didn't come out for twenty-four hours? I could have sworn you were starving him."

"He was showing me his stamina," Abigail said loftily.

"His stamina?" Margaret cackled. "That's a new word for it."

"You're just jealous," Abigail said with lofty disdain, walking out the door. Sticking her head back in, she added, "And horny."

"And horny," Margaret mimicked. She made a face at the now empty doorway.

Damn Abigail for being so clever. Damn Reid for addicting her to the delights of his flesh and then tormenting her with its withdrawal. What was it he'd said a mere two nights after the kidnapping…?

Forty

"No, Margaret." Reid had taken Margaret's hands from under his shirt and held them pressed together in front of him. "We mustn't anticipate our wedding day."

"What do you mean, we mustn't anticipate our wedding day?" She had grabbed his belt as he edged away from her on her couch. "What were we doing before?"

"What we did before Granddad and Amy were kidnapped is something that never should have happened, and won't happen again until we're married."

"Are you *crazy?*" She glanced around her little living room as if the answer would pop out of the walls.

"Not at all. I've never wanted to marry a woman before. I didn't know how to behave correctly. But that's all over. Now I know what to do." He watched her closely as he made his grand announcement. "I'm going to court you."

"Court me?" she asked in a daze. "What do you mean, court me?"

"Convince you through mutually pleasant means you want to marry me and consummate our relationship within the bonds of matrimony."

"What was all this?" She spread her hands to indicate their present dishevelment. "You certainly led me to believe we'd be *consummating our relationship*"—she spat the words—"this evening."

"This is one of the mutually pleasant means I was speaking about." He tucked in his shirt. "I agree, we got a little carried away. But the emotions of the past weeks contributed to that. Confronting a kidnapper and all."

Searching her mind for some way to counter his ridiculous logic, she stuttered, "You haven't asked me to marry you."

"I was going to," he assured her. "But every time I started, it was the wrong time. I planned to ask you at the house in West University. I planned to show you the puppies and ask you. So I've decided to let you do the asking."

"What? You want me to ask you?"

"I'd say that was clear enough. I'm buying the house for us. I got us a dog. I love your child. I've done all the offering. Now it's your turn to offer for me. If you want me, you're going to have to ask me." He nodded as if he was making sense.

"I don't believe this." She sagged against the arm of her couch. "You want to marry me, but I have to ask you?"

"That's it," he said approvingly.

"And if I don't ask you?"

"Then you can't have me."

She clutched one of the pillows tight in her fists and thought it an inadequate substitute for his neck. "You're going to be mighty frustrated."

"So are you." His lascivious wink made her wrap her fingers around the pillow and wring it. "Once I broke down your walls, I discovered a very easy woman."

"What?" She sat straight up.

"Oh, come, darlin'. I know you're not likely to become the town nymphomaniac, but with me, you're a pushover."

"*What?*"

Leaning forward, he ran his hand up her thigh as he nuzzled against her ear.

She knew what he was doing, and why, and she tried to remain untouched. But she melted like a snow cone in a heat wave.

When he pulled back, she was clinging to him, and he said, "See?"

Her eyelids fluttered open, and she looked at the man above her. "You're trying to control me with sex," she accused.

"That, too." He smiled, that all-teeth barracuda smile, and jumped back before she could hit him.

"You bastard. Is this what you told the Guarneri boys?"

"Yep."

"It's okay," she reassured. "You can back out on it. You can tell them you were drunk."

"On two beers," he reminded her.

"You'll stick with that story through thick and thin, won't you?"

"You believe it, too, don't you?"

"Yes." She was disgusted. "I talked to your grandfather when he got home from the hospital, and he told me the oil rig story."

"That's my girl." Reid stood up and away from her and strolled to the door. "After you propose, we'll try making love a new way."

She cocked her head inquiringly.

"In bed."

"Say, that is an idea." She didn't try to contain her sarcasm.

"Just don't take too long to propose," he warned. "Or I'll be forced to turn up the heat."

She was quick enough to smack him in the back of the head with the pillow and shout, "You owe me one hundred fifty bucks for the two bets you lost."

But that had been a temporary satisfaction. In the twelve days since, he had stuck with his resolution. All the black lace garter belts in the world hadn't changed his mind. He'd walked out on her seductive striptease. Sexy underwear, then no underwear, earned her a swat on the behind and an order to get dressed.

Now she was reduced to constant exercise and cold showers. She got a momentary feeling of achievement every time she ran into Reid in the gym or the pool. She wasn't the only one who was suffering—but he was holding up better.

He had a goal in mind; he relentlessly pursued it.

She had no goal but escape, and that was not a goal—only an avoidance.

Trouble came during the day, when Amy brought her patterns and cloth swatches and asked which one would be appropriate for a bridesmaid's dress.

And again when Mr. Jim talked to Manuel, in loud and longing tones, of his great-grandchild and how he longed to hold it in his trembling old arms.

Trouble came at night, when she lay in bed and remembered, in vivid, Technicolor reruns, just how good Reid had been to love. Lust was a pallid word for what she felt. After every date, his kisses, his caresses, moved her to a frenzy. She was always gasping, desperate, when he pried her hands away from his body and left her in a puddle of desire.

When she slept…the dreams would make a sailor blush.

She walked around trying to scratch an itch she couldn't seem to reach.

The staff jumped when she snapped at them, not understanding her foul mood.

Now that Abigail had figured out Margaret's problem, the staff would understand. Abigail would make sure of that.

With a sigh, Margaret slid off the stool. She'd go and exercise again.

Forty-one

Pool or gym? Margaret debated, as she clattered down the stairs to the gym. With a shrug she opted for both. Perhaps if she were tired enough, her dreams would be quiet and restful.

That plan had never worked before.

But it should, damn it.

Flipping on the light, she rummaged through the closet for her swimming suit and her shorts. It made her angry that her body, which had been trained to obey her, should now obey Reid.

Who did he think he was, anyway?

She snatched her clothes out and slammed the door shut.

Making all the rules, changing all the rules, being the perfect jerk one minute and the perfect gentleman the next. Laughing at her because she was off balance. Trying to convince her that she should ask him to marry her when nobody had said one word about love. He'd hinted that he cared. He'd hinted that if he could take the chance on her, she could take the chance on him.

But he'd never reassured her.

She kicked off her shoes.

He made her so mad. So smug and sure he could manipulate her.

She took off her jacket.

The constant highs and lows were making her dizzy—she, who'd been level-headed for so long.

She started to unbutton her vest, then stopped and stared at her hands. They looked so…so flesh-toned. She must have gotten too much sun.

Her legs. They looked so…so colorful. Usually, her whole body glowed a sickly white beneath these fluorescent bulb monstrosities. Usually…

She looked up and did a double take.

"What? When? Why?" She stammered to a stop.

There was no one around to answer her questions, and she didn't even know what to ask. Above her, on long tracks set on the ceiling, were lights. Real lights inside real frosted peach glass covers. The fluorescent tubes that had so bothered her were gone, removed with nary a trace.

She strained her eyes, circling below the spot where they'd been hung. Nothing. Whoever had removed and replaced them had done a marvelous job. And quickly, too, since lately she'd spent most of her time down here. Sniffing, she detected the smell of paint and plaster.

"Well." She sat down on the mat and stared up. Then she reclined on the mat and stared up. "This is amazing," she told the ceiling. "Who do you suppose did that? Why do you suppose someone did that?"

But she knew who'd done it. She even knew why.

Reid had done it because he remembered how she hated fluorescent lights. He knew they reminded her of hospitals, death and grief. He knew, illogical though it might be, she'd never shake that association. So like the arrogant jerk he was, he'd changed the lights, without a word to her, without any thought to the cost or the trouble.

The man wanted her to be happy.

Admitting that Reid was a *thoughtful* arrogant jerk put her in a difficult position—the position of having to propose.

Why should she, really? When she offered him marriage, she'd be giving in to a man already too indulged. He was spoiled. He was audacious. He radiated sensual magnetism, and women fell like nine-pins at his feet. She'd be falling, too, just like the rest.

But at least when she fell, it would be with such a thump and wallow, he'd never see another woman beneath him—in any manner.

Her eyes narrowed as she considered the women who wanted him.

He was a charmer, true. That brown-red hair, cut too short; those sherry-brown eyes, liquid with expression. That slashing bone structure that wasn't handsome, but so striking. It wasn't his looks that brought the women to attention.

It was the heat of his gaze, his open appreciation, the way he focused his whole attention on the woman of his choice; *those* were the reasons a woman wanted him.

When he met her, what a ghastly man he had been. Pushy, obnoxious, protective of his grandfather. Suspicious of her—and she wasn't sure if she'd forgiven him for that. Asking questions merely to torment her, and succeeding only too well.

If I were ill, would you abandon me?

How cruel to make her face the fears that ruled her life. That one question had torn the blinders from her eyes, had forced her to face the truth. If Reid were sick, she could run to the ends of the earth and never escape the pain...because she loved him. Loved him with the hot pleasure of a girl, with the calm sureness of a woman. Loved him enough to trust that the joy of their lives would overcome the adversity.

That was something else he'd returned to her: the memories of Luke, alive and healthy, with no shadow on him. Because of Reid, she could remember Luke with a sweet sadness and not a tearing pain.

All because of Reid.

That man, that swashbuckling barracuda of a man, was kind and loyal. He wasn't a one-dimensional leader, with a single-track mind. He was a colorful, multitalented genius who was the other half of herself.

So all right. He'd won. But she would win, too, and in more ways than one. She'd have her man, to care for and cherish. She'd have a father for Amy; a man who fostered a sense of family and never displayed jealousy of the Guarneri family.

If anything, he got along with them too well.

Grimacing, she picked up her jacket and shrugged it on.

Her brothers-in-law would celebrate tonight.

As she prepared to surrender, her restless body proclaimed victory. She'd roped and tied a man who celebrated sex. After they married, she'd take him to bed and work him until he screamed. She'd show him what a real woman could do when faced with an irresistible force. In fact—she held her panties between two fingers and debated, than flung them aside. Maybe if she caved in and proposed right away, he'd cave in and she'd get lucky right away. Chuckling, she checked her tie and put on her shoes.

There. If she was going to propose, she'd do it right. Trotting up the stairs and down the hall, she stopped at the first bouquet she liked. An eclectic mixture of lilies and ferns, it graced the entry with its lofty beauty. She lifted the flowers out of the vase and wiggled them to rid them of the excess moisture. Water dripped on the solid wood floors, but she was beyond caring. With an elegant flip, she shook out a lace doily and wrapped the stems. Clearing her throat nervously, she walked to the study door and lifted her hand to knock.

Before her knuckles made contact, a loud banging shook the front doors.

Startled, she glanced around. *Where was Simon?*

No one was in sight.

To arrive at the front door, visitors had to be allowed in the gate by someone in the house. So how had a stranger managed to sneak up the driveway without being apprehended by the still vigilant security? There should be someone here to greet…whoever it was.

The pounding came again.

Margaret marched to the front door. Two weeks before, the press had swarmed over them, tramping on her lawn, kicking over her flowerpots, demanding interviews and photo opportunities. In the way of news, the Donovans had become an old story, but lingering caution made Margaret peer through the peephole.

Through the convex glass, she could see two distorted faces peering back at her.

A smile broke across her face, and she jerked open the door. "Pierre! What are you doing back in Houston? Chantal! How was your trip to France?"

Chantal looked totally enchanting, of course. Her brief, sleeveless dress, so appropriate for the Houston autumn, flattered her figure. Her battered suitcase rested at her feet beside her expensive briefcase. "France was wonderful, but our time was fleeting." She bent a glance of unholy amusement at Pierre. "If only we hadn't been called back early."

Pierre glared at Chantal, but replied to Margaret. "I came back to do a favor for a friend, and to go to a wedding."

He looked so acutely uncomfortable, Margaret smiled. "Your own?"

"Comment?" he asked blankly. "What?"

"Your own wedding?" Margaret indicated them with a wave of the hand. "You're acting so oddly, I though that you and Chantal…"

Pierre relaxed and exchanged an understanding glance with Chantal. "We are, as they say, just good friends," he said with a grin. Then his grin faded, and he wiped his hands on his pants as if his palms were sweaty.

Margaret held the door wider. "You're hot, and I'm a dreadful hostess...I mean...butler. Come in."

Shifting from foot to foot, they made no move to enter. They kept nudging at each other until Chantal said, "You said you'd ask her."

"Ask me what?" Margaret queried.

Pierre rolled his eyes heavenward and muttered a few words in French, then—"Are you Amelia Margaret Guarneri?"

Startled and confused, she agreed, "You know I am."

Leaning down, he drew an envelope out of his briefcase.

Margaret accepted it. She looked inquiringly at him.

He drew a deep breath, bracing himself for some unpleasant duty. "I've been asked, in my capacity as a law officer, to present you with this summons to court."

Her jaw dropped, and she stared at the unopened envelope drooping in one hand and at the flowers drooping in the other. "What for?"

Taking several rapid steps backward, Pierre told her, "Reid Donovan is suing you for palimony."

Margaret lost her dignity. "*What?*" she shrieked, advancing on him. "He's doing what?"

Pierre crossed himself.

"Reid Donovan is suing you for palimony," Chantal repeated kindly. "Will he be bringing a patrimony suit against you soon, too?"

Like an avenging fury, Margaret rounded on Chantal. "What kind of smartass comment is that?" She saw the camera Chantal held, heard the click of the shutter. "What are you *doing?*"

"Recording the fact the papers were served on you." Chantal smirked. "Maybe I'll sell these pictures to one of those sleaze magazines. I could get good money for it."

"Maybe your heirs could," Margaret snarled. She extended her hand, palm out. "Give me that camera before I smash it."

"What will you do if I give it to you?" Chantal mocked.

"Smash it."

Chantal tucked it behind her back. "No way." She looked over Margaret's shoulder. "Reid, I'm glad you brought suit against this woman. She obviously has violent tendencies."

Flinging herself around, Margaret confronted Reid.

He stood behind her wearing a black suit, a white shirt, and the reddest power tie she'd ever seen.

"Something tells me," Margaret said, clutching the lilies with white knuckles, "you were expecting this."

He ignored her, smiling at Chantal with his most innocent smile. "I see Pierre told you about my suit against Ms. Guarneri."

"Yes, and I think it's shameful the way she's treated you." Chantal clicked her tongue. "Shameful."

Margaret suddenly realized it was a joke. It had to be a joke, and she was...was playing into Reid's hands. She chuckled weakly. "Stop this nonsense right now. You've all had your laugh. Now let's go in and sit down..." Her voice trailed off as three pairs of eyes reproached her.

Pierre shook his head. "The summons is real."

She looked doubtfully at the envelope.

"Read it," Reid advised.

Tearing the seal, Margaret skimmed the convoluted legal document. She'd never seen a summons before, but this certainly appeared to be genuine. Bewildered, she asked, "Why would you bring a palimony suit against me?"

"Yeah, Reid." Chantal drew her iPad and a stylus. "I'm a reporter. Tell me why you've brought a palimony suit against Margaret."

Noting Chantal's brisk and efficient manner, Reid asked, "Going to sell the story?"

"To somebody," she answered ambiguously.

He leaned toward her and confided, "In that case, I'd be delighted to tell you why I brought this suit. The reasons are unmistakable. At the beginning of our relationship, Ms. Guarneri indicated she wasn't interested in marriage, and I agreed for obvious reasons." His demeanor flipped from one of sorrow to efficiency. "Am I going too fast for you?"

"Not at all," Chantal assured him.

Flipping back to sorrow, he glanced wistfully at Margaret. "As the relationship progressed, I wanted more, yet Ms. Guarneri continued to insist on an uninstitutionalized union."

"Uninstitutionalized?" Margaret said.

"I insisted that until we got married, we'd keep our relationship pure—"

"Good God." Shaking her head, Margaret sank her face into her palm.

"—But she's been putting pressure on me, and I don't know how long I can hold out. You see, I love her and I want her to be happy. I've finally realized she wasn't interested in making an honest man out of me"—Reid's lower lip drooped—"and so I've brought this lawsuit. Ms. Guarneri has been living with me without benefit of matrimony while enjoying my body. She owes me support."

"Owes you support? Owes you support?" So angry she could scarcely draw breath, Margaret glanced about her in appeal.

Pierre stood with his arms crossed on his chest, grinning like a hyena.

Chantal wore an expression of indulgent amusement.

Margaret looked behind her into the entryway.

Mr. Jim sat in his wheelchair and Amy leaned against him.

Abigail stood with her arm around the bandaged Nagumbi.

Simon, the upstairs maid, the gardener, the chauffeur, and the cleaning crew stood in a clump.

"Can you believe..." Her voice died to a whisper.

Everyone, *everyone* was smirking.

Facing Reid, she saw a wounded countenance.

As they made eye contact, his face crumpled into wicked laughter. But he fought, composure won, and he returned to the sad and betrayed appearance of a basset hound.

Margaret was angry. She was furious, yet underneath it all was a vast and surreptitious merriment.

She'd told Abigail he was a jerk; if anything, she'd understated the issue.

What kind of man was Reid? Using her own sense of humor to create the kind of situation she couldn't back out of. Placing her in front of her family and friends to play a practical joke on her—a joke with its underlying serious message.

He had done this to get her attention.

He had succeeded.

Projecting her voice, she asked, "How am I supposed to support a man who makes more in a month than I make in five years?"

He sighed and confided, "I'm willing to live on your income merely to be close to you."

With precise movements, Margaret laid down the flowers and slid out of her formal black coat—and stomped on it. "I don't have an income."

"Why, darling." He laid one hand flat on his chest and gasped with ostentatious astonishment. "You mean you'd quit your job merely to avoid paying me my rightful support?"

"No." She stripped off her tie and vest and kicked off her shoes. "I'd quit my job so I can give you your just deserts."

He eyed her bare foot warily and stepped back. "What just deserts?"

She picked up the flowers. "I was coming to propose."

"Uh-oh." His face was a funny mixture of horror and ruefulness.

"I was going to go down on my knees. I was going to use the flowers to persuade you to accept my offer."

"I sense you've changed your mind."

"Oh, I'll use the flowers, all right." She pulled them back and whacked him across the chest with them. She followed him as he dodged and parried, protecting himself with upraised arms. "You're an unprincipled" — *whack!* — "rude" —*whack!*— "manipulative" — *whack!* She paused, out of adjectives.

"Unscrupulous?" he suggested.

"Unscrupulous scoundrel." *Whack, whack!*

"I was trying to get—"

"Murdered?" she suggested.

"Fair treatment," he protested.

Petals flew as she gave him one final whack and burst into laughter. "You'll do anything to get your own way."

He bared all his teeth in that barracuda smile and caught the mangled bouquet in his fist. He tugged.

She stumbled into his arms.

"That's why you adore me," he said.

"Adore you," she scoffed, wrapping her arms behind his head and tugging it toward her lips. "You want to truss me like a goat."

He laughed. "Yes, what's your point?"

"I'll bind you, too," she replied with determination. "You'll be tied on such a short leash—"

"As long as you're on the other end of the rope, I don't mind. Now ask me," he commanded. "Ask me loud enough for everyone to hear, and I might give you what you want."

"You know I'll be caving in for no better reason than that you're the man of my dreams."

"What kind of dreams?" He already knew the answer.

"My erotic dreams. You're a jerk."

"I know," he soothed. "Now ask me."

"Who'd want to marry you?"

"You do. Now ask me."

She smoothed the hair on the nape of his neck. Suddenly shy, her eyes dropped.

But he bent his knees, looked into her eyes, and smiled at her with such sweet understanding…

…That the words bubbled up from her soul. "Will you marry me?" she asked.

"At the first opportunity."

He let her bring his mouth to hers, and he let her kiss him while Chantal's camera shutter clicked, preserving forever the proof that Reid Donovan loved his lady in black.

The End

About the Author

Readers become writers, and Christina has always been a reader. Ultimately she discovered she liked to read romance best because the relationship between a man and a woman is always humorous. A woman wants world peace, a clean house, and a deep and meaningful relationship based on mutual understanding and love. A man wants a Craftsman router, undisputed control of the TV remote, and a red Corvette which will make his bald spot disappear.

So when Christina's first daughter was born, she told her husband she was going to write a book. It was a good time to start a new career, because how much trouble could one little infant be?

Quite a lot, it seemed. It took ten years, two children and three completed manuscripts before she was published. Now her fifty *New York Times* and *USA Today* bestselling novels—paranormals, historicals, romantic suspense and suspense—have been translated into twenty-five languages, recorded on Books on Tape for the Blind, won Romance Writers of America's prestigious Golden Heart and RITA Awards and been called the year's best by *Library Journal*. Dodd herself has been a clue in the *Los Angeles Times* crossword puzzle (11/18/05, # 13 Down: Romance Novelist named Christina.) *Publishers Weekly* praises her style that "showcases Dodd's easy, addictive charm and steamy storytelling."

Christina is married to a man with all his hair and no Corvette, but many Craftsman tools.

Virtue Falls is Christina's newest series
Visit Virgue Falls http://christinadodd.com/genre/virtue-falls-series

Chat with Christina on Facebook
http://www.facebook.com/ChristinaDoddFans
Tweet with Christina on Twitter! https://twitter.com/ChristinaDodd

Visit www.christinadodd.com for writing tips, book news, book sales, exclusive excerpts and to join her FREE mailing list
http://christinadodd.com/newsletter/new-books-to-add-to-your-e-reader/ for

Steal a Sneak Peek at Christina Dodd's **JUST THE WAY YOU ARE**, the first book in her "Lost Hearts" series, enhanced with bonus material!

"Come on," Hope said. "I'm going to be a lot more comfortable in the kitchen."

Griswald retrieved the chicken soup she had brought him and indicated she should precede him down a shadowy hall. "Why?"

"Mr. Givens's home is like a museum." She glanced back at him. "I'm afraid I'll break something."

He shrugged. "It can all be replaced."

"Really? So there aren't any genuine pieces of art here?" She walked backward so she could face him and shake this feeling of being pursued. "If I broke an antique, wouldn't I find myself washing dishes for the rest of my life trying to pay off the bill?"

"This isn't a restaurant. We don't charge our guests for breakage." He caught her arm and pulled her toward him. "But if you're worried, you might want to watch where you're going." He steered her around a small side table crowned by a tall, blown glass vase.

"I won't run into anything," she assured him. "You don't have to hang on to me."

He looked down at her, and his lids were heavy. "I like holding you."

"Oh." Oh, dear. That was a problem, because she liked it, too. From their telephone conversations, she knew him to be forceful and determined. Now that she saw him, now that he touched her, he created a longing that both compelled her and made her want to run as far and as fast as she could. If she were smart, she would run.

Obviously, she had lost all her smarts. And her conversation, for she couldn't think of one word to say as they walked along as close as lovers.

She couldn't think like that. Certainly not about a man she'd just met. A man…who was obviously ill. "You're running a fever." She halted. "Let me feel your forehead."

"My mother says you can't tell a fever unless you use your lips."

Darn. Her mother had always said the same thing. With a credible imitation of insouciance, Hope said, "Very well." Sliding her hand around his neck, she brought him close and pressed her lips on his forehead.

Cool. Startled, she tried in another spot, and another. He wasn't running a fever. Running her palm down the side of his face, she massaged his shoulder, passed her hand down his arm. "But you're so warm!"

"And rapidly getting warmer." He smiled, a slow stretching of his lips.

His first smile. Possibly ever, if she was any judge. And that smile made her realize—she was stroking him. Stroking him as if he were a great cat and she a lion tamer—and she knew very well she was nothing of the sort.

Not with this kind of lion. Not with this kind of man.

You can find *Just the Way You Are*, the first book in Christina's "Lost Hearts" series at all of your favorite on-line booksellers

40465365R00161

Made in the USA
San Bernardino, CA
21 October 2016